Ashes to ASHES

Ashes to ASHES

JENNY HAN & SIOBHAN VIVIAN

SIMON & SCHUSTER BFYR

NEW YORK   LONDON   TORONTO   SYDNEY   NEW DELHI

SIMON & SCHUSTER BFYR

An imprint of Simon & Schuster Children's Publishing Division

1230 Avenue of the Americas, New York, New York 10020

Text copyright © 2014 by Jenny Han and Siobhan Vivian

Cover photograph copyright © 2014 by Anna Wolf

For information about special discounts for bulk purchases, please contact
Simon & Schuster Special Sales at 1-866-506-1949 or business@simonandschuster.com.

The Simon & Schuster Speakers Bureau can bring authors to your live event.
For more information or to book an event, contact the Simon & Schuster Speakers Bureau
at 1-866-248-3049 or visit our website at www.simonspeakers.com.

Also available in a SIMON & SCHUSTER BFYR hardcover edition

Book design by Lucy Ruth Cummins

The text for this book is set in Stempel Garamond LT.

Manufactured in the United States of America

First SIMON & SCHUSTER BFYR paperback edition September 2015

4 6 8 10 9 7 5 3

The Library of Congress has cataloged the hardcover edition as follows:

Han, Jenny.

Ashes to ashes / Jenny Han and Siobhan Vivian.

pages cm

Sequel to: Fire with fire.

Summary: "Lillia, Kat, and Mary must deal with the fallout of what happened on
New Year's Eve in the conclusion to the Burn for Burn trilogy"—Provided by publisher.

ISBN 978-1-4424-4081-4 (hc)

[1. Revenge—Fiction. 2. Friendship—Fiction. 3. Grief—Fiction. 4. Guilt—Fiction. 5. High
Schools–Fiction. 6. Schools—Fiction. 7. Ghosts—Fiction. 8. Islands—Fiction.]

I. Vivian, Siobhan. II. Title.

PZ7.H18944Ash 2014

[Fic]—dc23

2014004241

ISBN 978-1-4424-4082-1 (pbk)

ISBN 978-1- 4424-4083-8 (eBook)

For Zareen Jaffery

"Therein lives the defect of revenge:
it's all in the anticipation; the thing itself is a pain,
not a pleasure; at least the pain is the biggest end of it."
—Mark Twain

Ashes to
ASHES

Prologue

MARY

I'M HIGH UP IN THE REAR BALCONY OF HOLY LADY OF the Sea, and it is pure agony. There aren't enough tears in the whole wide world. My sobs echo those of the congregation below me.

There is a brass urn on the white marble altar. And a sea of flowers. Roses and mums and lilies and snapdragons, a cross made of white carnations, wreaths with pink ribbons hanging down the front. So many flowers, even though it's snowing on the other side of the stained-glass windows.

I don't know when I got here. I don't know what day it is. I don't know the time.

An old lady takes a seat at the organ behind me and begins a sad hymn. Everyone stands up, and the preacher walks somberly down the center aisle, followed by two altar boys holding big wooden crosses. It is a struggle for my mom to keep up. I see her through my tears. Black pencil skirt, black sweater. She can barely stand. Aunt Bette supports her on one side, my father on the other.

I rub my eyes and look again. It's not my mom. It's Ms. Holtz. She's got the same curly hair, same petite frame as Rennie. The two people flanking her I've never seen before.

And the huge picture on an easel next to the urn is not one of me. It's Rennie in a yellow sundress, her hair down and curly and tousled from the offshore breeze. She's wearing an innocent expression, but she has mischief in her eyes. She looks about fifteen or sixteen. Younger than I remember her ever seeming.

This isn't my funeral. It's Rennie's.

It's so crowded that ushers have brought in extra folding chairs to put in the aisles and next to the confessionals. That's where I see Kat. Her father stands behind her. Pat squeezes her hand. I can tell by the way Kat's shoulders rise and fall that she's sobbing.

When Ms. Holtz passes the Cho family, she stops and reaches out with a shaky hand to touch Lillia's shoulder. She wants Lillia to come sit with her in the front pew. Lillia looks nervous, but Mrs. Cho gives her daughter an encouraging nod.

JENNY HAN & SIOBHAN VIVIAN

On her way to her new seat, Lillia passes Reeve and his family. His parents and his brothers and their girlfriends. They take up almost the whole row. Reeve's just had a haircut; the skin on his neck is pink. He's wearing the suit he wore to homecoming. Lillia doesn't look at him, and he doesn't look at her. Reeve starts flipping through a prayer book as she lowers her head and takes her seat.

I scan the rafters, the eaves, and the statuary.

Rennie? Are you here too?

I keep looking around, waiting for Rennie to show up. Only she never does. She's not here like I am.

What did I do to deserve this? To be stuck on Jar Island for eternity? Was it because I killed myself? I know how stupid it was. I just wanted to make Reeve feel sorry for what he'd done. I wanted to take it back as soon as I jumped off the chair with the rope around my neck, only I couldn't. It was too late. Can't God understand that it wasn't my fault? I never would have done it if it hadn't been for Reeve. He should be the one punished, not me.

The preacher asks us to bow our heads in prayer. I drop my chin and close my eyes. *Please let me leave this place. Let me find a way to heaven. Let me rest in peace.*

When I open my eyes again, the church is empty. The lights are out; the flowers are gone.

And I'm all alone.

Ashes to Ashes

Chapter One

LILLIA

IF IT WERE A NORMAL DAY, NADIA AND I WOULD BE listening to the local morning radio show. She actually laughs at the corny jokes they tell, at the slide-whistle sound effects. I don't think their banter is very funny, but I do like hearing the celebrity gossip. Sometimes, if they are doing a giveaway or contest, Nadia will call using both our cell phones at the same time to up her chances of winning.

But not today. Not the first day back at school since Rennie died. Today as I drive us, the radio stays off. We ride in silence, except for the *swish, swish, swish* of the wipers as they push the tiny snowflakes off my windshield.

Nadia tries to peel off her puffer jacket while keeping her seat belt buckled. "Can you turn the heat down? It's boiling in here."

I glance at the dashboard. I've got the dial set to high, plus my heated seats are cranked. It's because I can't get warm. My body's been cold since I heard the news. "Sorry," I say.

I pull into a parking spot and watch for a second as everyone slowly marches into school. It's like a silent movie. No one is talking or joking or laughing. I wonder, will school ever feel normal again, without Rennie here?

I'm sure not.

Sometimes, when I was annoyed with her, I'd tell myself that Rennie wasn't as big a force as she liked to think she was. That she didn't hold so much sway, so much power over our school. But now that she's gone, I know it was true. This place is dead without her.

Nadia unclicks her seat belt. "Do you want me to walk in with you?"

I shake my head. "I'll be fine." As Nadia reaches into the backseat for her book bag, I say, "You know, there are supposed to be grief counselors here today. If you feel like talking to anyone. I've heard Ms. Chirazo is nice."

Nadia nods, and she says in a timid voice, "You too, okay?"

I nod and say, "Of course," but I don't feel like talking. Not to anybody. I begged my mom to let me stay home sick today. Begged and pleaded. I haven't been sleeping well. At all, really. I lie in the dark for hours and hours, but I never fall asleep.

I grab Nadi by the sleeve before she's out of my car. "Hey. Don't worry about me. I'm fine." I know my voice sounds tired, weak, so I smile to compensate.

The worst part is—I know people will be feeling sorry for me. If only they knew the truth, that Rennie hated me before she died. That I betrayed her worse than anyone else could have. When I close my eyes, I keep seeing flashes of what happened in those last moments together. Her showing Reeve the pictures she'd found of me drugging him at homecoming. Her slapping me across the face. Her sobbing, hating me for betraying her.

And then there's Mary.

The thought of seeing her today makes me want to crawl into a hole. How am I going to tell her about Reeve? And what, exactly, am I going to say? That I made a mistake but it's over now? I've practiced it in my head so many times, but I still don't know the right words.

As I walk through the parking lot, I keep my eye out for Kat's car, but I don't see it either. I owe her a million phone calls. I'm sure she's pissed at me too.

I keep waiting for this to turn out to be a bad dream. To wake up and have things be the way they were. I wouldn't even care

JENNY HAN *&* SIOBHAN VIVIAN

if Rennie hated me for the rest of her life for what happened on New Year's with Reeve. Or if she never spoke to me again. All I want is for her to be alive.

I see her everywhere. The first-floor trophy case, where we'd hang out freshman year when it got too cold to sit outside by the fountain. The janitor's closet, where we'd hide notes for each other between classes. Her locker, sophomore year.

I feel the tears come, but I don't want to cry anymore.

I'm at my locker when Ash comes running down the hallway, pushing her way past people to get to me. "Lil," she moans, and she throws her arms around me, sobbing hysterically. I have the uncharitable thought that it's like she's in a movie about a girl who died in a car accident. Other people in the hallway turn and look at us.

I let her cry in my arms for a minute, and then I break away from her. "I'm gonna go get a juice at the vending machine," I say. "Do you want anything?" I'm not trying to be cold, but I can't deal with her right now. It's just too much.

She shakes her head. "I'll come with you, though."

"No, stay here. I'll be right back," I say. I give her a peck on the cheek and dart away. I'm halfway down the hall, thinking maybe I'll just keep walking, maybe I'll walk right out of here and go back home, when someone grabs my arm from behind me.

Alex.

"Lil," he says. "You hanging in there?"

"Yes." Just barely.

Alex doesn't look so good either. He has shadows under his eyes, stubble on his chin. He rubs his eyes and looks around and then says, "I keep expecting to see Rennie. It feels . . . really empty here without her. It's like nobody knows what to do anymore without her here to tell us."

That's exactly how it feels. Exactly. And it's such a relief that someone gets it. I let out a breath that comes out more like a gasp, and Alex reaches for me and I let him hold me, and it feels like his arms are the only thing keeping me upright.

I don't know what, if anything, Alex knows about the things that went down between Reeve, Rennie, and me on New Year's Eve, but I'm so thankful that he's here right now. This is who he's always been to me, the person who knows what I need, without me having to ask. Even when I don't deserve it.

Chapter Two

KAT

I BLOW OFF FIRST AND SECOND PERIOD, AND MR.
Turnshek, the school safety officer, finally catches me during
third. I'm smoking a cigarette underneath the stairs, where
I found Mary ditching a test that one time. I was hoping she
would be here. I came to school early this morning and waited
for her at her locker. I wanted to hear her excuse for why she
never called me or stopped by my house. By this time, she has
to know that Rennie's dead.

But Mary never showed.

Mr. Turnshek looks at me, aghast.

"I know, I know," I say, letting go of the smoke in my lungs before standing up. "Principal's office." I put the cigarette out on the wall. It leaves an ashy circle on the cinder block.

I've been going through nearly two packs a day since Rennie died. I can't even taste my food anymore, and the skin between my pointer and middle fingers is starting to turn yellow. I know it's bad; I should quit before I really get addicted. I tell myself that anyway, right before each cig I light up.

"You'd better believe it, DeBrassio," Turnshek says, his arms folded.

I guess part of me wanted to get caught. I don't know. This whole day has annoyed me. Everyone mourning, crying over Rennie. Everyone with arms around each other. It's like the whole school is propping each other up. Except no one's doing that for me. Most of the underclassmen don't even know that Rennie and I used to be best friends back in the day. They assume that I don't care that she's dead.

Or worse, that I'm happy.

I nearly lost it when I overheard one freshman cheerleader bitch mutter something under her breath when I passed her in the hall. I spun around and walked straight up to her, put my nose up to hers, and dared her to say whatever it was to my face. She practically crapped her designer jeans.

I shouldn't expect that dummy to understand what I'm going

through. But Lillia and Mary—they know my history with Rennie. Just because we weren't friends for the last few years of high school doesn't mean that her death isn't freaking ripping me apart. It doesn't mean that I don't need to talk shit out, have a good cry. After all, I was the last person to see Rennie alive. And at the end we were on good terms.

Not like her and Lillia.

I've texted Lil a bunch of times, but she hasn't written back once. She's probably been camped out at Rennie's condo with the rest of that crew, drying each other's tears. Either that or she feels guilty because I know that she left with Reeve that night. I'm trying not to think this way, but I wouldn't be surprised if she quit talking to me. Actually, she *should* keep a low profile. People must be wondering why the hell Rennie left her own damn party in the first place. If they found out why, shit would surely hit the fan.

I just hope Mary doesn't know. But her knowing is the only reason I can come up with to explain the fact that Mary has basically gone MIA on me too. I was so desperate for someone to talk to, I even drove by her house a couple of times. I never stopped, though. As much as I wanted to, I wasn't ready to answer questions about Reeve and Lillia. That's on Lillia.

Mr. Turnshek writes up a pink slip and sends me to the principal's office. But instead of walking there, I go see Ms. Chirazo.

The five guidance counselors are huddled around the

coffeepot. They made an announcement over the loudspeaker today, inviting anyone who needed grief counseling to come down. But the office is empty.

Ms. Chirazo spots me and steps away from the group. The rest of them give me dirty looks over their mugs. They know me as a troublemaker, I guess. But Ms. Chirazo never looks at me that way.

"Kat. Is everything okay?"

I hold up the pink slip. "I just got busted for smoking in the hallway."

"Oh, Kat. Why? I thought we were going to be on our best behavior, at least until we heard back from Oberlin."

I shrug my shoulders, because whatever. At this point I don't care if I get expelled. What's done is done. Picking at my nails, I say, "I used to be Rennie's best friend. For, like, my whole life. Until high school started, anyway. And then we hated each other." I realize that I'm gritting my teeth while I say it. Probably because I can't make sense of the idea that Rennie Holtz, who was always larger than life, was reduced to a pile of ashes in a fucking tacky-ass vase.

"I didn't know that."

"So it's like most people don't care how I'm doing, you know? How I might be handling this. And the truth is, I don't know how I'm supposed to act. I mean, should I be a hard-ass and pretend like it doesn't bother me? Should I scream in their smug faces that I was way closer to Rennie than any of them ever were? It's like a disgusting competition of who knew her best. And people think I'm last, when I should be in fucking first place." I glance around, and my eyes land on a vase full of dried flowers on the corner of the secretary's desk. I have the overwhelming urge to swat it off. I make a fist and bite down on it hard.

Ms. Chirazo seems to notice. A second later her hand is on my back, and she's pushing me into her office and closing the door.

"Kat, forget what other people think. You don't have anything to prove." She points at her door. "There's a reason why there are no students in this office today. People want to grieve with their friends, people who understand the connection, who don't need to be brought up to speed. You should surround yourself with the friends who know you best."

"I've tried that. My friends both blew me off."

"Then try again," she says matter-of-factly. "When you lost your mother, you were completely unreachable. It took time. It took people not giving up on you."

I move my eyes to the birds flying past her window. I wonder how long it will be until I feel normal again. When Mom died, I was depressed for an entire year.

Ms. Chirazo stands up. "I'm going to go talk to Principal

Tortola and see if I can't get him to excuse your lapse in judgment in light of current circumstances. In the meantime, sit here for as long as you like. The secretary will write you a pass when you're ready to go back to class."

I don't wait long. Just enough to scribble a note for Mary.

> *Yo. When you get this, find me.*
> *I miss you. Hope you're okay.*
> *—K*

I've just slipped the note inside Mary's locker when I notice that it's missing its padlock.

I open the door, hoping to see her jacket hanging inside, but the thing is freaking cleaned out. Not, like, the way some nerds do so they're neat and organized at the beginning of a semester. It's completely empty. Just my folded-up piece of notebook paper at the bottom.

I can think of two possibilities. Either Mary switched lockers or she switched schools.

No. There's no way she left Jar Island without telling us. Even if she did find out about Reeve and Lillia, she wouldn't dick out on me and not say good-bye. She knows I care about her. She knows I'm her friend.

At least, I hope she does.

Chapter Three

LILLIA

PEOPLE HAVE BEEN LEAVING FLOWERS IN RENNIE'S locker, poking them through the vents. I'm careful when I open the door, so the flowers don't fall onto the floor. The inside of her locker door has pictures of the cheerleading squad, her and Ash, her and Reeve. None of us. The one of us down by the beach is gone. It was the summer after ninth grade, and we were wearing sherbet-colored bikini tops and making silly faces into the camera. I wonder if she ripped it up or if she just threw it away. I haven't gone through any of our photo albums yet. I can't. It hurts too bad.

Methodically I start separating her personal things from the textbooks I have to return to Mr. Randolph. I throw away a package of doughnuts, a spiral notebook with only one page of notes inside, half a pack of old gum, and a fuzzy black hair tie. I falter when I get to her favorite lip gloss and her black compact mirror—would Paige want to keep this stuff? Probably not, but maybe just in case? I put that stuff into the cardboard box Mr. Randolph gave me, along with a long cardigan, a scarf, and a few binders.

"I was starting to think maybe you died too."

I turn around. It's Kat, with her bag slung over her shoulder. Her hair is piled on her head in a greasy bun, and strands are coming out the back, and she has dark circles under her eyes. She looks terrible.

"Sorry, bad joke," she says with a grimace.

"Hey," I say. "Kat, I'm so sorry I—"

Kat waves her hand, like *Forget it*, and I'm relieved. She hitches her bag up on shoulder. "Yo, have you seen Mary today?"

I shake my head.

"I went by her locker to put a note inside, and it was cleaned out." Kat chews on her fingernail. "Did you ever tell her what happened with you and Reeve?'

Biting my lip, I say, "I've been meaning to, but things have been so crazy . . ."

JENNY HAN & SIOBHAN VIVIAN

"Maybe she found out somehow and that's why she's been MIA." Kat shoves her hands into her pockets. "What's going on with you and Tabatsky now? Are you a *couple*?"

The derision in her voice makes me want to curl up and die. "No! We are definitely not a couple. We aren't anything."

"I'm not accusing you, Lil. I mean . . . it is what it is. I just want us to be real with each other."

I look around before I take a breath and start over. "That stuff with Reeve, it's over. It was just that one night and it hasn't happened again. And I'm not purposefully avoiding you guys either. I've been at Paige's every day with Ash and everybody, trying to get her to eat. She's a mess. All she does is sleep and cry. It's been really hard."

"Well, at least you've got people around you. I mean, who the eff am I supposed to cry with? Pat? My dad? They don't get it. I mean, sure, they feel sad about what happened to her. But nobody knew Ren the way we did." Kat's voice cracks on Rennie's name.

"I'm sorry," I whisper.

Kat wipes her eyes with her sleeve. "It's fine. Whatever. I just needed to say my piece." She grits her teeth and forces a smile, and it looks terrible. In a deadpan voice she says, "I feel better already."

I reach out and give her shoulder a squeeze. I'm going to

have to face Mary eventually. I owe her that. I close Rennie's locker door and hoist up the box of her things. "Let's go over to Mary's."

We take my car. As we get closer, Kat says, "Here's what I'm thinking. If Mary's home and it doesn't seem like she knows about you and Reeve and what happened on New Year's Eve . . . maybe you don't tell her."

I draw in my breath. "I can't not tell her." Can I?

"But like you said, it's over, and it would only hurt her. So there's no point, right?"

"I guess so." I don't want to hurt Mary. That's the last thing I want. And this thing with Reeve really is over. Maybe Kat's right.

I park in Mary's driveway, right behind her aunt's Volvo. It doesn't look like anyone's shoveled the snow; it's melting in patches. When I get out of the car, the bottoms of my boots crunch on broken glass. Kat and I look at each other, uneasy.

We go up to the front door and ring the bell, but no one answers. I have this weird feeling, like someone is watching us. It's the prickly-back-of-the-neck feeling I get late at night when the whole house is asleep and I go downstairs to get a glass of water. I always run back to my room fast.

Kat starts knocking on the door, hard.

"This is creepy," I whisper.

Kat keeps knocking until her knuckles turn red. "Shit." She presses up close to the window. "It looks like a tornado blew through there."

I press my nose up against the glass. Oh my God. The dining room chairs are knocked over; the entryway table is on its side. "Kat, Mary could be in serious trouble. We have to call the police!"

"The police?" Kat repeats. She's craning her neck, trying to see up the stairs. "Why don't we just break in ourselves and see what's what?"

"Because there could be an intruder in there! Who knows what we'd be walking into!" I grab her by the arm and drag her back to the car, where I take out my cell and dial 911.

Chapter Four

KAT

IT'S A FREAKING HALF HOUR BEFORE A COP CAR ROLLS up to Mary's house. So much for a goddamned emergency.

Lillia jumps out of the car and walks down the sidewalk to meet the officer at the walkway. I'm a few steps behind her when Eddie Shofull climbs out of the squad car like a damn cowboy.

"You've gotta be kidding me," I say.

Officer Eddie Shofull is all of twenty-two years old. He looks way more like a boy dressed up in a cop uniform than an *actual* cop. He used to be friends with Pat back in high school. Scratch that. Eddie used to smoke weed with Pat back in high school. After graduation, too. Basically until he joined the Jar Island Police Force. His father is a deputy sheriff. Jar Island nepotism at its finest.

Eddie glares at me. "What'd you expect, Kat? A detective?"

"Um, yeah. Considering we've got a missing-persons case here. Or a possible hostage situation."

Eddie rolls his eyes and radios in that he has arrived on the scene.

"Officer," Lillia says, and nudges me to the side. "Please. We haven't been able to get in touch with our friend. Her guardian had mental health issues, and we want to make sure she's okay."

Eddie looks over the tops of our heads at the house. "When was the last time you saw her?"

"Before New Year's Eve," Lillia answers quickly.

"Have you tried calling her?"

I throw my hands into the air. "Of course we've tried calling, you dumb-ass."

"*Kat!*" Lillia throws me a warning look before turning back to Eddie. "There's no answer, Officer. Her school locker was emptied out, and—"

"She probably moved."

Finally Lillia returns my look—that Eddie is a freaking moron. "Then tell me why her house is in complete shambles and there's a ton of broken glass in the driveway!"

Lillia takes him by the hand and leads him over to the pile. He clicks his flashlight onto the shards even though it's bright and sunny and we can see just fine. He crunches a few shards under his boot. "You can't tell when this glass was broken. It could have been months ago. Years ago, even."

"Years ago?" I scoff. "Come on, Eddie. You sound like a damned idiot!"

He narrows his eyes and puts a hand on his radio. "All it takes is one call, and you girls will both spend a night in jail for calling in a false report and insulting an officer of the law."

Lillia's eyes widen. She's totally falling for his fake-ass, weak-ass threat. "We're not trying to be disrespectful—"

"I am!" I shout.

"Please just check out the house, okay? Because if our friend is up there being tortured by her psycho aunt, and you didn't properly investigate, you'll be the one in jail!" And with that, Lillia folds her arms and purses her lips.

Eddie stares right back, and then slides his nightstick out from his belt. "Fine. I'll do a quick perimeter check. You two stay here."

But of course we don't. We follow Eddie as he walks around to the back of Mary's house. We both call out, "Mary? Are you there?"

Eddie walks up the back stairs and knocks hard on the

kitchen door with the butt of his nightstick. And, wouldn't you know, the thing pops wide open.

Lillia and I share a look before we push past Eddie and enter the house.

"You girls get back here!" Eddie shouts from the doorway. "I'm serious, Kat! Come on!"

"Mary?" Lillia calls out. "Are you in here?" Her breath makes tiny clouds. The heat is off. It's even colder in here than it is outside.

It's dead quiet.

And shit really is everywhere.

I walk around the kitchen table. "This is so weird." It looks like Mary and her aunt literally up and disappeared without any notice. Why else would there be dirty dishes left in the sink? There are empty plates on the table. I lean in close and see some mouse droppings.

"Kat, come on. Let's check upstairs," Lillia says.

Eddie groans and takes one step inside. "This is unlawful trespassing!" he whispers.

"You coming with us or not, Eddie?"

I pull my jacket up around my neck, and the three of us go deeper inside, through the hallway, through the living room. The place is still full of Mary's family's things. There are light-house and seascape paintings hanging on almost every wall and a bunch of family pictures on the fireplace mantel. I walk up to one. It's of Mary as a girl, posed with two people who I guess must be her mom and dad. She's barely recognizable. I remember her telling us that she used to be overweight, and I couldn't imagine it. But she was chubby. Big red cheeks, a double chin, round potbelly.

I can totally see Reeve picking on her, that bastard.

Lillia looks at the picture too. "Maybe this means she'll come back here eventually. Her family will want to get their things, right?"

"Maybe," I say. But I don't believe it. Looking around the rest of the room, I can see that most of it's trashed.

Lil and I make our way upstairs. Eddie's already there, pointing his flashlight up another set of stairs, probably leading to the attic.

We come to a bedroom and linger in the doorway. Unmade bed, closet doors wide open, clothes tossed about. Strangest of all, the entire floor is covered with hundreds of books open to random pages.

"This has to be her aunt's room," Lillia whispers.

Suddenly there's a hand on my arm. "The house is empty," Eddie says, pulling me back toward the staircase. "We're getting out of here. Move it!"

"Wait, Kat! Come look at this!"

I shake Eddie off and follow the sound of Lillia's voice into another bedroom.

It's the only one that's been completely emptied out. There's a dresser, a stripped bed, an empty bookshelf, and a bare closet. I walk to the window and look down at the spot where Lillia and I threw rocks to get Mary's attention when we came to visit her once in the middle of the night. That was the first time she told us about Reeve and what he'd done to her.

"She must have packed up her things." Lillia shakes her head. She can't believe it either. "I guess she really did leave without saying good-bye."

On our way out, Eddie pulls the back door shut and makes sure it's locked. Then he drives off. Lillia and I get back into her car. We should leave too, but we don't. Not right away.

"The last time I saw Mary, she was happy," I say. "Singing and dancing about you shutting Reeve down that night we both slept over. You know, she never showed up at Ren's party on New Year's. Maybe by that time she'd already peaced out. She got what she came for; she left on a high note."

"Maybe . . ." With a sigh Lillia turns on her car and heads to my house.

"Or, you know what? Things have been so crazy with Rennie's death. Maybe Mary came to say good-bye when we were both at the funeral." I fiddle with my seat belt. "Or it could be that something happened with her aunt. Like a family intervention and she didn't have time to come find us. Whatever it is, I bet she'll call us soon."

I can come up with a million excuses. The problem is that I don't buy a single one.

Chapter Five

MARY

FROM THE PEAK OF THE LIGHTHOUSE ROOF, JAR ISLAND looks small, like a play town with play people. That's where I'm perched, a seagull waiting out a storm. I'm as close to the sky as I've ever been, and everything is tiny. A man walking his poodle, a car driving up Main Street, a child crying for his mother. I'm too far away to care. What does it matter? What does any of it matter?

Before, I would have been afraid to be up so high. Now I'm not afraid. I'm not even sad. I'm nothing.

It's funny how my whole life, I never wanted to leave Jar Island, and now in death I can't. I remember when I first came back here, waking up on the ferry once it had reached Jar Island.

Or had I ever left? There was that time, after the first few days of school, when I'd had it with Reeve. I wanted to be back with my mom and dad. I packed up my suitcase and came down to the docks, ready to leave but unable to go. I didn't know why then, but now I do.

For some terrible reason I'm trapped here. I've been trapped here, maybe since the day I killed myself.

What I want to know is why. Why am I still here? Rennie got to leave. Is she in heaven? Or did she go straight to hell? Hopefully my dad is in heaven. He was a good dad. He deserves to be there. I wish I were with him.

It starts to snow. I'm not wearing a coat. I've got no socks, no shoes. Just me in a simple white dress. If I close my eyes, I can almost feel the cold wind whipping around me, I can almost feel the chill of the winter sea spray. Almost.

All those months of pretending, playacting like I was alive, like I was somebody. Only I didn't know it was pretend. I thought it was real. It felt real.

My friendship with Lillia and Kat, that was real. In their eyes I was alive. I never had friends like them before. It was the only time in my whole life when I felt a part of something.

They made me real. For a little while anyway.

If I let go of them, maybe then I can finally move on. To heaven, to hell, to wherever. So long as it's not Jar Island.

Chapter Six

LILLIA

SATURDAY NIGHT THERE'S A CANDLELIGHT VIGIL FOR Rennie in the courtyard outside the school. It's freezing, and the wind is blowing so hard people's candles keep going out, so they cut it short. Kat comes, but she leaves early.

After, Paige goes around telling everybody to come over to her place, that she cleaned out the gallery and found the leftover liquor and beer from Rennie's party. She says she wants to get rid of it. She says, "We can cry and drink and tell Rennie stories. Everyone can just camp out afterward and sleep there."

I've already slept over twice this week because Paige doesn't like to be alone on the nights when her boyfriend has to get back to his restaurant on the mainland. She makes me stay up all night with her, and it's a roller-coaster ride of her laughing one minute and then sobbing the next. But that's not the hard part. The hard part is sleeping in Ren's bed, because when I wake up, I still expect to see her there next to me.

When I get to the apartment, everyone's already there. Ash is sitting in Derek's lap in the armchair; PJ is lying on the floor with his hat over his face; a few girls from the squad are in the kitchen. Alex sits on the radiator flipping through a photo album. Reeve is next to Paige on the couch. She has a big shoe box in her lap, and she's passing around trinkets she's kept, like the tiny white dress Rennie was christened in. I can tell she's already drunk. Reeve barely looks at the stuff, just quick cursory glances. I go to the kitchen and fix Paige a turkey sandwich, because I'm sure she hasn't had anything to eat. From the couch I feel Reeve's eyes on me, but when I look up, he's already looking away.

I put the sandwich on a plate and bring it to Paige. "Try to eat a little."

Paige kisses me on the cheek. Her breath smells like whiskey and something sour. "You're my angel," she says, setting the plate down on the coffee table. "I planned on getting some snacks and things for you kids today, but when I went to the store, I felt everybody's judging eyes on me, so I left."

Frowning, Alex asks, "What do you mean?"

"All these Jar Island parents are convinced that I'm a terrible mother," she spits out. "They think Rennie got into that accident because she was drinking and driving. I have the police report. That had nothing to do with it. It was some kind of malfunction with the Jeep."

"My father said you could sue the car company," Ashlin says. "You definitely have a case."

Paige barely notices, and says, "Plus, you know Ren could hold her liquor. She's her father's daughter. But people would rather make up stories than believe the truth. They want to make me out to be an unfit parent. These people never liked me. They never accepted me."

I swallow and look at my lap. My mom has made a few comments just like that. Wanting to know if Paige regularly got us alcohol. I told her no, of course not. And it wasn't a lie. Rennie had her own connections. But Paige didn't exactly discourage us either. Still, she always made sure we were being safe, that no one would drive if they'd been drinking.

Paige glances at Alex. "Sweetie, I'm not trying to be a bitch, but your mother is a perfect example. I know she's let you kids drink at your house. But it happens at my gallery and suddenly I'm a lowlife?"

"I'm so sorry," Alex mumbles, his face red.

"No, no, no, no, sweetie. Please. It's fine. You kids know the truth, and that's all I care about. So let's have a good time tonight, okay? For Rennie." She pats the seat next to her. "Reevie, scoot over for Lil," Paige commands.

Reeve moves as far away as he can, and I sit down. "Take a look at this," Paige says, and she hands me a picture of Reeve and Rennie from kindergarten. They are both dressed up because it's the first day of school. Her curly hair is in pigtails, and he has on a plaid button-down shirt and is missing a front tooth. I can't help but smile.

"It's so cute," I say. I pass it to him, careful not to let my fingers touch his.

Reeve stares at the photo, swallows hard, and then hands it back to Paige. "Keep it," she says. Then, taking a sip of her drink, she continues, "You know, I always thought you two would get married one day."

He freezes. I see the pain in his face, the guilt. I see everything he's trying to hide.

Ash pipes up, "Rennie used to say that if you guys got married, she wanted to get a picture with you and all your brothers throwing her into the ocean in her wedding dress."

Paige chokes back a sob, and Reeve shoots Ash a look.

Sitting next to him on the couch, I'm too aware of everything. Every time he shifts his weight, or speaks, my heart beats double and it's hard to breathe, or concentrate. When Ash suggests we watch an old cheering video we made, I jump up to go find it on Rennie's laptop, and it's a relief not to be in the same room as him.

I sit at Rennie's desk and open up her computer. There's a memory stick already in the USB port. I open it and scroll for her videos, and then I see the file called "Homecoming," and my whole body goes hot. I click on it, and there they are— magnified pictures of me, drugging Reeve's drink. Quickly I drag the whole file over to the trash, which I then empty.

"Did you find it, Lil?" Ash calls out from the other room.

"Not yet," I say back, trying to make my voice sound normal and not guilty and disgusted with myself.

"Hurrrrrry!"

I do a search on her computer for "Homecoming," in case she has it saved there, too, but there's nothing, and my heart rate finally starts to slow down.

I go back to the living room. "I can't find it," I say.

Ash makes a sad face. Wistfully she says, "I guess we'll never see it again."

Then it's quiet. Paige goes into her room to lie down, and the rest of us just sit around in awkward, sad silence.

"Hey. Why don't we play a drinking game," Alex finally says. "It can be called . . . 'Remember When.' And everybody has to tell a memory of Rennie, and if you remember it, then you drink. Or . . . if you don't remember it, you drink."

"That's a great idea," I say, standing up. I get cups for everyone, and Ash grabs a bottle of cinnamon-flavored vodka from the cardboard box on the kitchen table.

Alex goes first. He raises his cup and says, "Remember when Rennie tried to convince me to get my eyebrows waxed?" He starts laughing. We all do.

"Didn't she make you an appointment somewhere?" Ash says, snorting with laughter.

"Yup. She totally did. At a nail salon, I think." Alex shakes his head. "Thank God I figured out she was joking before it was too late."

We raise our cups and swallow, and then I refill everyone's glasses.

"Remember when Rennie broke into the teachers' lounge and stole Mrs. Penfeld's precious coffee mug? The one with the cat in the argyle sweater?" Ash says. I raise my glass and sip, along with almost everybody else.

Not PJ, though. His mouth drops open. "She did not."

"Oh, yes she did," Ash says. "Don't you remember her bringing it to parties sometimes?"

PJ shakes his head. "Dude. Holtz was fearless."

I'm smiling, but all the while my mind is racing, because it will be my turn soon, and I can't think of anything. I have so many stories about Rennie, it feels like my whole life on Jar Island has been about Rennie, and yet I can't think of even one thing. I'm so panicky, I could cry.

Alex nudges his chin toward Reeve. "You're up."

Reeve shrugs his shoulders. "Pass."

Ash tries to sweet-talk him into sharing something, but he won't. She's persistent, but it only makes Reeve shut down even more. The muscles in his shoulders are bunched up, and he's two seconds from getting up and walking out of here, I know it. I throw Ash a warning look so she'll stop.

"PJ, you go," I say, and PJ launches into a story about Rennie sneaking into the boys' bathroom, and everyone starts to laugh, and the tension of the moment before fades away. Our eyes meet, and I can tell Reeve is grateful. Right before it's my turn, I get up and go to the bathroom, and I don't come out until I'm sure they've moved on to the next person.

After midnight some people have left and some are passed out in the living room and in Rennie's bedroom, I guess because everybody started drinking so early. I am on Paige's bed with Paige and Ash. They are both asleep, but I'm just lying here. I finally get up and open the bedroom door.

In the living room the TV is on and Reeve is cleaning, tying up a big recycling bag. I watch him for a few seconds, and I suddenly feel such longing for him in my heart, I ache. I'm about to say something when Alex comes out of the kitchen. I step back into Paige's room before they notice me.

I hear Alex say, "How are you holding up?"

I can hear the surprise in Reeve's voice when he says, "I'm all right."

"Come on, man. I know how much you cared about her." Alex pauses. "I'm still pissed at you for going after Lillia—"

"That's over."

It hurts to hear him say it, but it's time.

Then Alex says, "If you ever want to talk—I'm here for you."

There's this long beat, and I'm holding my breath, hoping. Hoping that Reeve will let him in. Alex has always known how to talk to Reeve. His opinion is the only one Reeve has ever really cared about besides Rennie's.

Gruffly Reeve says, "I'm good. But thanks."

I let out the breath I was holding. Then I hear Alex say, "All right," and then a few seconds later the front door opens and closes.

I step out, thinking it's Reeve who left. Only it wasn't.

Reeve looks up and sees me standing there. "Oh, hey," he says, startled.

"Hey," I say. I busy myself picking up plastic cups.

We work in silence. When we're almost done, I hear a muffled sound, and I look up and see Reeve, his back to me, his shoulders shaking. He's crying.

I go completely still. For a few seconds I'm not sure what to do for him. Then I realize I do know. I don't look at him when I say, "Just go. I'll finish up here."

Reeve takes a ragged breath. Then he gets his coat, says "Bye, Cho," and leaves. When he's gone, I burst into tears.

Chapter Seven

KAT

I CAN'T GET MARY OUT OF MY HEAD.

So Monday morning, I cut first period and go looking for Ms. Chirazo. Maybe she can tell me something about where Mary went. Just because Mary isn't locked up in the attic with her freaky aunt doesn't mean I have the best feeling about what could have happened to her. The guidance secretary doesn't see me come in, she's on the phone, so I just walk straight into Ms. Chirazo's office.

She's not there.

I wait for a few minutes, feeling stupid. I'm not sure what

Ms. Chirazo is going to be able to tell me. I bet there are privacy laws and shit that she won't be able to go against, even if she is cool with me. There aren't even any student files on her desk. Everything's on her computer. I lift my ass off the chair and peer at the screen. It's open and on, no password required.

Fuck it. I jump into her chair. If I can look up Mary's student records, maybe there will be some contact information. Either for Aunt Bette or for her parents. Mary might have gone home to them for the holidays and decided not to come back. If that's the case, I'll call her or write her a letter. Better yet, Lillia and I can take a road trip to visit her.

I open an icon that says "Student Transcripts," and I type in "Mary Zane" and then hit enter. An hourglass pops up as the computer searches the records. It takes forever because this computer is as old as shit.

Nothing.

I try it again with "Zane, Mary." And then just "Zane," in case maybe "Mary" is short for some weird name I don't know. No dice. Weird. I plug in her address and search again. But each time, nothing comes up.

There's no record of her at all.

What the hell?

I hear a pair of sensible shoes outside the door, and I have just about half a second to get out of Ms. Chirazo's chair and back into the one on the other side of her desk.

"Kat?"

"Hey." I feel like Ms. Chirazo knows I was up to something, because she gives me this weird, distrusting look. I've gotten that look hundreds of times, but never from her. "I wanted to stop by and make sure that whole smoking thing from last week was taken care of." I clear my throat. "I should probably get to class."

"Yes," she says slowly. "Good idea, Kat."

After school I meander over to the Preservation Society office in White Haven. It's my first day back since the holidays. The decorations have already been taken down—the wreaths, the electric candles flickering in each of the windows, the balsam greenery they had me wrap around the banisters and the door frame.

If I had driven straight over, I would have been on time, but I sort of cruised around the island for a bit with my windows down, because, well, I don't know. I guess I hoped that the fresh air would clear my head. Except it didn't. I'm as much of a mess as the piles of dirty slushy snow along the road.

I trudge up the stairs, reeking of cigarettes, my boots soaked clear through, and my nose running snot like crazy. Hopefully they'll take one look at me and send me home, but as soon as I'm through the door, Danner Longforth jumps out of her office and points at the clock on the wall with a bony, manicured finger.

Danner Longforth is one of the youngest women working at the Preservation Society. I bet she's not even thirty. She's married to a super-old rich guy who lives near the Chos. I doubt she's ever had a real job. She gets way too excited about office supplies — paper clips and shit.

"Katherine." Her voice is as thin as her body, and she holds the *n* sound of my name until she's standing directly in front of me. "You were supposed to be here thirty minutes ago."

It catches me off guard. Danner isn't my superior or my boss. In fact, I didn't even think she knew my name. "I—"

"I know you don't think so, but we do important work here." She waves at the wall next to us, where a bunch of framed proclamations with fancy calligraphy and gold foil seals are hung up. "Our efforts have been recognized by the governor for the last six years running. And if you want to remain in the privileged position of volunteering here, if you want to receive the kind of recommendation letter that will make your college application shine, you'll need to earn it. And the very least of your obligations here is to arrive on time." She folds her arms and purses her lips.

I stare at her and, in as flat a voice as I can manage, say, "There was a prayer service after school today. For Rennie Holtz, the girl who died over New Year's."

It's a lie, but whatever. Bitch needs to check herself.

"Oh," Danner says quietly, and fiddles with one of the many rings on her fingers. "Well, why didn't you just say that?"

"When? You were too busy reaming me out."

I instantly worry that I've gone too far, that Danner will fire me on the spot. But she doesn't. She has this fuzzy camel-colored sweater-wrap thing on, and she pulls it tight around herself. "You were that poor girl's friend?"

I feel my lip curl. Who is she to ask me that? "Yeah," I say through gritted teeth. "Yeah. I was." And it's true. At the very end I was Rennie's friend.

"I see," she says, and then lowers her eyes. "Well, I'd like to apologize to you, Katherine. I shouldn't have reacted that way. It's a crazy time of year for us here, and I already feel like I'm behind on everything." She sighs. "Please take today off if you need . . . but if you could manage to give me an hour or two, I'd greatly appreciate it."

"I'll stay for a bit," I say, and then turn to head down to the basement. That's where I scan the old documents and deeds and newspaper clippings for the Preservation Society archives. But Danner touches my shoulder and keeps me from walking away.

"Actually, the archival project is on the back burner for now. Our focus will be on the annual benefit happening this March. I don't know if your parents have ever attended one"—I watch her look me over, realizing there's no way—"but this will be an excellent experience for you. I'll make sure I put it in your recommendation letter. Admissions boards really respond to charity projects."

I want to laugh. Charity projects are working at a soup kitchen or volunteering at a battered-women's shelter. Not running errands for a bunch of rich ladies pretending like they have jobs.

But I do need a stellar recommendation to get me accepted to Oberlin. That's the one bright spot I've got to hold on to. A future away from this island, from the hurt and the pain and all the bad memories.

When I think about it that way, I can't blame Mary for wanting to leave.

"What's this benefit for?"

"To raise money for this year's preservation efforts. It's a huge formal dinner dance at the old city hall building, plus a silent auction. Last year we received almost half a million dollars, which we put toward the purchase and renovation of Jar Island landmarks."

A prom for rich people. Jeez.

Ashes to Ashes

Danner trots back to her office and then returns with several pieces of paper. "Okay, Katherine. I need you to double-check these invitation addresses against the ones in our Rolodex. Evelyn worked on them this morning, so there shouldn't be too many left for you. We need to make sure each one is correct before we send the final list off to the calligrapher. He charges per envelope, and we can't afford to waste money on preventable errors."

I'm about to tell Danner that they could save money by, um, not spending money on dumb shit like that. I mean, this is supposed to be a fund-raiser, right? But Danner's already headed into the glass-walled conference room, where a table full of ladies are heatedly discussing something. Probably arguing about waiter outfits.

I lock eyes with Evelyn, who's the oldest lady by far at the office. I doubt they'd let her work here if she weren't filthy rich, and I bet they hope she'll throw some money to the Preservation Society when she kicks off. Evelyn's working at a computer, her hand tentatively going for the mouse like it might come to life and bite her wrinkly fingers.

I take a seat at an empty desk and flip through the list. I only have three pages to check before I get to the end of the alphabet . . .

Erica Zane?

Mary's last name. Could this be her mom?

There's no address listed. Just a phone number.

I'm so excited, I can barely dial. What if Mary picks up the phone? What will I say?

I don't have to worry long. As soon as I punch the last number, I hear three chimes and a recording that this number is no longer in service.

Where have these Zanes gone to?

I check the rest of the addresses and wait for Danner to be done in the conference room. As soon as she is, I'm on top of her, pointing at Erica Zane's name.

"I couldn't find an address for her in the Rolodex. And this phone number is out of service. What should I do?"

Danner's lip curls. She takes a black pen and scratches out the name. "Don't worry about that one. She shouldn't be on the invite list."

Well, damn. My only lead is a bust.

Chapter Eight

LILLIA

PAIGE TEXTS ASKING ME TO STOP BY AFTER SCHOOL. When I get there, the door's unlocked, so I let myself in and call out, "Paige? It's Lillia."

I stop in the kitchen first. There are dishes neatly stacked in the drying rack, freshly washed. Paige hates doing dishes. That was always Rennie's job. It must have been Reeve. Ash told me he's been helping Paige out too. I turn around and see that he tied up a bag of cans and bottles for recycling and set it near the front door.

"In here, Lil!"

I find Paige in her bedroom, still in her robe and pajamas. She's packing her clothes into a cardboard box. She looks up at me, and her eyes have that zombie look to them that she gets when she takes her sleeping pills.

"Are you moving?" I ask her. This is the first I'm hearing of it. But I guess it makes sense. Paige always said she'd leave Jar Island after Rennie graduated. The only reason she stayed this long was because Rennie begged her.

"I'm out of here before the end of the month. Rick wants me to go live with him. I can't stay on this island, not without my girl. There's nothing left for me here." Paige wipes her eyes, and in a dull voice she says, "You should take a look around Ren's room, see if there's anything you want to keep of hers as a memento. Like maybe that necklace you gave her. I would have buried her in it, but—" She breaks down and starts to cry, and holds her arms out to me, so I go to her. She holds on to me tight. "Stay for dinner, okay?"

I don't want to. I know that if I say yes to dinner, Paige will push me to spend the night, and I can't. I can't wake up in Rennie's bed alone again. But it's not about what I can or can't do. It's about what I have to do. Being kind to Paige is my penance, a way to right the wrongs I did to Ren. "Sure, I'll stay," I say.

I go to the bathroom to call my mom. When I tell her I won't be home for dinner, it's clear she doesn't like it, because she is silent for a minute. Then she says, "Lilli, this is too much for you. You're only a child yourself. You need to rest."

I wish I could. But I can't. I don't deserve to. So I whisper, "Mommy, this is the least I can do for Rennie. Please."

She sighs heavily. "Make sure you eat something healthy. And send Paige my love."

When I come back out, Reeve is in the kitchen on the phone, quietly ordering Chinese takeout. He rubs his temples like he has a headache. "Can you make the General Tso's extra spicy?" he asks. I know that's how Paige likes it, how she and Rennie both liked it. Reeve hangs up his phone and gives me a nod. "Hey."

"I—I thought you'd left."

"I just got back from taking some of Ren's furniture over to Goodwill. Paige needs me to help her patch the walls where Rennie hung stuff up, so she doesn't lose her security deposit." He looks down at the floor.

There's an awkward silence between us. It feels like it goes on forever. "Why don't you go home? I can stay and have dinner with her and you could patch the walls tomorrow."

"Thanks," he says, and that one word is like a stinger in my heart.

I go find Paige. "Reeve's heading home, so . . . it'll just be us for dinner."

Frowning, she says, "No, he can't leave." She hurries into

the kitchen, with me trailing behind her. "Don't leave, Reevie. The food's already ordered, and I want both my kids with me. I won't have you for much longer."

He nods, and I think how tired he looks.

While we wait for the food, Reeve goes into Rennie's room and starts taking apart a bookshelf. I clear off the kitchen table, wipe it down, and set three places with paper plates and napkins.

The buzzer on Paige's door isn't working, so when the delivery guy arrives, she has to run downstairs to pay him. I call to Reeve that the food is here, and when he comes into the kitchen, he looks around for Paige. Then he leans against the table, clears his throat, and says, "Hey, I got into that prep school in Delaware."

My eyes widen. "What? Are you serious? Benedictine?"

"Yeah. I found out yesterday."

I beam at him. "Reeve, that's amazing!" Before I can stop myself, I jump up and give him a hug. At first he feels stiff, and I start to straighten up, to pull away. What am I doing hugging Reeve, in Rennie's kitchen of all places? But then Reeve pulls me in closer. And I let him.

He inhales deeply, his face buried in my hair. In a low voice he says, "Thanks for your help. I never would have thought to do this on my own." I get goose bumps all over.

"Forget it," I say back, and I feel like I'm going to cry. I know this is wrong, so very wrong, but I don't want to let him go.

Reeve doesn't want to let me go either. If anything, he pulls me even closer. His arms tighten around my waist, and I drop my head against his chest.

Then I hear a door close, and we spring apart. I spin around, and it's Paige, walking into the kitchen with a big plastic bag. She has a funny look on her face, and she says flatly, "I think they forgot our egg rolls."

I quickly walk toward her, take the bag from her hands, and check the receipt stapled to it. My heart is beating super quick. "I can't tell if you got charged or not." I try to sound normal, but I know I don't.

"I probably forgot to order them," Reeve says. "I'm gonna go get washed up."

"All right," Paige says, but she's not looking at him. She's looking at me.

Reeve ambles off to the bathroom, and it's just Paige and me. "Do you want me to call the restaurant and see if they'll come back with the egg rolls?" I ask.

"Actually, I think I may have lost my appetite."

Oh no. No, no, no. "Paige, I—"

"I'm going to take another sleeping pill and try to pass out. You should just go home."

My eyes dart down the hall to where the bathroom door is

still closed. Oh my God, why won't Reeve hurry up and come back out here? He can smooth-talk his way out of anything, but not me. I'm hopeless. I stutter, "Well, i-is there anything you want me to do before I go?"

"Nope. I'm all set." The words are sharp. She smiles a thin smile that doesn't reach her eyes. "Thanks for everything."

My mouth feels dry. "Sure. Well, I can come back tomorrow."

"Don't bother."

My stomach knots. "Paige, please. It isn't what you think."

"You don't owe me an explanation." There's the slightest emphasis on the word "me," and I know who she's thinking of, and it makes me want to die.

Chapter Nine

KAT

Dad's working late in the garage. He needs to finish up the canoe orders from this past summer. Tourist season basically kicks off in another month and a half. As soon as the snow is gone and the grass starts growing, they'll be here in droves looking for things to spend money on.

So Pat and I are in the kitchen together making tacos. We've got it down to a science. I'm cooking strips of flank steak. Pat's at the kitchen table filling up bowls of toppings—shredded cheese, sour cream, red onion, black beans, wedges of lime. He's very particular about the size of the onions. Anyway, the tortillas are getting warm in the oven and the yellow rice is going in the rice cooker.

"Hey," I say, turning away from the pan. "When you cook the steak, don't press down on it with the spatula. It dries it out." I don't know if Pat's listening or not, because he doesn't look up. So I kick his chair with my foot. "Actually, you're not even cooking it. Not really. You just want to sear it so the middle stays pink. Dad hates well-done meat. If it's well done, he won't eat it."

Pat makes a face. "You made me fuck up my onion dice. And whatever. I don't ever cook the steak."

"Well, soon you will, unless you want to go on a taco fast while I'm at college." It's crazy to think about. This time next year I won't be living on Jar Island.

"Don't bum me out on taco night, please." And the thing is, Pat actually does sound sad. My eyes fill fast with tears. Pat sees it. "Don't," he warns.

"I'm not," I say, and wipe my eyes. But of course more fall.

"Don't!"

"I'm not!" I scream. "It's the damn onions, dick!"

Pat laughs under his breath. "Yeah, okay. Look. I'll change the subject. Eddie Shofull stopped by the other night and told me some story about how you and Lillia called in a missing-persons thing and made him break into a house."

I busy myself with the steak. "What was he doing here in the first place?"

Pat gives me the eye. "What do you think?"

I shake my head. "That little pot-smoking pig! You know, he threatened to put me and Lil in jail for insulting an officer."

"Dummy. But wait. What was going on?"

I sigh and turn down the heat. I don't even know where to begin. "You remember that girl I brought to Ricky's basement on Halloween night?"

"The one who helped herself to one of my beers and then didn't drink a damn sip?"

"Oh, shut up. I gave you money for both of us. Anyway, yes. That girl. She . . . she basically disappeared."

Pat shrugs. "Not surprised. She was weird."

"She wasn't weird." But even as I say it, I know I'm lying. Mary was weird. I love the girl to death, but she wasn't exactly normal.

"She was too. Okay, not 'weird' as in 'freaky.' But . . . she seemed like she'd never been to a party before."

"She probably hadn't. She's very sheltered."

I pull two pieces of steak out of the pan and put them in Shep's food bowl. He loves steak. But he barely sniffs them. He doesn't have much of an appetite these days, poor old dog.

Pat says, "You say 'sheltered.' I say 'freaky.'"

I'm about to slap him upside the head, when my cell phone rings. The name on the screen surprises the shit out of me.

Lind.

JENNY HAN & SIOBHAN VIVIAN

I haven't talked to the boy since Rennie's New Year's Eve party. I hope he doesn't want to ask me anything about the shit Rennie was screaming at him about Reeve and Lillia. If Alex wants that scoop, he ain't getting it from me.

But I pick up anyway. I'll always pick up the phone for Alex. Tentatively I say, "Hello?"

"Kat! Dude! I got in! Well, not exactly in, exactly, but I'm close. I mean, they didn't reject me!"

I hold the phone a few inches away from my ear. "Fool, what are you talking about?"

"USC! I applied to their songwriting program, and they e-mailed and asked me to send in a demo! They call it a remote audition."

"Wait. For real? You sent in an application after all?" The last I'd heard, Alex had been too chickenshit to apply to a music school. He was going to either Michigan, because of his dad's connections there, or maybe Boston College.

"What can I say, Kat? You're pretty persuasive. So will you help me figure out which songs I should send them? Which ones are good, which ones suck? I want your honest opinions."

It's a tempting proposition. I've always wanted to hear Alex's music. I mean, there were those few songs or poems or whatever in that notebook we stole from his car back in September, but I bet there's more. I could just say yes right now, but I want to draw this out. I'm not above fishing for a compliment or two. I've been so down in the dumps lately.

"Why would you care what I think?"

"Because you know music. You've seen so many bands play. You know what's good and what's not. There's no way this is happening for me unless I have your help."

"All right, sure. I'll try."

"Awesome. Oh, wait up. I'm a self-absorbed dick. Have you heard anything from Oberlin?"

I would tell Alex the truth, that I got pushed into the general pool, but I can't. Not with Pat here. He and my dad still think I'm already accepted. "Hey, Al, I got to go. I'll talk to you at school, okay?"

I end the call as Pat pushes that last perfectly cut red onion into a bowl. Then he holds up his hand. "Taco time?"

I slap it back. "You know it." And for a second I think, if I don't get into Oberlin, it will suck, but it won't be the worst thing in the world.

Later that night I'm in my bedroom, working my way through a box of old CDs that I haven't listened to in years. I'm pulling aside ones I think will be up Alex's alley, mostly stuff I was into freshman year.

Listening to this old music is like being in a time machine.

I remember each CD I bought from Kim at Paul's Boutique. I concentrate on finding songs I think he'd do well to emulate—kind of folksy guitar stuff but with an edge.

I'm leaning back, eyes closed, listening to a song, when there's a knock at my door. I say come in, expecting to see Pat, but it's not him. It's Lillia. And she looks upset.

"Lil. What happened? What's wrong?"

She starts pacing around my room, literally wringing her hands like a lady in a Victorian novel. "Paige just caught me and Reeve hugging. And she basically told me off."

"What?"

Lillia flops down onto my bed and curls into a ball. "I promise you, we've barely said two words to each other since Rennie died. We were both over there today by accident, and then, when Paige left the room, he told me that he got into a prep school for his postgrad year, so he can have another shot with college recruiters, and then the next second we're hugging each other."

I roll my eyes. "So what? You guys hugged. Big deal." Trust Lil to turn a piddly hug into some soap-opera drama.

"It wasn't just a hug, okay? It's never just a hug with us. Like on New Year's Eve, when we were in his truck." Lil shivers. "We get near each other and we lose our heads."

I lean forward in my chair. Now she's getting to the good stuff. "Did you two have sex that night?"

"No! No, nothing like that. But it was probably the most intense make-out session of my life."

A wistfulness crosses her face for just a second, and then it disappears, and my heart drops. Damn. I'm happy that Lillia's gotten past what happened to her last summer with those college fucko rapists, enough to have a fun night letting loose with a guy. But it sucks that it happened with someone she can't actually be with.

"If Paige hadn't walked in . . . I'm scared of what could have happened." Lil closes her eyes and shakes her head. "I mean, we were in Rennie's kitchen! How could I do something like that?"

I hold up my hand. "Say no more. I know exactly what this is."

"What?"

"My sophomore year I was hooking up with this dude from the motocross circuit. I'd only ever see him on Pat's race days. He was a lot older than me. Like, I think he may have been twenty."

"Eww!"

"Don't *eww* me! He was hot. But he was also bad news. He definitely had a girlfriend. He might've even been married, I don't know. I knew that if my brother found out, he'd kill me. But, like, I still couldn't stop, you know? We'd run into each other near the bike trailers, and I'd tell myself not to look at him, and the next thing I'd know, we'd be up against a chain-link fence, going at it. It was like a gravitational pull."

Lillia nods her head vigorously. "That's exactly how it feels."

"You can't go near Reeve, Lillia. Especially not when it's just the two of you, alone. The force, it's too strong. You've got to shut it down."

"Shut it down," Lillia repeats. "Yes."

"Shut it the fuck down, because if you don't, it's only going to bring you trouble. Think about Mary, what she'd say if she knew."

"It would kill her." Lil shudders. "So you were able to stop seeing that guy?" she asks hopefully.

"Uh, well. I mean, yeah. After he moved to Italy to join this pro racing club." I wonder what ever happened to that guy. Fuzz? Fez? I can't remember. Lillia groans. "Lil, we only have, like, four months left of school. And then you're gone, baby, gone. You can do this."

"I *have* to do this," she corrects. Staring up at my ceiling, she says, "I just hate that Paige thinks badly of me now."

"Don't take it personally. Paige loves to stir up shit, you know that. She's a drama queen. That's where Rennie got it from. She's just pissed right now that Ren's gone, and she wants to take it out on somebody."

Lillia nods, but I can tell she's still bummed out. I get it. I'd probably be bummed out too.

She hangs around for a while longer. I fill her in on what's going on with Alex and play her a few of the songs that I'm putting on his mix. "Lindy must really trust you," she says, putting her jacket back on. "He doesn't play his songs for anyone else. I hope they're good enough for him to get in."

"Me too. He was so excited on the phone, like a kid on Christmas."

Before Lil leaves, she says, "I almost forgot—I have something for you." She unzips her purse and holds out a strip of black-and-white photos. They are of me and Rennie, as little girls, from the photo booth in the ice cream parlor. Rennie has her hair in two pigtails, and I've got mine long and straight, with bangs cut blunt across my forehead.

"Rennie's old nose," I say, laughing. "It wasn't even bad."

Lillia looks over my shoulder. "I told her that a hundred times, but she'd never listen."

In the first shot we're both smiling at the camera. In the second we're smiling at each other. In the third we're both back to looking at the camera, but this time Rennie's giving me bunny ears. The fourth one is blurry, because there are tears in my eyes.

Chapter Ten

MARY

I OPEN MY EYES, AND EVERYTHING SLOWLY COMES into focus. I'm lying on my bedroom floor, staring up at the wooden beam stretching across the ceiling. The one that I . . .

I push myself up onto my knees. How long has it been since I was sitting on top of the lighthouse? An hour? A day? A year?

I crawl on the floor over to the wall and sit with my back up against it.

This room was once full of my things. A closet packed with dresses and skirts, sweaters and shoes. A bookshelf lined with paperbacks. I had school notebooks and pencils and homework.

A quilt on my bed. Pretty trinkets I arranged on my dresser just so when I moved back to Jar Island.

It looked like the bedroom of any teenage girl.

Except now I see the truth. The empty closet. The bare bookshelf. A stripped mattress without pillows or sheets.

I used to think that this was the room I lived in. But it's not. It's the room I died in.

It kills me all over again, thinking back to how knowing the truth weighed on Aunt Bette. I basically drove her crazy. Her dead niece, haunting her house. Except I didn't know that was what I was doing. I really, truly believed that I lived through my suicide attempt. I thought I was alive.

I look down at myself, at the clothes I'm wearing. I'm the Mary I should be, seventeen, in a navy-blue sweater and a pair of jeans. Thin. But how? How did I fill this room up, my life up, with things that don't actually exist?

I close my eyes, concentrate hard, and try to put my things back in my room the way they were before New Year's Eve. The quilt, the clothes in my closet, my pink terry-cloth robe. I envision everything in my mind. I need something back. One little thing. A stuffed animal. One of my old books. I can't exist like this.

When I open my eyes, the room is still empty and dark.

And I swear I feel my heart break.

I get up and walk out of my room, down the hall, and linger in the doorway of Aunt Bette's room. It's total chaos from when my mom came and took her away. The floor is covered with her collection of those old occult books.

I remember the fight we had, after I found out she was doing those weird spells on me. Burning those herb bundles in teacups, making string webs on our shared wall, trying to trap me in my room. She was afraid of me, of what I might do. She knew I was the one who'd caused that fire at homecoming, even though I didn't.

I take a step inside, then a second, then a third. I hold my hand over a red cloth book teetering at the top of the stack closest to me, and wiggle my fingers. It flips opens to a random page. I used to think I had special powers, that I could move things with my mind. I was kind of right about that, I guess.

Some spirits are prone to unrest. Often they stay close to this world to resolve things they left unfinished.

Yes. Yes! That's it. Exactly.
I flip to another page.

Under no circumstances should one ever inform a spirit that they are, in fact, deceased. It is better for them to

remain ignorant of their plight and ignorant regarding
the extent of their capabilities, which they will almost
certainly use maliciously.

I stare down at the word "maliciously." It scares me. What I could be capable of. But these books are my only hope. And that's so much better than feeling hopeless.

Chapter Eleven

LILLIA

ASH MEETS ME BY MY LOCKER AFTER SCHOOL AND says, "Derek and PJ were talking about going to the basketball game tonight."

"We're playing off island, right?" Ash nods. I don't like basketball, and I don't think our team is very good, but the idea of getting away from Jar Island for the night sounds like a plan to me. There's just one thing keeping me from saying yes. "What are the other guys doing?"

"Alex has some school project thing he's working on. And Reeve's doing something with his brothers. So it'll just be us four, and we can fit into one car that way. I'll pick you up at six."

"Okay. Great."

Ash is late, as always. I'm outside on the curb waiting for her. Just for fun I put on a Jar Island varsity sweatshirt and tied my hair up in one of my cheerleader ribbons. When she arrives, almost twenty minutes late, I climb into the front seat. We pick up Derek next, and then PJ.

I expect Ash is going to head straight to the ferry, since the next one leaves in a few minutes, but instead she makes a left and speeds toward T-Town.

"Derek," Ash says, rolling through a stop sign. "Text Reeve and tell him to be outside in five minutes. If he's not there, we're leaving without him."

I lean forward. "What? I thought you said he wasn't coming." If I'd known Reeve was coming, there's no way I would have said yes.

"I guess he changed his mind," Ash says with a shrug.

I pray that Reeve isn't outside, that we will leave without him, but he's sitting on his front stairs as we pull up. I flip down the visor and touch up my lipstick so I don't have to make eye contact with him.

As soon as we get to the other high school's gym, I say that I have to go to the bathroom just so I can make sure that we don't end up sitting next to each other on the bleachers. On my way back I see two girls standing with Reeve at the bottom of the stands. I can tell he's not interested in talking to them, because he keeps looking over their shoulders. But I still feel a pang of jealousy as I walk by, until I hear one of them mention the Montessori school.

Oh God. What if it somehow gets back to Mary that I'm here with Reeve?

I push the thought away. I don't even know where Mary is. And I don't think she keeps in touch with any of the Montessori kids from back in the day. I climb the bleachers, take a seat between PJ and Derek, and keep really focused on the basketball game, even though it's insanely boring.

After the game everybody starts piling into Ash's car, and I immediately go for the front seat again, but Derek shakes his head at me. "No way, Lil. You're the smallest one here. You don't get shotgun again."

"Derek!" I protest. He *is* tall, though—like, basketball-player tall. Ash has to get on her tippy-toes to kiss him. "Come on. Be a gentleman!"

"Backseat, baby," he says, pulling the seat forward so I can climb in. Reeve and PJ are crammed into the back, and there's barely room for the two of them, much less me.

My eyes meet Reeve's. "But . . . there's no room."

Reeve tips his head back against the seat. Looking straight ahead, he says, "Cho, just get in. We're going to miss the ferry home."

"You can sit in Reeve's lap," Ash advises me. "Or stretch out on top."

This is basically the opposite of what Kat told me to do. Reluctantly I climb in between the boys. I perch as lightly as I can, half on Reeve's thigh and half on PJ's. PJ doesn't move—he's looking at his phone—but Reeve shifts as far away from me as he can and holds on to the handle above the window. "You can scoot back a little," he says, his voice gruff.

"I'm fine," I say. To Ashlin I say, "Let's go."

Ash starts the car, and we zoom out of the high school's parking lot. Ash is always speeding. She's gotten, like, a million speeding tickets in just the one year she's been driving. The car is quiet except for Ash and Derek talking to each other in low voices. Suddenly the light turns red, Ash slams on the brakes, and I start to fly forward, but Reeve grabs me by the waist with both arms.

"Ugh, why do they have a stoplight on this road anyway?" Ash complains.

My heart's pounding in my chest. Even though he doesn't have to, Reeve's still holding on to me tight, and just for a second I feel him sigh and fall his forehead against my back, but then, abruptly, his arms drop away from me. I think I can hear his heart beating fast too.

After the ferry ride back to Jar Island, Ashlin drops me off first. My mom's light is off, and Nadia's in her room doing her homework. I stop in to say good night, and we talk for a few minutes. I don't even know what we're talking about, because all I'm doing is thinking about him. And then Kat's voice is in my head, telling me to *shut it the eff down. This will only lead to trouble.* She's right. I know she is.

I go through my nighttime routine of a bath, drying my hair just a little bit and then brushing it. I put on my big Harvard sweatshirt and thick socks and get into bed, and then I just lie there in the dark for what feels like forever.

And before I can talk myself out of it, before I can go through all the reasons why not, I'm crawling out of bed. I'm fumbling around for my leggings and my bra and my big puffy coat. I'm stuffing my keys and my phone inside the pocket, and then I'm creeping out into the hallway. It's dark; everyone's asleep. I crack open Nadia's door just to make sure, and she is.

Then I'm tiptoeing down the stairs, creeping out the back door, and running fast to my car. I don't turn on the headlights until I'm out of the cul-de-sac. I don't know what I'm doing. He might not even be awake. This is crazy.

As I drive, I keep thinking I should turn back around. I keep thinking it, and yet I don't do it.

All the lights are off at Reeve's house except for in his room. I pull out my phone and text him, my hands shaking.

Are you awake?

He writes back instantly. *Yeah.*

I'm outside.

Reeve's face appears in the window, and then it's gone. I get out of the car and wait for him, shivering. I don't have to wait long. He's out the front door and running toward me in sweats, no coat.

"What's wrong?" he pants. "Did something happen?"

I shake my head.

His brow furrows. "Then why—why are you here?"

"I don't know." I lift my shoulders and drop them. "I guess . . . I just wanted to see you." Reeve is staring at me with a bewildered look on his face, and I feel my cheeks get hot. I turn away from him and back toward my car. "I shouldn't have come."

Reeve grabs my arm. "Wait," he says, and I spin back around, and before I can tell myself not to, I pull his face toward mine and I'm kissing him. He hesitates for a split second, and then he's kissing me back, and I feel a jolt inside me. I lean back against the car, and I pull him with me. I can see the puffs our breaths make in the cold night air.

"I miss you," I whisper between kisses. Then I look up at him, and my pulse quickens as I wait for him to answer.

A cocky smile spreads across his face. "Course you do. You can't get enough of me."

I stiffen. I come over here in the middle of the night against my better judgment, and he's joking around like it's nothing? Is everything a joke to him? I stand up straight and try to push him away, but he doesn't let me. His voice gets serious as he says, "I miss you, too. You know I do. I . . . I just don't know how to act. Everything's so fucked up."

I sigh. "I wish . . ." I stop, and Reeve pushes my hair out of my eyes.

"Your hair's wet."

"I just had a bath," I say, and he nods.

"What were you going to say?" he asks me. "What do you wish?"

"I wish it didn't have to be like this. It's so . . . complicated." More than Reeve even knows. "We haven't talked about Rennie once."

He looks down at the ground. "I don't want to talk about Rennie right now."

I'm about to say, *If not now, then when?* It's already been two weeks since she died, and I think maybe we'd both feel better if we talked about her. But Reeve leans in close to me and nuzzles his face against mine. "Why is your skin so soft?" His breath tickles my cheek.

I laugh, for what feels like the first time in forever. "I don't know, because I'm a girl? All girls are soft."

He kisses my cheek. "No, you're different. You have the softest skin of any girl I've ever known. And you always smell really good." He's kissing his way down my neck. "What is that smell?"

"Bluebells." I'm shivering, and it's not because of the cold. His hands are at my hips, under my coat. I have to lean against the car to keep my balance. "Bluebells and . . . burnt sugar." It's so hard to think.

"Yeah, that's it. Sugar. My grandma used to have a thing of brown-sugar bath salts in her bathroom. . . . One time I dumped the whole bottle into the toilet because I wanted to see if it would fizz." Reeve kisses me, his mouth open against mine, and I have that feeling I get when I step into the bath, warm all over. I let out a sigh. Softly he asks me, "Do you want to come inside for a minute?"

I whisper back, "What, are you going to sneak me up to your room?"

He grins. "Yeah. Why not?"

I put my hands on his shoulders and tilt my head up at him.

"Sorry to break it to you, but I'm not your girl Melanie Renfro. I don't do that." For the first time in my life, I wish I was that kind of girl.

"I know you're not like Mel," he says, and I feel a slight twinge of jealousy. It sounds so affectionate. So intimate. *Mel.* Then he says, "You're not like any other girl I've ever met."

I can feel myself flush. Shyly I say, "I don't want your parents to see me."

Reeve kisses me again, with the confidence of a boy who knows exactly what he's doing. His hands move under my sweatshirt, and I don't even care that they're cold. I just want him to keep on touching me. When he's touching me, everything else fades mercifully away, and I'm not thinking about what I did to Rennie, what I did to Mary. It feels good to forget, even if it's just for a moment.

When I shiver, he stops abruptly and says, "You should go. It's cold out here and your hair's wet."

"Okay." I start to stand up straight.

"Wait . . . five more minutes."

"Five more minutes," I agree, pulling him toward me again.

The next morning everybody's eating doughnuts by the vending machines, and I sneeze three times in a row. Reeve's eyes meet mine and he smiles a secret smile, but I don't smile back.

I force myself to turn away, like I didn't see. Because I shouldn't have gone to Reeve's house; I shouldn't have kissed him. I won't make that mistake again.

Chapter Twelve

MARY

I'm asleep more than I'm awake now, if you can even call it sleeping. It's not restful, and I don't have dreams. It's just darkness.

When I'm awake and alert, I put everything I have into reading Aunt Bette's books, hoping they'll tell me something. Tonight I got about halfway through a book about how ghosts interact with the living world.

I don't have enough energy to finish it. But I need to understand how I've been tricking myself. I use what little energy I can muster, and then I close my eyes and focus.

When I open my eyes, it's morning. I'm no longer at home. I'm standing in front of Jar Island High School, in the fountain. It must still be winter, because the water is shut off.

A bell rings in the distance. I walk to one of the heavy steel doors. Once the school day starts, the janitors lock them so outsiders can't get in. It's a security measure. Through the window I watch a few last stragglers sprint down the hallway to their classrooms.

If I were a real girl, a living girl, I'd have to go to the main office and sign in at the front desk. But I'm not. I pass through the door like it's nothing. Like it's air. And I'm on the other side.

I've probably been doing that all along. Only I didn't let myself notice. I think back on the days I spent here this school year, going to classes I thought I was enrolled in, doing homework I thought was assigned to me. Even dreaming of where I'd apply for college next year.

Except I'm not a student here. I never was.

The clock says 10:35. If this were a normal day, I'd be in Spanish class with Señor Tremont, so that's where I go.

Señor Tremont's door is wedged open, so I walk right in. He's sitting on top of his desk. The fluorescent classroom lights are off, and he has a video going on the TV. It's a Spanish soap opera called *El Corazón Late Siempre*. It means "The Heart Always Beats." Señor Tremont normally has us watch an episode on Fridays.

Okay. It's Friday. And it's winter. But January? February?

I have no idea.

I glance out at the room, at the desk where I used to sit. It's an empty desk in the back, one that was probably never assigned to anyone. I just sat there. I pretended it was mine. Just like I pretended I was alive.

That's why whenever I raised my hand, Señor Tremont never once called on me.

That's why I never got a report card sent home, or a test handed back, or my name up on the bulletin board.

No one could see me.

I feel so completely stupid.

A fiery anger begins to simmer inside me. I used to hate feeling angry. I used to fear it. Except now . . . it feels good. It feels like *something*.

I take a couple of steps so I'm standing in front of the television, blocking everyone's view. But not everyone is watching the show. A few girls are whispering behind a notebook. Alex Lind has his forehead down on the desk, but I know he's not asleep, because his left leg is bouncing up and down. Another kid is drawing black circles over and over again on the sole of his sneaker.

I open my mouth and scream. Scream as loud as I can.

And no one hears me.

Ashes to Ashes

Shaking, I press down on the channel buttons. I can actually feel them underneath my fingertips.

The channels start changing, and everyone in class snaps to attention.

"*Ay, diosmío,*" Señor Tremont says. He stands up and comes over to the television with the remote. I move my hand to the power button and click the television off and on. "This . . . I don't understand."

I'm laughing now; I can't help it. Señor Tremont looks so confused, and the rest of the kids do too.

And then, with every last bit of strength I've got left, I push my body into the television cart and knock the entire thing over. The screen bursts into a million pieces on the floor. And the crazy thing is that doing it doesn't make me feel tired. It's the opposite. It has filled me back up with energy.

Just then the bell rings. I walk out into the hallway like everyone else.

"Mary?"

Her voice comes from far behind me, from the other end of the hallway.

Kat.

"Yo! Mary!"

I take off, keeping my back to her, and then step through the door of the janitor's closet and wait to hear if she calls my name again.

She doesn't.

Lillia and Kat have always been able to see me. They believed I was real, that I was seventeen. They were able to see the things I'd imagined too. But why?

A minute or two later I sneak back out of the classroom. I see Lillia and Kat talking at the end of the hallway. Lillia's holding a folder, maroon and embossed with gold foil letters. Boston College. I wonder if she's been accepted. Lillia will be gone in a few months. Kat, too. Then I won't have to hide from them. That's a relief. But it also breaks my heart.

When they leave, there won't be anyone left who can see me.

Then I'll truly be gone. Gone for good.

Chapter Thirteen

LILLIA

AFTER SCHOOL ASH AND I RIDE IN HER CAR OVER TO her house to work on our English project. It's sort of the worst, being partnered with Ash, because she's lazy, but I know she'd be hurt if I partnered up with someone else. We're in her room, supposedly doing research, but whenever I glance over at her computer screen, she's looking at gossip blogs.

I'm cutting and pasting an article to read later, when my phone buzzes. It's Reeve. *Can I see you tonight?*

Oh no. No, no, no. This is exactly what I was afraid of, and it's my fault. I was weak.

I have to be strong now.

I can't. I'm studying over at Ashlin's.

:(

His little sad face makes me want to smile, but I don't let myself go there.

A few minutes later Ashlin's phone buzzes from across the room. She picks it up and squeals. "Derek and the guys want to come over and hang out," she says. "Our sauna's not working, but we could take a hot tub break!"

I bite my lip. Reeve. I could kill him.

"Ash, we can't. This is due on Monday. If the guys come over, you know it's not going to be a short break. It's going to be all night." And then I pick up my phone and text Reeve.

Not cool.

Ash nods. "You're right, I know you're right. I'm just having a hard time concentrating." Plaintively she says, "Are things ever going to feel normal again?"

"I don't know." And then, because that sounds so depressing, I add, "I hope."

Ash picks up her phone to text Derek, and I feel bad. I haven't been a good friend to her lately. So I close my laptop and say, "Ash, it's fine. The guys can stop by. We're almost done anyway."

Ash's face lights up. "Yay!" She jumps up and starts rifling through her bikini drawer. She gasps suddenly and lifts one up for me to look at—it's Rennie's. "Ren left this the last time she was over here."

I remember when she bought it, last summer at the bikini store near Java Jones. It's tiny and black, and she loved it because it made her boobs look bigger. "I—I'll just wear one of yours."

"But mine won't fit you," Ash says, dropping the bikini back into her drawer.

"Then I'll just dip my feet into the tub." I'm not wearing Rennie's bikini. It's too eerie.

"Wait!" Ash digs into her drawer again. She holds up a skimpy navy-and-green tie-dyed one with the tags still on. "The top was way too small for me, but I never got around to returning it. It'll fit you perfectly."

Relieved, I quickly undress and put on her bikini. Ash comes around and ties the tie around my back tighter. "It looks great on you," she says. "You can keep it."

"Thanks, Ash." Ash and I have never been super close. There was always Rennie in between us. She always had to be most loved. And we did love her most. We both knew we'd pick Ren over each other. But Ash is a nice person, and I feel lucky to have her.

After we're both changed, we put on Uggs and bathrobes and go outside to turn on the hot tub. Ash goes back in to get a bottle of wine from her parents' cellar, and I'm testing how hot the water is when Alex walks up.

"How's the water?" he asks me, peeling off his peacoat. He pulls his sweater over his head, and I go over and turn on the jets.

"Pretty hot," I say.

Alex throws his clothes onto a lounge chair. He looks around to make sure we're alone, and then says, "Hey, can I talk to you about something?"

"Sure."

He slides into the water. "There's something I've been wanting to say to you for a while, but I didn't want to bring it up at the wrong time."

It's suddenly very hard to swallow.

I look around for Ash, but she hasn't come back yet, and there's no sign of Reeve and Derek yet. So I slip off her bathrobe and quickly step inside the hot tub. The hot water pricks my skin. I put my hair up into a high bun so it won't get wet. "Umm. Okay."

"I know you and Rennie had a fight the night she died." I go still in the water. "I just want to say that you shouldn't let that be the thing that defines your friendship. I mean, friends fight. It happens. Look at me and Reeve. Things have been weird with us ever since . . . ever since Christmas." Alex colors, and I can feel myself blush too. "But I know we'll hash it out at some point. The same way I know that if Ren hadn't had that accident, you guys would have too."

No, we wouldn't have. Rennie would never have forgiven me for taking Reeve away from her, not in a million years. Alex doesn't know her like I do. I mean he *didn't*, he didn't know her like I did. But it's nice of him to say, and it's so Lindy of him to say it. I offer him a smile and say, "Maybe."

He can tell I don't mean it. He says, "Listen to what I'm telling you, Lil. Rennie loved you. And you loved her. It would have worked out. When people love each other as much as you did, the love doesn't just go away. No matter what."

Tears spring to my eyes. Alex sounds so sure, it gives me hope, even when I have no right to hope for anything. If I'd had the chance to explain, to try to make Ren understand, could we have gotten past it? We were best friends. More than best friends. We were like sisters. That has to count for something.

"Alex . . . thank you for saying that." I really, truly mean it. He reaches over and gives my hand a squeeze, and the tightness inside me feels a little bit loosened.

We're still talking when Reeve arrives. I don't look at him, but I can feel his eyes on me. He strips down and lowers himself into the water and sits at the corner opposite Alex and me. "What are you guys talking about?" he asks.

"Nothing," I say, staring down at the foamy water. It gurgles and bubbles like soup that's about to boil over.

"New bikini?" he asks me.

I give him a funny look. "It's Ash's. She gave it to me."

"I like it."

What is he doing? Especially in front of Alex, of all people. Alex is watching Reeve with narrowed eyes now.

Ash and Derek come out of the house with the wine and beach towels. When they climb into the hot tub, Alex scoots closer to me to make room, and our shoulders touch. Alex bumps my shoulder again, this time on purpose, and he smiles at me, and I smile back. A true smile.

"Do you have any beer, Ash?" Reeve asks suddenly.

"Yeah, there should be some in the fridge," Ash says, stretching out her arms. "Just make sure you replace them with the beers in the pantry, or my dad will notice."

"Get me a beer too," Derek says.

Reeve gets up. "Cho, come help me."

I don't look at him as I say, "I'm not getting out of the water. It's too cold."

Reeve frowns at me, which I pretend not to see. Then he steps out of the hot tub and stalks off to the house. He can be mad all he wants, but if he thinks I'm going to sneak away with him with our friends right outside, he's crazy.

To Alex I say, "Your skin's getting red."

Alex groans. "The plight of the fair-skinned Irish. That's why I have to marry you, Lil, so I can stop this vicious cycle. Our kids would be so good-looking."

Uncomfortably, I giggle. "As long as they get my fashion sense," I say, stretching out my legs so my toes float above the water. "And my dance skills. You have no rhythm whatsoever, Lindy."

Later, when we're all out of the hot tub and it's time to go home, Alex offers to drive me to school for my car. Reeve's putting his sweater back on, but I know he's listening to every word. I say, "No, that's okay. Ash and I have more work to get done tonight."

Alex looks disappointed, but he leaves, and so do Reeve and Derek. Reeve doesn't even look at me when he goes.

Upstairs in Ash's room, I go over to her bed to open up my computer, and I look out her window. Reeve's truck is still here. He's waiting for me. Reeve needs to understand that he and I aren't happening, not ever.

Quickly I look down at my phone and say, "Uh-oh, my mom's texting me. She wants me home."

Ashlin looks up from her computer. She's in the process of buying a new cashmere sweater. "Just give me two secs, and I'll drive you back to your car."

"No, that's okay. The guys haven't left yet. I'll get one of them to take me." I grab my bag and my computer and give Ash a hug, and then I'm running down the stairs and out the front door.

I climb into Reeve's truck, and for a moment we're both silent. He has a scowl on his face. "What's the matter with you tonight?" I ask.

He fumes. "I wanted to see you, I wanted to have fun, and I walk in on you and Alex cozy in the hot tub, and you won't even tell me what you were talking about." He makes an annoyed face, which gets me so mad.

"We were talking about Rennie!" I burst out. "And, Reeve, you never want to talk about her!"

Reeve turns white. "What good does it do to bring up the past? She's dead. Talking about it isn't going to bring her back. This thing between you and me is separate from that."

"No, it isn't. We're the reason Rennie died, and it's eating me up inside. She never would have been driving around that night if it weren't for us. She'd have been at her party, where she belonged—"

"Stop!" Reeve shouts. I jump. He's breathing hard. "I don't want to do this right now, okay? I can't. So just—stop. Don't say anything else. Please."

"Okay." He's shaking. I smooth my hand over his back until his breathing slows down. "It's okay."

Before I can say another word, he's got me pushed up against the window and he's kissing me. And I'm kissing him back.

When we get to the school parking lot an hour later, I pull down the visor mirror and try to fix my hair. It's a mess.

Watching me, he says, "You're the only thing that's keeping me going."

My hand stills.

"I can't not see you," he says.

I don't look at him, I can't. "If we're going to do this, no one can know. It can't be like what happened tonight. We need to be careful."

Quickly he says, "Okay. I'll do whatever you want. However you want to do it. I feel like I can't breathe when I'm not with you, Cho."

And then I'm in his arms, and we're kissing again. Just like before.

Chapter Fourteen

KAT

AT THE END OF THE DAY, ALEX WAITS FOR ME AT MY locker, and then we head to his car. He's talking about who-the-hell-knows-what. I'm not listening. Instead I'm taking mental note of the people watching us together. I think back to how worried I was back in September, on the first day of school. It's funny, the stuff I used to think was a big deal. Now I realize that none of it fucking matters.

"Have you heard a single word I've said?"

I turn to face Alex. He's got his navy wool beanie hat pulled down super low over his ears, but a lot of hair still comes curling out the sides. It's turning dark again, now that's it's full-on wintertime, with just a few flecks of rusty red.

"Honestly, no, because you've been talking nonstop since the bell rang."

He laughs, like I've said something hilarious, and then chugs the last of his water bottle. It crinkles in his grip. "I'm nervous, Kat." I think for a second he's joking. But there's something about his voice that makes me know it's true. It's low and kind of deep-sounding. That and he doesn't look at me when he says it. Instead he keeps his eyes focused straight ahead.

"Nervous? About what?"

"That you'll hate everything I play."

"Oh, shut up," I say, even though I'm a little worried about that too. What if Alex's music really does suck? I mean, he rocked his "Baby, It's Cold Outside" solo during the Christmas tree lighting. But I've never heard his original stuff before. And that's the kind of program he's applying for at USC—songwriting. I've already come up with a few stock compliments in case shit is really rough, but he'll probably see right through them. I don't have the best poker face. If his songs blow, should I still encourage him to do this? Or would it be better to tell him the hard truth, that I don't think he's good enough, like the judges on those stupid reality show music competitions do?

Ugh. I never should have agreed to this in the first place.

"Well, we could always do it another day. Or . . . like . . . never."

"I want to do it," Alex says. "We're doing it."

"All right."

We get into the car, and Alex turns the key and starts it up. His stereo kicks on loudly to the CD I burned for him.

"I like everything you put on here," he says, turning it down. "But I don't sound anything like these guys."

Uh-oh. I give his arm a friendly squeeze. "You don't have to. You just need to sound like . . . you." Whatever that means.

An hour later I'm sitting on the edge of Alex's bed, sipping soda from a cold can. He's on a wooden stool across the room. He has his head down, strumming his guitar. He doesn't even look at the notebook he has propped open on a music stand. He knows the words by heart.

This is the third song he's played for me. And they've all been about the same thing—actually, the same person.

Lillia.

Which, yeah, I've known that he has a thing for her. But damn. The kid's in love. From the sound of it, he's been in love for a long time. Maybe forever.

He lets the last note vibrate out to quiet. And then Alex sets his guitar down and wipes his brow. "Those are the three I'm thinking I'll submit." He picks up a pencil to take notes. "Okay. So. First thoughts."

I tell myself to keep my mouth shut, about a thousand times, rapid-fire in my head. *Don't be an asshole, Kat. Just focus on the music.* I lean back and try to say it as casually as I can. "Do you have any other songs? Or do they all sound like those?"

His face wrinkles up. "What do you mean?"

"Nothing. Forget it."

"You don't think I can take it? I can take it. Tell me. What do my songs all sound like?"

I start talking fast. "Fine. I'm only being critical like this because this is an application process, and the people who are going to listen—"

"Just say it!"

"They all sound like junior high love songs about Lillia Cho, dude."

Alex's mouth drops open, and his whole face turns bright-ass red. "What?"

I start ticking points off on my fingers. "The first one was about a black-haired girl who comes to your window at night. The next, a dark-haired girl who doesn't know you exist."

"Now, wait a second, Kat. I—"

I don't wait a second. I keep going. "And what was that last one? A rich girl who holds your hand on the gritty streets of Boston? I'm sorry but . . . seriously?"

He stands up fast, so fast that the stool tips backward onto the floor. Alex's eyes are stormy, and he has them lasered on me. "I know you don't like Lillia for whatever happened between you guys in the past, but I'd appreciate it if you could try to be objective and keep your comments about the song and not the person."

The hell? "Excuse me, Alex, but Lillia and I are actually cool with each other. This isn't about her. It's about you showing some range. I'm trying to help you, remember?"

"I have other songs." He picks up his notebook and holds it out. "I have a whole notebook full."

I shrug. "Great. Can't wait to hear one."

Alex flips through a few pages and then frowns.

"Ha!" I give my knee a slap. "I knew it!"

"It's not that." He lets out a deep sigh as he turns around and rights the fallen stool. "Shit," he says under his breath, and plops down onto it. "It's pretty much exactly that."

I see his confidence wavering, and it makes me feel like a dick. I shouldn't have called his music "junior high." That was messed up. "Look. It's not that your songs aren't good. They are. They're sincere and, um, heartfelt. Which is Alex Lind to a T! But thematically speaking, they do sound the same."

"Forget it, Kat. Don't blow smoke up my ass." Alex flops into the chair. "And if you and Lillia really are friends, then you must know if something's going on with her and Reeve."

I force a swallow. "What do you wanna know?"

"They left the New Year's Eve party together." He won't look at me when he adds, "Plus, Lil told me they did kiss before. I mean, she said she regretted it, but—"

"She *does* regret it," I correct.

"I get this weird vibe from them lately. I don't know."

Lillia definitely doesn't want anyone to think she's dating Reeve, because she's not. A couple of random grief hookups do not a relationship make. But I can't tell him they *aren't* together either. Not after my conversation with Lillia. "Are you pissed?"

"I mean, yeah, I'm not happy with Reeve. He's my best friend. Was my best friend. Shit. I don't even know."

Oh Lord. I don't want to have a Lillia therapy session with Alex right now. I try to keep him focused on the task at hand. I tap the letter from USC and say, "Here's what you need to do. Pick your favorite one of those last three songs, and then round out your demo with two others that sound different."

"Actually, there is something new I've been working on." He picks his guitar back up, opens his notebook, and flips to one of the last pages. "It's rough, but it's starting to come together. . . ."

The first three songs were super-quiet and whispery, but this one explodes from the first note and fills the whole room with sound. Alex's hands are flying over the strings of his guitar, and it's like everything is vibrating.

From what I can gather, it's a song about crashing and burning and living like there's no tomorrow. It's about Rennie.

And . . . it's awesome. Truly freaking awesome.

When he finishes, I give him a standing ovation. "That's what I'm talking about, dude!"

"You liked it?" He blushes. "I actually wrote it the night I heard from USC. After what happened to Rennie . . . It's like, life's too short. I don't want to have any regrets, you know?"

I nod. "Good for you. I bet Ren would be happy to hear that."

"Thanks. I'm glad you and Rennie had a chance to make up before the accident. You two went way back, and yeah, you had your issues with each other, but it's good that everything was forgiven."

"Yeah. True dat," I manage to say, even though the back of my throat is suddenly itchy. For weeks that's all I've wanted to hear from somebody. "Seriously, Lind. The song killed."

Now Alex is the one who's not listening to me. He's off in his own world. "I think I'll call it 'No Regrets.'"

"'No Regrets.' I like the sound of that."

"You know what? Me too."

Chapter Fifteen

LILLIA

REEVE AND I FIND TIME TO SEE EACH OTHER WHENEVER we can, always in secret. I've gone to his dad's office and helped him reorganize their filing system; he's come to the barn and watched me ride Phantom. Phantom likes him because he always brings apples. I told Reeve to stop, that it would spoil him, but Reeve sneaks them when he thinks I'm not looking. One night we just play cards in the back of his truck and listen to the radio.

We never talk about Rennie. Sometimes we don't even kiss. But what Reeve said about needing to see me to breathe—I feel the same way. Like if I'm away from him too long, I'm underwater.

After one of my riding lessons, Reeve invites me to his house for dinner later that night. I get nervous for a second that he's told his family about us, but he says his mom just wants to thank me for helping him get into prep school.

So now I'm at Jean-Jacques Patisserie, staring down at all the cakes and tarts in the glass display case. There are so many beautiful cakes to choose from. A mille-feuille, which is sort of a crepe cake with layers of pastry cream; a chocolate-raspberry bombe; a tall white chocolate cake with real gold sprinkled on top like it's a Christmas ornament. I'm thinking the white chocolate cake because it's got the wow factor, but then I remember how I made a mess of things the last time I went over to Reeve's to meet his family. How I wore my fancy blue dress and I bought that huge poinsettia arrangement, and Rennie opened the door in a football jersey, and she looked like she belonged and I looked so out of place.

I should have just gone to Milky Morning and gotten a cookie tray. It's too late for that now.

I stand there debating for so long that the saleslady comes over twice to ask if I need help. "Do you have anything more . . . rustic?" I ask. "Or, like, homey?"

The saleslady frowns. "Homey? Let's see, we have a beautiful strawberry tart with a pistachio brûlée."

"Umm . . ."

"Or how about a peanut butter–chocolate mousse cake?" she suggests.

Eagerly I nod. "Yes, yes!" Peanut butter is definitely homey.

She opens the display case and pulls out the cake with a flourish, and it looks like something my mom would describe as "truly decadent"—ganache was poured on top, and it has hardened into a shell, and there are chocolate shavings piled high like a modern sculpture. Chocolate-covered peanuts border the cake like a pearl necklace. This is the least homey cake I have ever seen.

I shout out, "Wait! I'm so sorry. Can you wait just one minute? I just need, like, two seconds to consult with my friend."

The saleslady looks annoyed, but she gives me a fake smile, and I fake smile back and turn around and whip my cell phone out to call Kat. She would know what I should bring to the Tabatskys.

She takes forever to answer. "What up, what up, Lil."

"Um, so, remember how I helped Reeve get a postgraduate year at a prep school?"

"No. I mean, you mentioned that it happened, but not that you helped him."

"Ugh. Well, I didn't really help him. I just gave him the idea." Kat's quiet, so I just keep going. "Anyway, his mom is so happy about it that she wants me to come over for dinner." Hastily I add, "Just as friends. So, like, if you were going over to his house for dinner, what would you bring for dessert? If it was between a peanut butter–chocolate mousse cake and a strawberry tart?"

"Lil."

My heart thumps. "Yes?"

"Did you or did you not shut that shit down like we discussed?"

The lie is right there on the tip of my tongue, *Yes, of course,* but I'm having a hard time saying it to Kat. "Well, basically. I mean—"

Kat groans. "*Girl!* What did I tell you?"

"Kat, please," I whimper. On the other side of the room, the saleslady clears her throat and looks at the clock. Crap. The bakery is going to close soon. "Please. You can yell at me later, but for now will you just help me? Which is less fancy, peanut butter–chocolate mousse cake or a strawberry tart?"

Sighing, she says, "Umm . . . shit, I don't know, Lillia. Reeve's family is all dudes. Just, like, get a few gallons of cheapo Neapolitan and throw it at them, and they'll lap it up like dogs."

"Do any of them have any nut allergies or dietary restrictions?"

"Are you kidding me? Those guys don't have freaking nut allergies. They're animals. They grew up eating dirt and blood and roadkill. If any one of them had a nut allergy, the other brothers would beat it out of him."

I stare at my phone in horror. Dirt and blood and roadkill? "You're scaring me," I whisper.

"Just buy the peanut-butter whatever and be done with it. And, Lil, after this dinner's over, you and me are gonna have a talk. Aight?"

"Aight."

I've never met a boy's family before, like as a girlfriend. Not that they know I'm his girlfriend. But still.

Before I can ring the bell, Reeve's already opening the door for me. He's wearing a navy-blue turtleneck sweater that I've never seen before, and his hair is combed nicely. He takes the cake out of my hands, sets it on the entryway table, and sweeps me into his arms for a bear hug. He lifts me up in the air for a second before he puts me down. "I'm so glad you're here," he says, smiling big.

I try to smile back, but I'm so nervous. I can hear the TV on, and men's voices shouting at it. Reeve picks up the cake box with one hand, and with the other hand he leads me into the kitchen, where his mom is taking dinner rolls out of the oven. I've met Mrs. Tabatsky before a bunch of times, at football games and when we've all hung out over here. And then at the hospital when Reeve got hurt.

She's wearing an apron, and when we walk in, she beams at

me. "Hello, Lillia. I'm so happy you could join us for dinner." She has a faint Boston accent.

"Thank you so much for inviting me, Mrs. Tabatsky," I say, talking too fast. "Is there, um, anything I can do to help?"

"No, honey. Just make yourself comfortable with the boys." To Reeve she says, "Reevie, take her coat."

Reeve sets the cake box on the counter and helps me out of my coat. "What's in the box?" he asks me.

"It's a cake," I say.

"That was so thoughtful of you," Mrs. Tabatsky says. "And it's from Jean-Jacques, no less! Ooh la la!"

Reeve rolls his eyes and puts his arms around his mom. "My mom's not used to the finer things. Don't worry, Mom. When I'm big-time, I'll buy you as many cakes from Jean-Jacques as you want."

Mrs. Tabatsky laughs. "Lillia, you're my witness. He said as many cakes as I want! So, what kind of cake is it, anyway?"

"It's a peanut butter–chocolate mousse," I say, and both their eyes light up. For the first time I notice that Reeve has his mom's eyes.

Reeve has three brothers. The oldest is Luke, who I've only met once or twice. Luke set a bunch of sports records at our school—he played football and baseball, and the newspaper called him Jar Island's Bo Jackson. He played football in college, but he got injured, so now he works with Reeve's dad at the landscaping company. Next is Pete, who moved off island pretty recently. Then Tommy, who I know the best, because he's only a couple of years older than us. Tommy used to get in trouble all the time at school. The stories about him are legendary. During gym, when Tommy was only fourteen, he used to take Coach's car out for joyrides. He did it for a month before he got caught.

Reeve's dad and his brothers Tommy and Luke are sitting in front of the TV, drinking beers and watching a hockey game. Of Reeve's three brothers, Luke looks the most like Reeve. They're both dark-haired, green-eyed, have the same proud nose. Tommy has lighter hair, and he's shorter but more muscular.

Fun fact: Tommy was both Rennie's *and* Kat's first kiss.

Reeve and I stand in the doorway for a few seconds before Reeve shoves Tommy's knee and says, "Make room for Lillia."

Tommy stuffs a handful of potato chips into his mouth and scoots over, and there are crumbs scattered over the couch cushion. I'm trying to decide if I should sit on them and pretend I don't see or if I should clean them up, when Tommy winks at me and sweeps the crumbs onto the carpet. Reeve glares at him. "I just vacuumed in here, you Neanderthal."

Tommy ignores him. He pats the cushion, and I sit down next to him. Reeve squeezes in on Tommy's other side. Tommy raises his eyebrow at me. "So are you and my little brother a thing, or what?"

I almost choke. "Nooo. We're just friends." I look over at Reeve, but he's looking straight ahead at the TV.

"Just friends, huh?" Tommy leans closer to me. "Nah, I don't think so. The kid is whipped over you. He spent hours cleaning up the living room before you got here."

Reeve is scowling. "Really?" I say.

From the La-Z-Boy Luke chimes in, "Oh yeah." He takes a swig of beer. "He had the Swiffer out and a duster and a fucking can of Pledge."

"Shut it, you guys," Reeve warns. He's getting red, which is so adorable, I can't even.

Tommy's just getting started. "You know how long it took Reevie to get his hair looking like that tonight?" Tommy pretends like he's looking in the mirror, primping and smoothing down his hair, which makes me giggle.

Reeve says, "Tommy, what are you even doing here? You moved out, remember?"

Tommy reaches over and messes with Reeve's hair, and Reeve shrugs him off. "Aw, is Baby Reevie getting embarrassed in front of his girl?"

"Yeah, I'm embarrassed that I'm related to you," Reeve retorts, his eyes focused on the TV screen. "And she just told you, she's not my girl."

"Then I guess she's fair game." Tommy winks at me. "What do you say, Lil?"

I know he's only teasing, but I can feel myself blush.

"Don't waste your breath, Tom," Reeve says. "Cho only talks to guys with IQs in the double digits."

"No wonder she ain't with you, then." Tommy reaches over and play-slaps Reeve upside the head, and Reeve launches himself at Tommy and they start wrestling around. I jump up so I don't get caught in the fray.

Mr. Tabatsky looks over at me from his armchair, unfazed. "You'd think they were raised in a back alley," he says. "How are your parents doing, Lillia?"

"They're great," I say.

"Tell your mom to let me know if she needs me to take down any of the trees before the next snowstorm," he says.

"I will," I say.

Breathing hard, Reeve collapses onto the sofa and pats the seat next to him, which Tommy has now vacated. Tommy grins at me from the floor. "Sit down, Cho," Reeve says.

I sit down next to him. "So where's your cat?" I ask him. "I want to pet it."

Reeve's brow furrows. "Cat? We don't have a cat. My mom's allergic."

Oh, Ren. Of course she lied about the cat! I smile to myself.

"What?" Reeve asks.

"Nothing," I say. It's crazy, but at moments like these I really miss her.

We sit down at the dining room table. Mr. Tabatsky is at the head, with Luke on his left and Mrs. Tabatsky on his right, and I'm down at the other end with Reeve and Tommy.

"Mom did her scalloped potatoes, which means she wants to impress you," Tommy tells me. "They're her specialty, so you better eat a lot."

"Hush, Tommy," Mrs. Tabatsky says, swatting at him. She slices pot roast and slides it onto my plate. "It's not every day Reevie brings a girl home."

I suck in my breath. So he never brought over Teresa or Melanie. I'm not like his other girls. I'm pressing my lips together and trying not to smile, when Reeve says, "I told you, Mom. It's not like that. Cho's just a friend from school."

I stare down at my plate. *Just a friend from school.*

"All right, all right, Reevie. Cool your jets," Mrs. Tabatsky says. "Lillia, we're so glad to have you over tonight. We've been wanting to thank you for everything you did to help Reeve when he was injured." She looks across the table at Reeve's dad, who is chewing his pot roast. "Mr. Tabatsky and I obviously don't know much about prep schools and fifth-year opportunities. We're so glad he had you to guide him."

Gruffly Mr. Tabatsky says, "When those college scouts scattered like cockroaches, I thought Reevie was done for. But now he's got a second chance to play ball again." Nodding to himself, he says, "I can't wait to slam our front door in their faces when they come calling after they see what Reeve'll do next season."

"We're not slamming the door in anybody's face," Reeve's mom chides. "But we're gonna make them work for it, that's for sure." She dimples. "My baby is a star."

"He ain't all that, Mom," Luke says. "Don't forget your firstborn." He points to his trophies lining the top shelf of Mrs. Tabatsky's china closet, and Tommy laughs so hard he almost spits out his milk.

Mrs. Tabatsky silences them with a glare and turns to me again. "It's all thanks to you, Lillia."

Guilt stabs my heart. It's all thanks to me that Reeve almost lost everything in the first place.

"Who wants more potatoes?" Mrs. Tabatsky asks.

Immediately I say, "I'd love some more," even though I'm not finished with my first helping yet. I'll eat every single bite on my plate and more if it means I'll stay on Mrs. Tabatsky's good side.

After dessert Reeve walks me outside. We're almost at my car when he says, "Let's go for a drive."

We get into his truck and drive to the woods.

I can tell something's wrong. I reach out and touch his hair in the back, where it's soft and curls against my hand. He likes it when I touch him here. But he doesn't melt against my hand the way he usually does. He stays rigid. "What are we doing, Cho?"

I go cold. "I don't know."

"This doesn't feel right. I don't like lying to my family. I want to introduce you as my girlfriend." Reeve goes quiet, and then he says, his voice halting, "I got into another prep school. . . . It's an all-boys school called Graydon. It's an hour outside Boston."

I sit up straight and turn to look at him. "Really?" Benedictine is all the way in Delaware.

He's watching me closely. "BC's still your top choice, right?"

"Yes. I think so."

"So . . ." Reeve shrugs his shoulders. "Then that's where I'll be."

"But what about Benedictine?"

"It's too far away. I don't want us to be so far apart." I'm staring at him, and he colors. "I mean, unless that's what you want. I'll do whatever you want to do. If you don't want to try for a long-distance thing, or if you do . . . it's . . . whatever. I'm just laying out options." He swallows. "It's as good a school as Benedictine, too. Plus, their coach played pro ball back in the day. But . . . you know, like I said, it's just another option. No pressure. I don't have to decide right away."

My heart is thrumming in my chest. This thing with me and Reeve . . . it doesn't have to be a secret forever. I lean forward and press my lips against his. "Yes, yes, yes, yes," I whisper against his mouth.

He pulls back, and his face breaks into a grin. "Yeah? Are you sure?"

"Sure, I'm sure!" The thought that this—we—get to continue, that he wants it to—it's everything.

Reeve lets out a breath and relaxes his shoulders. "Okay, cool. Awesome. So we'll just bide our time until graduation, and then we're out of here." He pulls his phone out of his coat pocket. "You need to get home soon."

That he was nervous and unsure of me, it's so sweet I could die. I want to give him something of me in return.

My hand is shaking as I unzip my coat, reach behind under my sweater, and unhook my bra. I pull it out of my jacket arm-hole, and I'm glad I wore a pretty one today—sheer pink with a dove-gray bow in the center. Reeve has stopped breathing and is watching me like a boy in a trance. He doesn't take his eyes off me, and all of a sudden I feel like a queen. I take his hand, and

I slide it underneath my sweater and up my front, all the way to my heart. "You can touch me," I whisper, and I let go, and he cups his hand around the curve of my breast. I wonder if he can feel my heart pounding against his hand. It's beating so hard and so fast, he must. I know he's been with other girls, that this is nothing new. But the way he looks at me, like I am a revelation, a treasure to behold, it takes my breath away, and there's nowhere else I'd rather be than here.

Chapter Sixteen

KAT

I CRASH INTO MY HOMEROOM SEAT, TUCK MY headphones into my ears, and lay my head down so my cheek is on my desk. Then I press play and turn the volume up and up and up, basically as loud as it can go. The kids milling around hear it too, because they turn and look my way for a second. Then they go back to their business of being annoying, and I go back to my business of ignoring them.

I close my eyes and try to fall asleep, but the fluorescent lighting in here is just too awful. It colors the backs of my eyelids acid yellow. So I'm forced to watch the girls parade into the room like a silent movie scored by my favorite punk band from Germany, Umlaut Suicide.

I don't know exactly when this became the thing at our high school, but every February 14 everyone with boobs dresses up like a literal living Valentine. Red pleated skirts, pink fuzzy sweaters, white kneesocks with hearts running up the backs. They do their hair up special, barrel curled or braided with ribbons or pinned up with sparkly barrettes. I shift myself and bury my nose in the arm of my hoodie, because the smells of all the different perfumes make me want to barf.

The boys, they don't wear anything special. They have a different responsibility today.

Since the first of the month, there's been a mention every single morning about placing orders for the rose sale run by the student council.

Yellow roses are symbols of friendship, sold for a dollar a stem. Pink roses are for crushes, at three dollars a stem. Red roses mean true love and are sold for a whopping five bucks a stem. On the morning of Valentine's Day, a student council person goes to each homeroom and delivers the flowers, and then the girls compare who got the most.

It's, like, the biggest affront to feminism, like, ever.

Back when I was a freshman, anyone could buy whatever

color rose they wanted for someone else. But the "rules" have changed over the years as the girls have gotten more competitive. Now you can only buy red roses for a person of the opposite gender, unless you're gay, because we are very progressive. It's effing ridiculous, if you ask me.

Now, I'm not trying to shit on the very idea of Valentine's Day. I'm a fan of love. I'm a sucker for romance. Truth be told, when I'm home alone, I usually channel surf to the sappiest movie I can find, one where the sound track is just violins and there are, like, big passionate kisses at the airport, or on some rocky beach. Or, best of all, in a hospital bed.

It's Valentine's Day played out inside our high school that's utter bullshit. I mean, I don't think I could find even one or two couples in the whole school who are really, truly in love.

Love is not a big show of spending fifty bucks on some bullshit flowers as part of a fund-raiser for school. I've seen plenty of girls get a red rose from their boyfriends, and then they're screaming at each other ten minutes later in the hallway.

They don't know what love is. They're just hopped up on hormones.

I'm sure some people think I'm bitter because I've never gotten a rose. First off, none of my guy friends are going to waste their money on dumb shit like that. You can get better roses at the dang gas station for half of what our school

JENNY HAN & SIOBHAN VIVIAN

charges, and they won't be wilted by eighth period either.

I've gotten my fair share of tokens of romance. Like my sophomore year, when Vincent Upton drew a heart on a pack of cigarettes and cut off my padlock with a hacksaw he'd stolen from the shop room so he could put the pack in my locker.

So whatever.

All throughout homeroom everyone's eyes are on the door, waiting for the flower delivery person to come by with their cart. And when ours comes with a big white box, I pull my hood up over my head.

A few minutes later there's a tap on my shoulder. I lift my head up, and there is the flower girl with a pair of cardboard angel wings on her back and an arm full of roses. I tug out my headphones. "Yeah?"

"Can you move back a little?"

I rock back in my chair, and she sets twelve yellow roses on my desk along with a card.

I look around. A few other girls have gotten a red rose or maybe two. But no one has a bouquet in any color.

I feel my cheeks heat up as I pick up the card. The delivery girl is standing expectantly, like I'm going to read it out loud or something. I give her a bitchy look and she leaves.

The bell rings, and then I gather up the flowers and the card and head to my locker. I stick them inside because I'm not parading that shit around for everyone to see. And later, once the next period starts, I discreetly open my card.

Dear Kat,

It was hard to hear, but you were right—my Lillia Cho oeuvre was definitely junior high material. If not for your musical kick in the ass, I don't know if I would have ever found the guts to quit writing songs about Lillia and just tell her how I really feel.
Here's to having "No Regrets." (See what I did there?)

Rock on,
Your friend,
Alex

Oh shit. Shit, shit, shit.

Chapter Seventeen

LILLIA

BECAUSE IT'S VALENTINE'S DAY, I'M WEARING A SALMON-pink sweater and tomato-red cigarette pants. My mom says I look like something out of a 1960s Italian *Vogue*, and she insists that I wear my hair pinned up on the side with her pearl pin. I've always liked to dress up special for Valentine's Day, but now everyone does it and it's slightly annoying.

The student council starts delivering roses during homeroom. It's part of it—you get your flowers in the morning, and then you carry them around all day for everyone to see. Red for love, yellow for friendship, pink if you have a crush on someone.

Rennie and Ash and I always send each other two yellow ones and one pink.

Last year I set the record for most roses ever received by a girl at Jar High. Twenty-four! A dozen from my dad, Rennie's three, Ash's three, one from Alex, one from PJ, one from my chem lab partner, Tyler, and three from a group of freshman guys I gave a ride home to once after school because they missed the bus.

I already know I won't be getting a rose from Reeve, and it's not just because we're keeping things on the down low. It's a point of pride for him—that he wouldn't ever waste his money on something so cheesy and meaningless. I've heard him give the speech every year, how Valentine's Day is complete bullshit. Also, in the past he's always had more than one girl he was flirting with at a time, and it would have been drama if he'd sent a rose to just one girl or to all the girls. So his policy is to send none. Junior year, Rennie begged him to send her a rose, and he still refused "on the principle of it," and she wouldn't speak to him for days.

Jamie Cochran, a junior girl from the squad, comes into our homeroom with an armful of red roses.

Jamie stops at my desk first. She drops a dozen onto my desk and keeps moving. I open the card, and it reads, *Happy Valentine's Day to my darling. Love, Daddy.*

Jamie goes back to her pushcart in the doorway and comes back with a big armful, all different colors. She walks around the room, plucking out stems and handing them to the other students. And then she heads back to my desk.

Jamie hands me the last bouquet in her arms, three roses—two yellow and one pink—which I know are from Ash. She walks back to her cart and picks up an enormous bouquet of roses, all red. It's so big, she has trouble carrying it. She stops in front of my desk and hands them to me, all of them. "Fifty red roses," she announces loudly, and I hear people in the room gasp. "Looks like you win most roses again, Lillia!"

What!

As soon as Jamie walks away, I tear open the card.

I've wanted to say this for a long time, only I didn't have the guts. But life is too short. So here goes. I'm in love with you, Lillia. Always have been, always will be.

Alex

Whoa. I can't believe it. I put my hands on my cheeks, and they are warm. I always knew Alex had feelings for me, but never in a million years did I think he'd put himself out there like this. It's just . . . beyond.

And I'm going to have to let him down.

As soon as the bell rings, I scoop up all my bouquets and race to my locker. I have to hide Alex's roses before Reeve sees. I stuff them all inside as quick as I can. Some of the stems break, and a few petals fall out onto the floor. I stoop down and pick them up and put them in my purse.

PJ, Derek, and Alex are already at the lunch table when I get to the cafeteria. I spot Reeve in the lunch line.

I slide into the seat next to Alex. "Hi," he says.

"Hey," I whisper back. I mouth, *Thank you.*

He mouths back, *You're welcome.*

I glance over at Reeve again. He's picking out a Jell-O at the counter.

Alex leans in and touches my arm. In a low voice he asks, "Did you read the card?"

I nod and make myself smile. "Can we talk later?" I want to do this so carefully, and in private.

He nods, and I can feel my heart break a little bit.

Ashlin comes running up to the table just as Reeve sits down with his lunch. She throws down her lunch bag and shrieks, "I heard someone sent you *fifty* roses, Lil!" My mouth goes dry. "You lucky bitch! Who was it?" She sits down and reaches around PJ to whack Derek on the shoulder with her bag. "Derek only sent me five! Cheap bastard."

"Um . . ." What do I say? My dad?

Ash giggles and swivels in her seat. "Was it you, Lindy?"

Alex is just smiling. I can't even look at Reeve.

That's when Jamie comes running up to the table with a single red rose in her hand. "Lillia, I forgot to give this one to you in all the craziness this morning." She hands me the rose and a card and walks away.

"Open up the card!" Ash demands.

Everybody's looking at me now. Slowly I open the little red envelope. The card says, *First time I bought a rose for anyone other than my mom. Congratulations, Cho.* I can feel my cheeks heat up. "It's from my dad," I say at last.

"Oh my God, you're a horrible liar, Lil," Ash says with a laugh. She reaches across the table and snatches the card out of my hands.

Desperately I say, "Give it back, Ash."

The smile on her face fades as she reads. She puts two and two together immediately, her eyes moving from Reeve to me and back again. "Is this a joke?"

Beside me Alex has gone rigid in his seat. He looks from Reeve to me. "So you guys are together."

I'm such a coward. I can't even answer him. All I can do is look down at the table.

Then I hear Ash whisper, "Oh. My. God." I look up at her,

and she's staring at me with round disbelieving eyes. "Lil?"

I open and close my mouth. I don't know what to say to her.

Rubbing his hands through his hair, Reeve says, "Um . . . yeah. We are. We didn't want it to come out like this, but, yeah."

Alex quickly gathers up his lunch tray and stands up. "Feel free to throw those roses away if you haven't already."

Reeve reaches out to him. "Hey, dude, listen—"

Alex doesn't let him finish. He gets up and leaves and doesn't spare me a second look.

The entire cafeteria has gone quiet. Everyone is staring at us.

"Tell me this isn't happening," Ash says. She's talking only to me. "Tell me you and Reeve are not a thing." When I don't say anything, when seconds pass of me still not saying anything, she hisses, "Ren's body isn't even cold!"

I feel all the blood drain from my face.

Sharply Reeve says, "What'd you say, Ash?"

Ashlin shrugs a defiant kind of shrug, and Reeve narrows his eyes at Derek in warning. "You need to put a muzzle on your girl."

Derek brushes him off and keeps on eating his sandwich. "Chill out, Tabatsky."

Ash is shooting daggers at me, and PJ just looks dumbfounded. I feel sick to my stomach. I want to explain, but what can I even say?

"Anybody else have shit they want to say?" Reeve says. "If so, say it now to my face, because I'm not dealing with any whisper-behind-the-back bullshit."

"This is sickening," Ash spits out. Then she bolts up and leaves our table. Derek follows her. PJ shakes his head sadly, and he gets up too. Now it's just Reeve and me at our end of the table. Reeve blinks. I know he wasn't expecting that.

He pulls my chair closer and hugs me to him. I guess he can feel how nervous I am, because he says, "Don't worry. We aren't doing anything wrong."

We both know that isn't true. If we weren't doing anything wrong, why were we sneaking around all this time?

"I'd do anything for you, Cho." Reeve squeezes my hand. "You're with me, right?" There's an urgency in his voice, a weakness I'm not used to hearing.

Am I with him? Are we really doing this? I'm scared what people will think, what my sister will think. My parents. Ash. But it's too late to worry about all that now. There's no going back. And I do want to be with him. So I let him hold me. But I still can't get the look on Alex's face out of my head.

Chapter Eighteen

KAT

I'M HUSTLING OVER TO THE CAFETERIA WHEN I RUN right into Alex. He looks like he wants to murder somebody. Uh-oh. "Hey, Alex—" I say.

"I can't talk right now, Kat," he says, and steamrolls past me. So much for no regrets.

In the cafeteria Reeve and Lillia are sitting at their table alone. She's got one long-stemmed red rose on the table in front of her. I know Alex is gone, but where are the rest of their friends? There's, like, three trays of uneaten food left behind. I plop down in the seat across from Lil, where there's a chicken sand-wich and fries.

I help myself to a fry and glance over at Reeve. I don't partic-ularly want to dish about Alex's feelings in front of him. "Hey, Reeve, can you get me a drink?"

He makes a disgusted face as I eat another fry. "There are five open sodas in front of you. Why don't you mooch off one of them?"

Ugh. I turn my chair away from him and lower my voice. "Did shit just go down?" Pointing to the single rose, I say, "Is that from Al?" I was expecting something bigger. Though maybe he did a rose and, like, sang one of his songs for her or something.

Lillia shakes her head and hands me the card that came with the rose.

"Oh." I say. "Wait. I thought you and Reeve were keeping things on the down low?"

Reeve looks from me to Lillia. "Wait a minute—DeBrassio knows about us?" I give him a Cheshire cat smile. "I thought we were keeping this a secret from *everyone*!"

Defensively Lillia says, "First off, I only told Kat, and I swore her to secrecy. And what right do you have to be mad at that? I'm not the one who sent you a valentine in front of everyone!"

I dip a fry into some ketchup and nod my head in agreement. "She's got a point."

Reeve lets out a frustrated sigh. "I thought I could send you a rose and it would get lost in all the other ones you get in homeroom and you'd be the only one who knew. I definitely didn't expect it to be delivered in the middle of lunch with everyone around."

"No. I mean . . ." Lillia picks up the rose and puts it to her nose. "I know it was an accident. I just wish you hadn't been such a jerk to Derek."

"What else could I do? I'm not going to sit here and not say anything while Ash is a bitch to you." Reeve glances at me before he says, "It's none of their business anyway."

"Ash was a bitch? What did that bobblehead say?"

Lillia's chin trembles. "Ash said that Rennie's body isn't even cold. And then everyone just—they just got up and left."

I lean forward and drag a fry through Lil's ketchup. When our eyes meet, I can see how truly upset she is. Poor kid. I do feel bad for her, but, well . . . she had to have known that being with Reeve, in secret or not, came with a whole lotta baggage. I give her arm a squeeze. "They'll come around," I say, but I don't know if that's true. I just want to make her feel better.

"Kat's right. They will. They're just shocked," Reeve says, and pushes some of Lillia's hair behind her ear. "And now everyone knows. We don't have to sneak around anymore. It's honestly a relief."

Lillia and I share a look. *Almost* everyone knows. And that is a relief. Thank God Mary isn't here to see this.

Reeve pulls Lil's chair close to him and kisses the top of her head. It makes me feel better that she's smiling, even for a second. I know it makes Reeve feel better too. You can see it all over his face.

Chapter Nineteen

MARY

When I open my eyes, I find myself inside the high school. Everyone's dressed in pinks and reds and whites. They're carrying roses, sharing kisses in the hallways.

Oh my gosh, it's Valentine's Day.

Valentine's Day? How can that be? How can a whole month and a half have passed? I don't think I understand what time feels like anymore. A long time or a short time, it all feels the same to me now.

I do feel something, though. Something magnetic. A pull. A current. A tide.

It takes me to the cafeteria.

And what I see eclipses any pain I've ever felt.

They're together. Lillia, Kat, Reeve. As thick as thieves. Kat's reaching for food, Reeve's swatting her hands away, and Lillia is laughing at both of them.

I tear at my hair. *Why?* Why am I being tortured like this? Forced to watch Reeve move on with his life, watch him get whatever he wants. Watch him take my friends, erase me from the world. He doesn't deserve to be happy. Not after what he did to me.

The edges of the cafeteria get white, and I begin to lose focus. Which is good, because I don't want to see this. I was wrong. I was so wrong about everything. We aren't friends. They don't miss me; they don't think about me. If they did, there's no way in hell this would be happening.

The very last thing that made me feel like I was human, just a little bit human, is gone.

I don't know how much time passes, where I go, what happens to me after. I come to on my bedroom floor to the sound of laughter. It's coming from outside, but strangely, it sounds like their lips are right next to my ears.

Kids laugh in two different kinds of ways. There's the joyous, silly kind that happens when you're getting tickled by your mom or chased around the backyard by your dad.

And then there's the mean, teasing kind. The cruel kind of laughter that isn't funny at all.

That's what I hear, and it brings me right back to my Montessori days.

I quickly push up off my stomach and walk to the window. There's a group of kids down on the street below, right in front of my house. I bet they're coming from the park up the road. Four of them are closing the gap on one boy who's by himself. He's walking backward as best he can, though he almost trips on the curb, because he doesn't want to turn his back on them.

I close my eyes, and in a flash I'm down on the curb.

The one boy who's by himself, the unease on his face makes my stomach hurt. He's ten years old, maybe eleven. I can't tell exactly because he's tall for his age. Taller than the other kids who are taunting him, but that doesn't matter. He's trying not to look scared, but I know he is. I can feel his heart drumming. His hair is long and shaggy and a bit greasy, and he keeps flipping it out of his eyes by jerking his head. His jeans are dirty and they don't fit him so great. His cheeks are dotted by a few ripe red pimples.

Poor thing.

The other four kids, three boys and one girl, have the energy of a full-blown mob.

"I know you want to kiss her, Benjamin," the blond-haired boy says. "I saw you staring at her ass."

"I was not," the tall boy, Benjamin, says. And then he realizes that he's been backed into the bushes that edge my property. The other kids quickly surround him. He wipes away some sweat from his temple with his sleeve.

I step between two of the boys and stand next to Benjamin. Even if he can't see me, I hope he can feel me next to him. I hope he can tell he's not alone.

The ringleader boy tips his head back and laughs. "Dude! I saw you do it! Are you calling me a liar?" He glances over at the girl standing next to him. "Betsy, he's calling me a liar."

Betsy doesn't look all that into what's happening, but she's not exactly stopping it either. She just shrugs her shoulders.

"I'm not calling you a liar, Seth," Benjamin says carefully. "I'm just saying that you're wrong."

Seth slings an arm over Betsy's shoulder. "So if Betsy tried to kiss you, you wouldn't do it?"

"No."

Betsy rolls her eyes at that, and I feel the pang of hurt inside Benjamin. My hand goes to my chest, where my heart would be beating if I were alive. I can really, truly feel it. His hurt, as if it were my own. I've felt this way before. The first day of school when I hid in the bathroom. Kat and Lillia were both so upset, their pain radiating through the stall door.

Seth lowers his head menacingly. "So you're saying that my girlfriend is ugly?"

"No! I'm not saying that!" Benjamin is clearly getting frustrated, and I don't blame him. "I wouldn't kiss her because I know Betsy's your girlfriend."

Seth nods to the other two boys, who suddenly produce a bunch of folded papers from their pockets. Seth takes them and holds them up, two fists full. "Then why have you been writing her love notes?"

Before he can stop himself, Benjamin looks at Betsy, slack-jawed. Like, *Why? Why would you do that?*

I grit my teeth. The sky darkens above us, and the wind picks up.

He pleads with Seth, "She started writing to me first!"

Seth nods. "Um, yeah, you dope. Because I told her to. We wanted to see what you would say."

I glance at Betsy, to see if she feels even a little bit bad about what she's done, the trouble she's caused Benjamin, but she's shaking her head. "Ben, I only wrote you, like, twice, and they were barely half a page. You wrote me every day, pages and pages. You've been obsessed with me since first grade. You even said so."

I feel the heat behind Benjamin's eyes that comes right before tears. His lip begins to quiver.

Don't cry, I tell him silently, and every muscle in my body tightens up. *Don't cry. Don't cry. They are evil. They aren't worth your tears.*

"Oh my God, look!" Seth sounds gleeful. "Crybaby's going to cry!" He steps closer and closer to Benjamin.

I can taste it. The desperation, the humiliation. The feeling of being so alone. It's sharp and acrid on my tongue.

I narrow my eyes on Seth and push my arm out fast. That's all it takes for Seth to fall backward. He hits the ground hard and cracks the back of his head on the curb. It makes a sickening sound. His hands both open up, and the letters fall out.

The other boys look as shocked as he is.

I glance behind me at the tree in my yard. The sky gets darker, and the wind kicks up even more, and the bare branches above us shake and shake.

"You guys!" one of the other boys shouts. "The tree's about to fall!"

Using my mind, I push harder and harder against the tree. The ground buckles.

"Look out!" someone shouts as the roots burst up through the dirt. Betsy screams, and the boys help Seth up and out of the way before the tree creaks over and snaps in half. The entire thing smashes through the bushes and falls across the street. That sends neighbors running out of their houses.

Benjamin looks behind him. He sees me, and his eyes go wide and scared.

He can actually see me. Just like Lillia and Kat in the bathroom.

"Don't be afraid!" I call out. "I'm here to help you!" I will help him, because there was no one there to help me.

He takes a step backward, and then another, practically tripping over his sneakers. "Thank you," he gasps. And then he turns and runs down the street.

"Let's get out of here," Betsy says, and turns to hurry down the street in the opposite direction. I lift my hand once more and use my energy to knock her forward, facedown onto the street.

She's as guilty as the rest of them.

She screams. The boys pick her up. Betsy's bleeding from the mouth, crying. And her hands are bright red and cut as well. She spits a tooth out into her hand.

Not so pretty anymore, are you, Betsy?

As they disappear around the corner, I realize it. This is my purpose. This is why I'm here on Jar Island. I am an avenger. An avenging angel sent down to right wrongs.

I am not weak.

I am powerful. More powerful than I know.

Me, Kat, and Lillia, we weren't ever supposed to be a team. All along it has been my responsibility and mine alone. My purpose.

It's why I'm drawn to Reeve. Because I have a job to do, a score to settle. And once I do, I'll finally be free.

Chapter Twenty

LILLIA

FOR THE REST OF THE DAY, ALEX IS ALL I THINK about. I have to talk to him. I have to tell him how sorry I am.

I leave my last class a few minutes early, before the bell rings, and I race over to his class and wait outside the door. When Alex walks out, I'm standing there waiting. I feel clammy and dizzy.

His face hardens and he keeps walking. I run up to him and grab his arm. "Alex, please talk to me!"

He jerks out of my grasp. "There's nothing to talk about." And then he walks away, and I just stand there, my arms hugging my chest.

I'm still standing in the same place when Reeve appears next to me. "Are you okay?" he asks, putting his hands on my shoulders.

"Yes."

Reeve looks down the hallway, in the direction where Alex walked. "I'm the dick, not you. I was his best friend. I knew how he felt about you. You're the only girl he's ever wanted. There's a guy code, you know?"

I know, because there's a girl code too, and I did the same exact thing to Rennie.

Reeve faces me, suddenly anxious. "He's probably going to try to warn you against me."

"There's nothing Alex could tell me about you that would change my mind."

Reeve nods, but he doesn't look convinced.

"I know everything there is to know about you!" In a teasing voice I say, "Let's see, how many girls have there been? Teresa, and Melanie Renfro, and that junior girl Tara, and oh, half the JV cheerleading squad. And who could forget the college girl at the doughnut shop who gave you free doughnuts every morning?"

"Cho, I only ever kissed that girl! And it was only one time, I swear."

I throw my arms around him and hug him to me tightly. I

burrow my head into the space between his neck and his shoulder. I close my eyes and breathe in his smell. I wouldn't go back on it even if I could. No matter what, I still choose Reeve.

"Everything will be okay," he says into my hair. "People just need the weekend to get over it. They'll come around."

Nadia is waiting in front of my car. "Is it true?" she asks me, her eyes accusing. "Are you and Reeve really together?" When I hesitate, she says, "You were supposed to be her best friend, Lilli!"

It cuts me to the bone.

"The worst part is that I had to find out along with everyone else at school. I'm your *sister*, Lillia. Don't you know that's supposed to count for something?" Her eyes well up. "You could have at least told *me*."

I whisper, "I'm sorry. I was scared of what you'd think of me. I want to be someone you can look up to, Nadi. And I guess . . . I guess I thought if you knew, you'd be ashamed of me."

She doesn't say anything, but she doesn't have to. She turns and starts to walk away, back toward the school.

"Nadi! Come on! How are you going to get home?"

But she doesn't come back.

Chapter Twenty-One

MARY

I THINK BACK TO THAT NIGHT WE MET AT KAT'S BOAT, down at the Jar Island Yacht Club. It was then that our revenge plans were born, when we entered into a pact to see this thing through. There were rules. We needed them. Otherwise, how could we trust each other?

Kat was the one who said it.

If you're in, you need to be in until the very end. If not, well . . . consider yourself fair game. It'll be open season, and we'll have a hell of a lot of ammo to use against you.

Each of us agreed. We made that promise to each other. Each

of us knew the terrible truth, that the people who know you best have the power to hurt you the worst. Rennie did it all the time. She was ruthless, a master at using people's insecurities against them. And Reeve. Reeve always knew the perfect way to hurt me.

Lillia and Kat may have forgotten what they promised, but I haven't. I'm not letting them off the hook that easily. They knew what they were getting into, and they both got something out of it too. I'm the one who was left hanging, and it's only fair that I hold them accountable.

I know so many ways to hurt them. I know who they love; I know their prized possessions; I know their secrets.

I am the last person they should have turned on. And they only have themselves to blame.

I'm sandwiched between the barn and the open door, watching through a knot in the wood as Lillia races with Phantom to the end of the riding trail. Despite his speed, she barely has to pull on his reins to make him come to a perfect stop. She leans forward and gives his neck a tender pat before climbing out of the saddle and hopping to the ground.

Lillia takes off her helmet and shakes out her hair, and even though the sun is barely out, her hair catches the glow. She's wearing tight black pants tucked into knee-high riding boots the color of caramel, a fitted wool coat, and leather gloves. Her cheeks are pink from the cold. She takes Phantom's reins and leads him toward the stables.

He pauses and turns his head toward me as they pass my hiding place. His muscles ripple and tighten, and his black eye trains on me. He lets out an anxious snort. But Lillia clicks her tongue and nudges him forward. They walk down the center of the stable to his pen at the opposite end of the barn.

I remember the day when Kat and I came here to hang out with her. It was one of the first times when we really felt like friends. We didn't need a reason to hang out. There was nothing to plan or scheme about. We just wanted to be together.

It feels like forever ago.

When Lillia ducks inside Phantom's stall, I creep out and hurry after her. Each pen I pass, the horse inside reacts. Whinnies and brays, hooves stomping and scraping the stable floor. I'm scared Lillia will hear the commotion and see me, so I break into a run and hide in the empty stall next to Phantom's.

I walk up to the shared wall. Phantom turns his head as soon as I'm there, but Lillia shushes him. She kneels down on the ground and begins loosening the strap of Phantom's saddle under his belly.

I lift my hand, ball it into a fist, and then flick my fingers at Phantom.

He immediately bucks up on his hind legs, knocking Lillia onto her butt. He brays, showing his teeth.

Lillia's stunned. "Phantom, easy, boy," she cries, then rolls onto her knees and gets to her feet. "It's okay. Everything's okay." She approaches him carefully and begins to rub his neck while she glances around, looking for what's spooking him.

I keep flicking my fingers at him, popping my fists open and closed.

Phantom whips his tail, snaps his jaws, and bucks up again. He lets out a terrifying whine and nearly comes down on top of Lillia. She steps out of the way just in time, but his hoof knocks into her forearm. She falls against the wall where I'm hiding and screams out in pain.

At this point all the horses are crying and bucking and shaking the entire barn.

One of the stable boys comes running. He grabs a rake from the side of the stall and brandishes the wooden handle at Phantom. "Easy, Phantom! Get back now!"

Lillia screams not to hurt him, but the stable boy isn't listening. Phantom rears up again, his ears pinned, and lunges where Lillia's cowering. Phantom's not attacking her. He's trying to get at me, on the other side of the wall.

The stable boy swings the rake handle like a bat, and it cracks against Phantom's neck so hard that the wood snaps in half. Phantom steps back and lunges again, leaving the stable boy with only a splintered wooden spear to wield him off.

He's about to jab when Lillia grabs him, pulls him out of the stall, and quickly shuts the gate.

"I could have calmed him down!" she screams, cradling her arm. "You almost killed him!"

"He almost killed you," the boy says, panting. "Is it broken?"

Lillia shakes her head. She has tears streaming down her face. She shrugs off her jacket. Her arm is bright red and swollen and already beginning to turn purple.

"He's never done anything like that before," she says, wiping her eyes. "I don't know what happened."

The stable boy runs off to get Lillia some ice. I hear her crying outside Phantom's pen. I know exactly what she's feeling. It's terrible when a friend you trust turns on you.

A heartbeat later I'm at the Jar Island Yacht Club, standing in front of *Judy Blue Eyes*, the Catalina daysailer Kat named after her mother. I expected to be more tired than I am, from all the stuff I did to Phantom, but I'm not. I feel strong.

One of Aunt Bette's books predicted this would happen as I grew more confident and increased my focus. The book phrased it like a warning, but to me it feels like something to celebrate.

It's clear that my ties to Lillia and Kat are what made me weak. Worrying about them and their problems. If I hadn't met them, maybe I would have come to these realizations a lot earlier. I'd already be free, in a better place.

Kat's boat is closed up for winter, with a tarp stretched taut across it and the sail tied tightly to the mast. With the smallest wave of my hand, every knot comes undone. The tarp and the sail snap from their tethers, and the wind carries them away like ribbons.

I lift my hands up and the waves begin to swell. The other boats tied up along the dock bob in the water. But they are nothing compared to Kat's boat. It's as if all the energy in the ocean is being pooled underneath it.

Finally the boat lifts high enough. I lower my hand fast, and the thing launches into the air, like the water was a rubber band that I just snapped. The boat hits one of the rocks and is pulverized into wooden splinters.

The dockworkers come running. They can't believe their eyes. I know one of them will eventually figure out whose boat that was, and they'll call Kat and let her know it's destroyed.

Sorry, Kat. But you knew what you signed up for.

Actually, I'm not sorry. Not one little bit.

They deserved to be punished.

Now, Reeve—he deserves way worse. He deserves to die.

Chapter Twenty-Two

LILLIA

REEVE'S TRUCK IS WAITING IN FRONT OF MY HOUSE on Monday morning. I run up to it and jump inside. "What are you doing here?" I ask him. He didn't say anything about picking me up when we were on the phone last night.

"Driving my girl to school," he says, kissing me on the cheek. "How's your arm?" I pull up my sleeve. I'm purple from my wrist to my elbow. "Damn."

"It looks worse than it feels," I tell him. That's a lie. It hurts like crazy. But it wasn't Phantom's fault. He'd never hurt me on purpose. Something spooked him.

I climb in and notice immediately that Reeve's truck smells good. Like, super good. Reeve passes me a white Milky Morning bag, and I open it. It's monkey bread and an organic apple juice. "Reeve! My favorite things!"

He grins a pleased kind of grin. "Where's Nadia?"

"She's getting a ride with Patrice," I say.

"Is she still mad?" Reeve puts the truck in reverse and backs out of my driveway.

I nod. "The only time she spoke to me all weekend was when my dad said he was thinking about selling Phantom for what happened, and then we both freaked out and begged him not to." I take a big bite of the monkey bread. "Thank you for my breakfast. Want some?" I dangle it under his nose, even though I know he's going to say no.

He makes a face. "Too sweet."

The closer we get to school, the more nervous I get about seeing everybody. I guess Reeve can tell, because he reaches over and takes my hand without saying anything.

We walk into school holding hands too. I try to let go, but Reeve just holds tighter. "No more hiding, Cho. That's a good thing."

Then I spot Ash coming down the hallway, and our eyes meet, and she just keeps walking like she doesn't see me. And all I want to do is run and hide. Reeve notices, of course, but he doesn't say anything about Ash. Instead he starts telling me this story about some soldier who had a dog in Afghanistan. He was a bomb-sniffing dog, and this guy was his trainer. Anyway, the story goes on and on and on, and it's hard to follow at points. Basically Reeve just rambles while I get my books out of my locker. Magically, the story ends just as I reach my homeroom door.

"You did that to distract me," I say.

"Did it work?"

I nod. It did.

"See you later, Cho."

But for Reeve "later" turns out to mean as soon as the first-period bell rings. He's there to escort me to class. And it happens like that, all day. I don't know how he does it, but no matter where his classes are, he's waiting outside my classroom door when the bell rings, ready to walk me to my next period. He doesn't leave me alone once.

At lunch it's just the two of us at the lunch table. I don't know where the rest of our friends are. But Reeve makes me laugh, he makes me forget, and the day isn't so bad. It's kind of good.

Chapter Twenty-Three

KAT

DURING MY FREE PERIOD I GO VISIT MY OLD EARTH-science teacher and play her the message that my boss at the yacht club left on my phone this weekend. His voice sounds frayed and choppy, like he's distracted. Or confused. But he claims there was a weather phenomenon like they'd never seen before. He called it a "flash tide." Apparently it was so worrisome, they radioed for the coast guard. Anyway, my boat was destroyed.

My boat was the *only* one destroyed.

"So what's a 'flash tide'?" I ask.

Mrs. Hilman shakes her head. "There's no such thing. The tides are the most predictable natural phenomena on earth. They don't have irregularities. You can literally figure them out to the minute."

"That lying bastard. I knew it!"

I bet it was some kind of fuck-up with the off-season skeleton crew as they moved around boats to prepare for the summer people coming back to the island. Someone probably crashed a yacht into mine, and now they're trying to cover it up. They must have been going way too fast, because there wasn't anything salvageable. He told me as much, but I still wanted to see it for myself. I tried to pick out a few bits of wood, ones where Dad had painted the name on the hull, thinking maybe I could glue them back together. But there was no way.

Mrs. Hillman gazes at me incredulously. "You didn't pay attention at all in my class, did you? You'd just zone out like this. We did an entire week on tides."

I don't bother answering her. What does it matter? My boat, the beautiful *Judy Blue Eyes*, is no more.

We have a senior assembly last period. A few former Jar High graduates are back home for spring break, and they're talking to us about their first-year experiences in college or some shit. Lil's sitting in the back, by herself, with an empty seat next to her. Reeve's, I guess. The rest of their friends are down front. Before the thing gets started, I shoot up there and steal the seat.

"How's it going?"

"Ash hasn't said two words to me. And Alex, he won't even look at me. But I think Derek and PJ are coming around. I mean, obviously Reeve and I didn't set out to hurt anyone."

I give her the eye. "Come on, Lil. Yeah, you didn't set out to hurt anyone but you knew exactly what would happen if people found out. Otherwise you wouldn't have been sneaking around."

"That's fair." She bites her lip. "But I can't help the way I feel."

I shrug. "Then fuck everyone. Who cares? You're almost out of this place anyway."

Lillia nods like I'm making sense, which I am, but then she sinks low in her seat. "I hate feeling like Alex hates me."

"Have you tried talking to him?"

"Yes. But he just walked away." She hangs her head.

"Then try again!"

"I feel like maybe I should give him some space?"

"Lil, don't do that thing you do where you just pretend that shit is fine and dandy. Remember, you got off easy because Mary isn't around anymore."

"I'm not!" she says emphatically. "He's just so mad, Kat. I've never seen him this mad before."

"Well, think about it. The girl he's loved forever and his supposed best friend have been secretly together under his nose."

"You're not making me feel better."

"Sorry. Your hair looks very shiny today."

Lillia pouts at me. And then she concedes, "It's a new conditioner."

As soon as I see Reeve making his way across the auditorium toward us, I stand up. "Later, Lil." I love Lil, and I do have her back, but I also can't help but think she and Reeve are just a bad idea.

Chapter Twenty-Four

MARY

I'VE IMAGINED WHAT REEVE'S BEDROOM MIGHT LOOK like so many times. At first I'm almost afraid to move. I just stand and look at everything, take it all in. I've never been in a boy's room before. Not ever.

Reeve's bedroom is in the attic of his house. I can tell by the pitch of the roof over my head, because it looks like I'm standing underneath the top of a triangle. On either side of the room there's a small circular window. I can see the bare branches of winter treetops outside, dancing in the wind.

His bed is a queen, and it's neatly made. There's a weight

bench in a corner, right in front of a large mirror. On the floor there's a range of dumbbells in two neat rows, from smallest to largest. And on the walls are a bunch of pages ripped out from exercise magazines. The pictures are of exercise routines, but also of football players in splashy poses, and some models. I wrinkle my nose at one he has of a brunette in a hot-pink bikini drinking beer from a big frothy stein. At least it looks like it's been up there for a long time, because the clear tape is yellow and peeling away from the wall.

Reeve's bedroom isn't completely clean. Dirty clothes spill out over the top of an overstuffed laundry hamper into a pile on the floor. His desk is covered in paper. And every single drawer in his dresser has been left open.

Reeve's at his desk. He hasn't started his homework. Instead he's just staring at a framed picture underneath his lamp. It's of him and Rennie, probably from freshman year. He's in his Jar Island football uniform, and she's in her cheering outfit. He's holding her like a strongman.

Reeve lets out a sigh. He picks up the frame, walks past me, and puts it into his very top drawer. He pushes it closed, but only halfway, and walks out of his room.

I tiptoe over to look inside the drawer. There are a few pairs of boxer shorts inside, but mostly it's random trinkets. There are army dog tags for someone named William Tabatsky. A couple of silver dollars. An article from the newspaper when Reeve was sports player of the week. And now the picture of him and Rennie. I feel something weird underneath the frame. Something vibrating. Humming. Warm. I'm not sure if it's a real noise or something only I can detect. I use my hand to guide away the picture frame, and then I find it.

The pocketknife.

He looked so bummed that morning on the ferry, I knew something had happened. I sat next to him and asked him what was wrong. Reeve just shook his head at first; he didn't want to talk about it. So I let him sit in silence, and we shared the pack of Pop-Tarts I'd bought from the snack stand.

Mom always fixed me breakfast, but I used to take some change from her change plate each morning so I could buy Reeve and myself a pack of Pop-Tarts to split. One time Reeve said that I should lay off the Pop-Tarts, that I'd probably lose weight if I didn't eat that kind of junk. I'd still buy them after he said that, but I'd only eat half of mine.

As we got close to the mainland, Reeve told me how his older brother Luke had taken back the pocketknife Reeve had stolen, the one Reeve had used to carve his name in the ferry seat. I didn't totally follow the story, but Reeve was upset. It had been their grandfather's. "Grandpap said he wanted me to have it," he told me. "But Luke said I was lying. He told me to quit being such a baby. And when I wouldn't, he told my dad and I got the belt."

Before, Reeve had told me stories about how his older brothers picked on him, but they always ended with some comeuppance, some prank or sneaky thing Reeve did to settle the score. But on that day there was no such happy ending, and that was usually the case when Reeve's dad got involved. He was a drinker and he had a temper, and it seemed, to me anyway, that Reeve got the worst of it. I couldn't imagine my parents giving me the belt. Ever. I turned to look at him, and he was wiping his eyes. Reeve was crying.

That night I asked my mom if I could have some of the money from my savings account. They'd started it when I was a baby, and every time there was a holiday or a birthday, I had to put at least some of the money in there for safekeeping. I didn't understand why, but Mom said that one day I could use that money for college, or for a trip to Europe or something.

She refused.

So when my parents went to sleep, I snuck downstairs and went into my mom's wallet. She had a bunch of money in there. I took a fifty-dollar bill.

That weekend I went down to the shops on Main Street. I knew this one store my dad liked to bring his antique coins to.

They had a lot of pocketknives there. The old man who owned the place didn't seem keen to help me at first, but I told him I was shopping for my father's birthday present and flashed him the fifty-dollar bill.

I ended up finding an old pocketknife that looked pretty close to the one Reeve had had. It had mother-of-pearl inlay in the handle and a lot of different tools you could slide out, like a can opener, a nail file, and a corkscrew. I knew it wouldn't be as special as the one from his grandfather, but I hoped maybe this one could be special in a different way.

When I gave it to him on Monday, he was really surprised. I had chosen not to wrap it. I just handed it over like it was no big deal with his share of the Pop-Tarts.

"Where'd you get the money for this?"

I was glad he could tell it was expensive. "Don't worry about it," I said. It was funny. My mom hadn't even noticed the money was missing. I was afraid she might ask me if I'd taken it. But she didn't.

Reeve didn't exactly say thank you, but I knew he was thankful. He was smiling super big, and he kept saying "Oh, cool!" over and over again as he fiddled with the features. He showed me what each little thing did. Even though the man at the shop had explained it to me, I pretended like I didn't know a thing.

* * *

There it is. The pocketknife I gave to Reeve. I can't believe he kept it. I concentrate hard and take it in my hand. It doesn't look like he ever used it. The blade is shiny and sharp.

I sink down to the carpet and I frown. It's not a keepsake. Reeve probably tossed it in here after I gave it to him, yet another thing Reeve wants to hide away and not think about. I'm not someone he wants to remember. I'm something to forget.

How funny, then, that I'll use it to kill him.

It's dark; the only light is the glowing face of the alarm clock on his bedside table. It's just after three in the morning. The wind is whipping through the bare trees outside, and a few of the branches scrape against the window. Reeve's asleep in his bed. I take quiet steps across the room, the knife in my hand, and move closer and closer to his bed. He won't even see it coming.

Reeve's lying on his back, shirtless, the covers tangled around his legs. I step closer to him and watch as his chest rises and falls in long, slow breaths. His hair is just slightly damp around his forehead. He looks more like a boy than a man, vulnerable and sweet and peaceful. It's too bad his insides are the opposite of his outside.

I slowly lower myself onto his bed. Reeve groans, and I

freeze. He shifts and rolls over onto his side, so he's facing me. I give it a second, just to make sure he won't wake up, and then lie down next to him, nose to nose, so that we're almost touching but not quite. He's so close to me, I can see the tiny bit of stubble on his chin.

I've always wondered what it would be like to kiss him. Back when I was fat and he was the crown prince of Montessori, I'd daydream about it all the time. His lips on mine. My first kiss. I creep closer. His lips are parted the tiniest bit, and I can see the slick pink insides of his mouth.

Why shouldn't I? I've earned the right to do whatever I want to him. I could do way, way worse.

I lean in over his face, my lips pouty and soft. I never should have kissed that boy David on Halloween night. I should have saved it for Reeve.

Just then he moves again, this time with a quiet mumble, and his lips lift into a smile.

I set the knife down. What's he dreaming about?

If someone who has passed on regularly appears in your dreams, it may be due to more than your subconscious longing. Some spirits are known to actively reach into the dream states of the living to pass along messages or to simply communicate that they still exist in an

active capacity. Therefore, it is advisable not to dismiss
any information regarding the afterlife obtained via a
dream or subconscious event.

I reach out and press my hand to his forehead. Reeve immediately shivers, and then, in a rush of energy, I'm pulled straight
into his mind.

Being in someone else's dream is just like Aunt Bette's book
said. Things look a little smoky. But I can definitely tell where
I am. Reeve's on a football field, dressed in a uniform that's
not Jar Island colors. The stands are full of fans, not unlike the
games I went to early in the season. He's in the middle of a play,
throwing the football downfield. The other players are blurry,
faceless.

Reeve cocks back his arm and lets a long pass fly. Instead of
watching it, he turns away from the field and walks over to the
sidelines, like he has every confidence the ball will land where
he wants it to. He's got a big grin on his face, and the crowd
roars. I guess because he was right.

I walk quickly alongside him and try to see where he's
headed. And then I spot Lillia in the stands, clapping happily for
him. She's in a tight black dress, her hair impossibly shiny, her
lips rose-petal red. It's the dress Kat bought her, to get Reeve's
attention. I've always thought Lillia was the prettiest girl at our

high school, but in Reeve's eyes she's more than that. She's sexy.

She stands up and throws her arms out, ready to embrace him, and calls out "Reeve!" breathlessly, like they've been apart for years and years.

Before Reeve can get to her, I step in front of him.

"Guess who?" I say.

He startles. "Excuse me."

I won't let him step past.

"Um, hello. I was talking to you. Don't be rude."

Reeve looks confused. "Do I know you?"

I lick my lips. "Yup. You and me go way back."

I reach up for his face and pull it down to mine. I force our lips together.

And then it's happening. We're kissing. *Kissing* kissing.

But only for a second or two. Then he pulls away, his brow furrowed with confusion. Behind us I hear Lillia calling for him.

He wants to drift past me and go to her, but I won't let him. I keep my body between them. "Reeve," I say, more loudly so that I drown out Lillia's voice. "Remember? From Halloween night? I bumped into you in the maze."

He finally focuses on me. "Yeah. I remember. You picked up my crutches for me. What's your name again?"

I can't wait to tell him. I smile my prettiest smile. "My name is Big Easy."

I have his attention now. He's frozen; his eyes are wide and alarmed. I show him the pocketknife, slide out the blade. "Look," I tell him. "You kept it." And then I try to kiss him again. I have to grab him by the back of his neck to bring our faces close together. But I can only get our lips to touch for the briefest of seconds before he's pushing away from me, panicked.

I glance over my shoulder and watch the bleachers where Lillia sits. Alex has appeared next to her and he whispers something into her ear. As he does, everyone in the stands drifts far, far away into the background, as if they are on a conveyor belt. Reeve sees this too, and he looks distressed.

"Please, Alex!" he screams, and reaches out for Lillia. "Don't tell her what I did!"

But they are gone. Finally he looks back at me. Reeve starts rubbing his eyes, as if he's about to wake up. "You need to stay a secret," he tells me.

I'm his secret. His shameful, terrible secret.

I scream, "You think you deserve to be happy, after taking my life? You honestly think you deserve that?" And my voice is so loud, it drowns out any other sounds.

Reeve looks stricken. "I didn't know you were going to—"

Pointing at him with the blade, I scream, "You didn't leave me any choice! You knew that I loved you, and you treated me like garbage!" I scream it so loud, the back of my throat burns like fire. Any decent human being wouldn't do that. It's crueler than cruel. It's heartless.

I turn my head slightly, and there are Reeve's teammates, rushing toward him with one of the big water coolers hoisted high in their arms. Reeve tries to back up away from them, and from me, but it happens too fast. They tip the cooler on top of us, and we're both splashed with ice-cold water.

Except something shifts. We don't get wet just from the water inside the cooler. It's an impossible amount, an ocean's worth. And the knife slips out of my hands.

Suddenly the water turns dark, dark blue, like midnight. We're in the water around Jar Island.

He's underwater with me, limbs flailing, mouth open in a silent scream. He tries to kick and swim up to the surface, where Lillia is peering down on us from the dock. But I'm not letting him. I grab hold of his arm, and I start swimming toward the blackness, toward the bottom of the ocean, tugging him down with me. Bubbles of air pour out of his mouth as he struggles to break free from me, but I'm not letting go. I'm Big Easy, fat and heavy like an anchor, sinking him farther and farther and farther away from the surface.

I open one eye and watch as Reeve thrashes around in the bed. It looks like he's having a seizure, just like he did at homecoming. He saw me that night. He whispered "Big Easy." He was afraid of me then, too. That the secret of me would come out. That everyone would know the truth, what a terrible, horrible person he is. Every muscle is taut as he writhes around, gasping for air. And his face—I swear he's turning blue.

I don't know why, but I pull my hand off his forehead. Reeve's eyes immediately fly open and he sucks in a huge breath of air. He's coughing and gagging, his eyes darting around the room. He clicks on his side lamp, sits on the edge of his bed, and tries to catch his breath. He's panting. He pitches forward and sinks his head between his knees. "You're dreaming," he pants. "It's only a dream."

He lies back down and, after a bit, falls back asleep. I curl myself next to him and listen to him breathe.

Chapter Twenty-Five

KAT

AFTER CHUGGING THE LAST DROPS OF ORANGE SODA in my can, I rewind the track about twenty seconds and click the playback button. The final strum comes on nice and loud—the very last note of Alex's third song—and I slide up the treble just a bit on the mixer, so you can really hear the dirty vibration of him pounding that guitar string. It's raw and messy, just like his lyrics.

We've each got one of my earbuds in, and we're both peering at his laptop screen, watching the levels bounce up and down and then turn, abruptly, into a flat line when the track ends.

Alex turns his head to me and whispers with a half smile, "Are we good?"

I hit save and pull out my side of the earbuds. "We are *so* good." I hold up my hand, and Alex high-fives me with a big grin on his face.

"You're freaking awesome, Kat."

"Tell me about it," I deadpan.

Alex asked me to mix his audition tape, even though I told him that I didn't know shit about music production. I mean, I sat in on plenty of bands screwing around at Paul's Boutique with recording equipment, back when I used to hang with Kim. She and I would add hand claps or screams or whatever was needed to the tracks, but none of the guys ever let either of us near the mixing board to tweak the sound.

But Alex insisted. So I told him what software to buy for his laptop and picked him out a pimp microphone that cost more than a year's worth of ferry tickets, and a new guitar pedal that we had to special-order from Europe.

He didn't hesitate.

I'm glad he's looking ahead and not moping around over Lillia and Reeve. He's been texting me like crazy with lyric tweaks and chord changes, and he's reworked all three of his songs according to my feedback. Everybody knows that the best music comes from bloodshed. Not one of those original

Lillia love songs made the cut. It's probably a good thing. He's moving on.

"Well, that's a wrap," I say. "And now you can join me in the hell of waiting for an acceptance letter." I'm about to shut his laptop screen, but Alex stops me.

"I'm going to upload them to the USC server right now." Soberly he adds, "Hopefully they take me, because I can't wait to get out of here. I don't really see myself coming back after graduation."

I let out a little snicker. "You sound like me. Anyway, what are you talking about? You're coming back. Your parents live here."

"For now they do. But my dad's always talking about what a hassle it is to commute from the island to work. And, I mean, my mom loves California. She's already talking about maybe getting a place in Santa Barbara while I'm at school."

Okay, that I do believe. Alex's mom is freaking obsessed with him. "What if you don't get in?" I hate to say it, but I have to, because nothing is a guarantee. Shit, I can barely sleep at night, thinking about Oberlin. "Would they move to Boston?"

Alex isn't hearing me. He keeps his eyes on the computer screen. "I'm not going to Boston. If I don't get into USC, then I'll go to Michigan. I want to be as far away as possible."

I get it. He might not be singing about Lillia, but Alex is

still hurting. But he's being a bit dramatic with this whole I'm-running-away shtick. I ignore it and grab my bag. "All righty, dude. I better bounce. I was supposed to be at Lillia's house hours ago."

"Have fun," he says sarcastically.

I should just go, but I can't help it. "Dude, don't be like that."

"Be like what?"

"Look," I say. "I know you probably feel like a dummy for sending those flowers on Valentine's Day, but I still think it was a good move."

Alex laughs dryly. "Yeah. I'm glad to know that I wasted my whole high school experience on people who don't give a shit about me."

I dig out my keys. I know Lil is trying to wait for the right time to talk to Alex, when he's cooled down some. Unfortunately, he's still white-hot. So instead I ask, "Has Reeve apologized?"

He gives me a look like I'm crazy. "Reeve doesn't say 'sorry.' It's not in his vocabulary."

"Right." That I can believe.

I'm at Lillia's house, and there's a movie on their big-ass TV, but we're not really watching it. Lillia goes into the kitchen and comes back with chips and salsa and hummus. "I got your favorite kind of hummus," she sings out.

Ashes to Ashes

"Thanks, Lil," I say, and I grab a handful of chips.

Nadia comes wandering into the living room in leggings and a cheering hoodie. She sees me lying on the couch but doesn't say anything. "What up, Nadi," I say.

Nadia doesn't answer me. She glares at Lil and snarks, "I didn't know you were having friends over. I was going to invite people over."

"Go ahead. We can hang up in my room."

"Just forget it."

"Easy, little girl," I say. "That's your big sister you're talking to."

Nadia rolls her eyes. If this were at school and not, say, Lillia's living room, I'd knock Nadia on her ass. But I'm a guest here, so I just help myself to another delicious chip.

Turning to Lil, she asks, "Are there any tortilla chips left?"

Lillia shakes her head. "No, but there are pita chips."

Nadia makes a huffy sound. Eyeing our Oranginas, she says, "Did you drink all the Orangina too?"

"I hope so," I say, taking a big swig. I can't help myself.

Lillia elbows me. "I think there's one left."

Nadia shuffles into the kitchen, and I hear her rustling around in the fridge. "I don't see it!"

"Look behind the deli meats," Lillia calls back. Nadia doesn't answer. "Did you find it?"

"No." Nadia comes back into the living room with a Diet Coke and a bag of pita chips. She snatches the hummus and stalks up to her room.

I'm glad I don't have a little sister. Pat can be a pain in the ass, but damn. As soon as she's gone, I say, "Yo, why's Nadia being such a bitch baby?"

"Sorry about that. It's not you. It's me."

"You gotta get her in line," I say, shaking my head. "Whup some ass if need be."

"She's still mad about the whole Reeve thing. She thinks it's a betrayal of Rennie." Quickly Lillia adds, "Which I know it is. Trust me, I know."

I want to say that it's a betrayal of Mary, too, but I keep that thought to myself because I'm here to make her feel better, not worse.

"So how is Alex? How are his songs? When will he hear something back from USC?"

"Um, which one of those do you want me to answer first?"

"Sorry. It's just been a while since we've talked."

"I know you're trying to give him time, Lil, but I'm starting to think that time ain't doing you any favors."

"Ugh." Lillia chews on her bottom lip. "Do you think I'm crazy for going through all this just to be with Reeve?"

"Look, I'm not saying I understand it." I shudder, because

God, Reeve can be such a dick. "But it's your bag. I'm not gonna judge you for it."

Lillia presses her foot up against mine and looks at me with big, grateful eyes. "I promise you, Kat, he's not what you think he is."

I snort. "How so?"

Her face goes all dreamy and soft, which makes me regret asking. Tipping her head back against the couch, she says, "He looks at me like I'm the only girl in the world."

I roll my eyes. "Eww. Forget I asked."

"Kat! Just listen for a minute. Please? I never get to talk about him like this."

"Fine, I'll listen. For a minute."

Lillia looks around, then leans in close to me and whispers, "He's an *amazing* kisser."

I pick at my cuticles. "How far have you guys gone, anyway?"

She covers her mouth and giggles like crazy.

"I've heard the boy has skills," I say.

Lil's cheeks go pink. "We haven't had sex or anything." Then she whispers, "But . . . I think I maybe want to."

I let out a whoop. "You hussy!"

Lillia swats at me, but I block her hand with a pillow. Then, suddenly, her face gets serious. "You've had sex with a lot of guys, right?"

I cut my eyes at her. "A few! Not a lot."

"Right, sorry, sorry," she says. She ducks her head, and her hair falls across her face. Worriedly she asks, "Do you think that Reeve minds? I mean, that we haven't done it yet?"

"Nah. It's like you said, the boy's crazy about you. Any idiot can see that. He might get blue balls, but whatever, he can just jack off, no big deal." Lillia makes a face at me. "What? I'm just being honest. There's no rush, Lil."

"I just wish Reeve was my first time and not that other guy."

I grab her foot. Hard, because this shit is serious. I ain't playing. "That other guy doesn't count. You never said yes to that other guy, so he doesn't count. Your first time is whoever you say it is. You got me?"

She nods.

The front door opens, and Lillia's mom steps inside, wearing an ivory coat with a funnel neck, and studded black leather gloves. She looks like Jackie O but with some edge. She drops her black bag onto the entranceway table and slips out of her heels. "Girls, sorry I'm so late!" she calls out.

I stand up. "Hi, Mrs. Cho."

"Kat!" Lillia's mom rushes over to me without even taking her coat off. She puts her gloved hands on my cheeks and says, "My God, look how grown-up you are! I haven't seen you in so long, honey." She sweeps me into her arms for a long hug, and

I lean into it. She still wears the same perfume, which is weirdly comforting.

Lillia says, "We were just watching a movie, Mommy."

"Oh, that's nice. You'll stay for dinner, won't you, Kat? I want to hear all about everything." When I hesitate, she says, "We'll order in from Red Hot! You always loved their Mongolian beef, right?"

"Stay," Lillia urges me, tugging on my arm.

I grin. "I do love that Mongolian beef."

Mrs. Cho claps her hands together. "Yes! Wonderful! And I have some really nice gelato, and this *decadent* salted caramel sauce. We'll do sundaes!" Putting her arm around me, she says, "It's good to see you girls together again. I'm glad you have each other to lean on."

Lillia and I look at each other. I hadn't thought of it that way, but she's right. We're the only two people who really knew Rennie; we're the only two people who understand that loss. And now Mary's gone too, it truly is just me and Lil.

Chapter Twenty-Six

MARY

I VISIT REEVE NIGHT AFTER NIGHT. I MEET HIM IN HIS dreams. Every time, I say it's the last time, that I need to end Reeve's life once and for all. But when it's morning I come back home, read some more of Aunt Bette's books, and wait until the moon comes out again.

I'm startled by the jingling of keys in the front door, and then a stampede of high-heeled shoes crossing the threshold into the foyer.

In a flash I'm standing at the bottom of the stairs. It's five women from the Preservation Society, dressed like they've just come from a fancy lunch, in fur-trimmed coats, heels and stockings, and quilted purses hanging from gold chains off their shoulders. They are huddled together like a pack, staring around, wide-eyed. One woman, the youngest, searches the wall for the light switch.

I stare at the switch as she clicks it on. Nothing happens. She tries again a few times.

"I guess they turned the electricity off already," she says.

No, you idiot. The electricity is still on. I'm just not letting you use it.

Since my mother took Aunt Bette away, the Preservation Society has come by too many times to count. Usually they stick to the outside, circling the house, making notes in their notebooks, cupping their hands around their eyes to try to peer into the windows.

They've never come inside before.

"I can't see a thing," an older woman complains. She takes a step and almost trips over a pile of mail that was shoved through the front door slot. Another white-haired woman catches her.

"Ooh, I've got an idea!" the young woman says pertly. She pulls out her cell phone and uses the screen like a flashlight. The place is still a mess from when my mother dragged Aunt Bette away. The woman's perky smile fades. "Oh my gosh."

The eldest woman is also the shortest. Her chest is covered

in a bib of pearls. "We'll leave the front door open and just stick to the ground floor." She steps over a buckled runner carpet. "I'm most anxious to see the state of the living room. I know the Zanes did some renovations, and I pray they were smart enough to leave the fireplace mantel intact."

What do these women think they're doing? I know they want to turn the place into some empty dollhouse with fake furniture that no one can live in, but this house has been in my family for more than a hundred years. There's no way my mom or Aunt Bette would ever sell it. Which means that these women are trespassing.

They move as a group into the living room. It's not in great shape. But Aunt Bette and Mom will clean it up when they come back this summer. I hope I'll be in heaven, or wherever, by then. But it still makes me happy to think that my family will live on in this house, that Aunt Bette and my mom still have each other.

"Polly, make sure you take lots of pictures. This will definitely show the people at the benefit why we need to raise those funds."

"We'll have to get our interior guy on this straightaway. Danner, take some notes, and we'll get a quote."

"All right. We need to call the water company and the gas company and get the utilities shut off during renovation. As for that, all the lighting fixtures must go. I don't think these built-in shelves are original, but we can look at the blueprints back in the office. We'll need him to repair the crown moldings and . . . oh good Lord. This wallpaper is atrocious!" The lady with the pearls actually rips a piece off the wall and flicks it onto the floor.

I helped my mother pick out that wallpaper. We both loved the tiny birds on it and the flecks of foil. It was really expensive. It had to be special-ordered from overseas.

Another woman is staring at one of Aunt Bette's paintings on the wall. She lifts it off and tosses it onto the floor, like it's garbage. "Danner, have them bring two Dumpsters."

They can keep dreaming. They can't remove anything or renovate without an owner's permission. I've heard my mother say that she'd rather sell a kidney than ever part with this house.

"Thank goodness Erica decided to donate the house. Another few months and this place would have to be condemned."

What?

There's no way. No.

"I'm surprised she wanted to hold on to it after her daughter killed herself in the room upstairs. If I were her, I'd never want to come back."

Danner holds up her pencil. "Ooh! Actually, this may sound

silly, but maybe we should look into having the place spiritually cleansed. I know a woman who does an excellent tarot reading in White Haven. She studied in India and—"

I feel like I'm about to burst out of my skin. And the house feels it too. Cracks bloom on the plaster walls; white dust sprinkles down like snowflakes. The women scream in unison.

They make for the front door, running through a gauntlet of spark and sizzle as I send bolts of electric current flashing out of outlets and light switches. Danner is the last one to the door, and I slam it and trap her inside before she can cross the threshold.

The other women outside are calling for her. Danner drops her notepad, grabs at the doorknob, and frantically tries to turn it to escape. I pucker my lips and blow some of the electrical sparks down onto the pages, making them catch fire. Their precious notes and measurements crackle into ash.

Shrieking, Danner peels off her fur coat, lays it down on the fire, and stamps the flames out. Then she picks her smoking coat up off the floor, and I finally let her open the door. She runs like mad down the walkway.

They might want this house, but they're not going to get it. Not while I'm still here.

Suddenly I'm standing in front of a beautiful old building. There's a bronze plaque next to the door.

I wonder if I've appeared here because I'm supposed to get back at these ladies. At Danner. I am here for a reason. I just need to find out what the reason is.

The office is closed up; there aren't any lights on inside. I guess the whole staff was over scoping out my house. I pass through the locked door and look around inside. Every detail is beautifully restored. The place must have been an old bank or some kind of store. The ceilings are high, and the place glows with the pink setting sun.

I feel myself pulled down the hallway, and I go with the current. Hanging along the walls are black-and-white photographs of Jar Island from long ago. It's like a museum. I stop at one photo, of a group of elected officials seated at a table covered in documents. Five men and one woman. She has to be my great-aunt, the first female alderman of Middlebury. She fought for the rights of the migrant workers on the island, to see that they were paid fairly and treated well by their employers. My family did such great things. I could have done great things too, if I hadn't . . .

No. Wait. I am doing great things.

I am avenging the lost, the downtrodden. I am punishing those who deserve it.

I pass by an open office door and see a picture of my house up on an easel. On the desk there are contractor plans, beautiful plans, no doubt, but it's not their right. The Preservation Society must have preyed on my mother, knowing she was so vulnerable.

They stole my house.

I snoop around on the desk. There's a seating chart from last year's fund-raiser. There's an X over the date, and someone's changed it to this year's date. I scan the table assignments. I see Alex, his parents. Lillia and her parents at the same table with the Linds. I remember Lillia once telling me how much fun she and Alex had together at the fund-raiser. But someone has put a Post-it next to Lillia's seat. It says *available*.

Well, that shouldn't be. If Reeve is so intimidated by Alex Lind, if he's so worried that Alex is going to steal Lillia away from him, then Lillia should definitely be at the benefit with Alex. I use my hand to lift that Post-it note off, and then I peel off the very top ticket in the pile.

Okay. Time to go make mischief.

But when I try to go, I can't. I'm still in the office.

There must be something else I need to find.

It takes some searching, but I finally spot a creamy white envelope in the outbox. I can see through it to the letter inside, like the envelope is glass.

To Whom It May Concern:

*I am writing to highly recommend acceptance
of Katherine DeBrassio to Oberlin College. I have
worked with Katherine for the last several months
on a preservation project here on the island and am
so impressed with the character . . .*

It goes on and on, full of praise, glowing praise, detailing what a hard and motivated worker Katherine DeBrassio is. How she'd be an asset to any college.

Ah. Yes. I get it.

It makes me extra mad, knowing that she's helped the place that basically stole our family house.

I pick the letter up between two fingers, blink, and the thing goes up in flames.

Chapter Twenty-Seven

LILLIA

EVENTUALLY EVERYONE COMES BACK TO ONE LUNCH table but Alex. I don't know where he eats. I tried to ask PJ about it once, but he just gave me a vague nonanswer, and I gave up. Ash isn't exactly warm to me, but she isn't outright ignoring me anymore either. I'll take what I can get. Alex is the one I can't stop thinking about. He's the one I have to make things right with. And Kat's right. Letting more and more time go by is only going to make a hard conversation even harder.

Friday night I don't get home until dinnertime because my riding lesson at the barn goes long. I run straight upstairs and hop into the shower because Reeve's going to be here soon to pick me up for a party—some junior girl PJ is talking to is throwing it, and Reeve thinks we should go and be social. I think it's because he knows Alex won't be there; he'll be at the Preservation Society gala with his parents. Alex's parents buy a table every year, and my parents always go. That's where they are tonight.

Last year Alex and I went. We sat with our parents, and we rolled our eyes and laughed at them on the dance floor. We snuck a glass of champagne behind the staircase, and we took turns gulping it down. I kept thinking he would ask me to dance, but he never did.

When I get out of the shower, I sit down at my vanity to comb my hair, and that's when I see the gala ticket, tucked in between my perfume bottles. I pick it up, hold it in my hands. My mom must have left it for me this morning. When my mom first mentioned the gala, it was right after Valentine's Day, when things between me and Alex were super weird. I told her I probably wasn't going, but I'm glad she didn't listen.

There's no way Alex will be able to ignore me in front of our parents! He'll *have* to talk to me. I leap into action, doing my makeup, putting my hair in a slicked-back bun. I don't have time to curl it or do anything special. I'm zipping myself into the only long dress I own, a slinky black strapless dress my mom gave me because it was "too youthful" for her, when I remember I'm supposed to go to that party with Reeve.

Shoot.

Before I really think it through, I text him that I'm not feeling well and I'm going to skip out on the party and rest. Reeve immediately texts back a concerned *Are you okay???*, which makes me feel horrible. But there's no going back now.

Dinner is being served when I arrive. I hurry over to the table, and Alex's mother, Celeste, jumps up as soon as she sees me. "Lillia! You look stunning!"

We hug, and then I slide into the empty seat next to Alex. His jaw is hanging halfway to the floor, and then he remembers he's mad at me and erases the surprise from his face and goes back to indifference. He looks very grown-up in his tuxedo.

My mom turns to me and says, "Lilli! How did you know there was an extra seat at the table?"

"Because you left me a ticket," I remind her.

"I did?"

"Yes, it was on my dresser."

My mom looks confused, and then Daddy says, "You look beautiful, honey. Just like your mom."

"Thanks, Daddy," I say.

When the adults are talking about one of the vacations up for silent auction, I whisper to Alex, "I came here to talk to you."

"Then you should probably go." Alex pushes his chair out and stands up. "Does anybody want anything from the bar?" Celeste gives him a reproving look, and he holds up his hands and says, "I'm getting a Sprite."

Alex disappears, and he doesn't come back until dessert. I've got a spoonful of cranberry gelato halfway to my mouth when Celeste says delightedly, "The band's started playing music again! Alex, ask Lil to dance."

I nearly choke. But it's the perfect thing. "I'd love to dance."

"No, thanks," Alex says, taking a sip of his drink. Whatever it is, it definitely isn't just Sprite.

Celeste narrows her eyes at him. "Alex Lind!"

Celeste keeps harassing him, and then his dad joins in, and my dad says, "Don't force the guy."

At this, Alex finally stands up without looking at me. "Do you want to dance?" He says it like it's the last thing he wants to do. I'm red-faced as I follow him out to the dance floor. Stiffly he takes my right hand, and I put my other hand on his shoulder, and we don't look at each other at all. We both look straight ahead. Halfway through the song I know time is running out, and I start practicing in my head what I'm going to say. *I care about you so much. You've always been such a good friend to me. . . .* No, that's not right. *You're one of my best friends—*

"Reeve's going to hurt you. That's the kind of guy he is. But maybe you know that already." I start to pull away from him, so I can see his face, but Alex holds me still. "I want you to know one thing."

My heart beats painfully hard inside my chest. "What?"

"When he breaks your heart, I won't be there waiting. I'm done." And then the song is over, and Alex lets go of me and walks away.

I make some excuse as to why I have to leave, but I can't remember what I tell my parents and the Linds. And I don't wait for permission. I just mumble something, grab my clutch, and go.

My hands shake the whole ride home. Once I'm in my driveway, I don't get out of the car right away. I'm lost in that moment, hearing Alex's voice. *When he breaks your heart, I won't be there waiting. I'm done.*

I've wanted to have it both ways. Both boys. I've never told Alex no, not really. Because I like the way he makes me feel. Because . . . maybe I do have some feelings for him. Maybe that's why this has been hurting me so bad. It's why I don't care about Ash or PJ or anybody else being mad at me. Because none of that's important compared to the thought of Alex hating me.

I'm finally getting out of the car when headlights shine behind me. I turn around, thinking it's my parents coming home early. But it's not. It's Reeve.

He shuts off the engine and jumps out of the truck, holding a plastic bag. He stops short when he sees me. In my dress, with my red lipstick and my hair done up. He frowns in confusion. "Why are you all dressed up?"

I step toward him, and then I falter. "I—I went to that Preservation Society benefit tonight."

"I thought you said you didn't feel well." Realization is dawning over his face. Realization and hurt. He holds out the bag to me, which I take. I open it, and there are candy bars inside.

"I'm sorry," I say, wringing the bag in my hands. "I should have told you I was going. I just—I wanted a chance to talk to Alex alone."

"You mean without me around."

"No. I mean, maybe." I bite my lip. "Alex is really important to me—"

Incredulously, Reeve says, "More important than me?"

"Of course not!"

"Then what the fuck, Cho! You lied to me so you could go to some party with him?" He's panicky. Pacing.

"I just wanted to talk to him, to try to explain—"

Reeve shakes his head. "So now what, you two are buddy-buddy again?"

"No."

"But you wish you were."

"Reeve, just because you and I are together, that doesn't mean I'm cutting him out of my life." I swallow hard. Not that it matters anymore, because he's already cut me out of his.

"Well, what did he say?" He's suddenly quiet. Nervous.

"Nothing."

He takes a step toward me. "Tell me, Cho. He had to have said something."

"Reeve, I . . ." I struggle for what to say. Should I be honest and tell him the terrible things Alex said about him? Every second that passes, Reeve looks like he crumbles. And then I realize he's afraid I'm going to break up with him. "I want to be with you, okay?"

Reeve's face clears, and he grabs me and hugs me so tight. Reeve is the one I am with. And if this is really going to work with us, I need to set these feelings for Alex aside for good. I have to let him go, because he's already let go of me.

Good-bye, Lindy.

Chapter Twenty-Eight

KAT

I TEXT LILLIA TO SEE IF SHE WANTS TO HANG OUT, and she suggests Scoops. When I get there, she's sitting at a table waiting for me. She waves me over like mad even though I can clearly see her.

"What kind of ice cream do you want?" she asks. "My treat."

I raise my eyebrow. Why does she want to treat me? Whatevs. I'm not passing up free ice cream. "Sweet. I'll take a scoop of Moose Tracks and a scoop of mint chip."

"You got it." Lillia jumps up and goes to place the order. I look at my phone until she comes back.

When she sits back down, she has three cups of ice cream. "Whoa, Lil. I know I'm a pig, but I can't eat all that by myself."

"It's not just for us," she says. Sucking in her breath, she says, "Don't be mad, but I invited Reeve to meet us here."

"Lil," I whine. It's one thing if Lil wants to be with Reeve, but I don't see why I should have to waste an afternoon with the kid.

"You know, I was talking about you the other day, and Reeve was like, 'We should hang out with Kat more often! She's really cool!'"

I snort. He never said that. Lillia can't lie for shit.

"Okay, okay, fine. He didn't say that. But here's the truth, Kat. You and Reeve are the two people I care about most in my life, besides my family." She fixes her puppy-dog eyes on me, all beseeching. "And it's important to me that you have a good relationship with each other. I know you guys have history, and we all have history with Mary, but can't you let some of that go and start off fresh? Or, at least try to? For me? I mean, that's what Mary's probably doing. She's starting fresh somewhere, letting the past go. Don't you think?"

Oh, gawd. No wonder Lil has every guy I know eating out of the palm of her hand. This chick is impossible to say *no* to, and I'm not even a dude. She's right. I think a lot of my current Reeve disdain comes from knowing what he did to Mary.

But Lillia seems so sure that he's a good guy. Maybe I have him pegged wrong. And Mary must have found closure, or else she'd still be here.

I sink back into my chair. "Fine, but if he pisses me off, I walk."

"Thank you, thank you, thank you!"

"Does he know I'm here, or did you trick him, too?"

"He knows," she assures me.

I'm shoveling a spoonful of Moose Tracks into my mouth when Reeve walks into Scoops and ambles over to our table like he's a damn king. God, he doesn't even have to speak, and he's already annoying me. He gives Lil a kiss, and then he grins at me and says, "What up, DeBrassio."

I nod at him. With a mouthful of ice cream I say, "'Sup."

Nobody's saying anything, so Lil starts chattering about her horse, Phantom, and practicing different jumping obstacles. Personally, it's boring the shit out of me because I have no idea what any of it means, but Reeve's nodding and listening like he's actually interested. He yawns a couple of times, though, deep sleepy ones. The third time Lillia frowns at him. "Are you even listening to what I'm saying?"

"Yes."

"Then what did I just say?" she challenges.

"You were explaining what jumping over a crossrail means."

He demonstrates by setting up an obstacle course with the napkin dispenser and some straws. He raises his brows at her smugly. "See?" He leans in toward her and opens his mouth and says, "Ahh."

Inwardly I groan. I don't know why I have to sit here and be a witness to their foreplay.

"You have your own ice cream," she says. "You can feed yourself."

"But I like yours better," he says, and pouts.

"I'm not sharing. You don't deserve it. You were yawning the whole time I was talking, right, Kat?"

I shrug and keep eating my ice cream. I'm already plotting what excuse I'm gonna give so I can get out of here.

"Sorry, babe. I'm just tired," he says.

"You do look kinda rough," I say to Reeve, who frowns. With my spoon I gesture at his face. "You've got circles under your eyes."

"I've been sleeping for shit lately," Reeve admits, rubbing his face. "I keep having weird dreams."

"What kind of dreams?" Now I'm interested. I love hearing about freaky dreams. "I have a book that tells you the meaning of different dreams."

"That's so neat," Lillia says. "Reeve, tell her about your dream and she'll interpret it."

Reeve quickly shakes his head. "I don't remember."

Lil licks her spoon. "What do you mean, you don't remember? You just said your dreams were weird."

"I don't know. I don't remember them, okay?"

"God, get defensive, why don't you. I thought it'd be fun. Jeez." She looks at me and makes a face.

I get up to go to the bathroom, and as I duck down the hallway, I hear Lillia hiss, "Can you please perk up and at least try to make an effort with her?"

I stop behind the corner to hide and listen. This sounds like it's gonna be good.

"I'm serious. Kat's my friend and it's important to me that she like you."

Aww. That means a lot. Maybe I could try to make more of an effort too.

"Okay, okay."

"She already has a terrible impression of you, and you're making it worse. The dream thing was the perfect in!"

Damn. He wasn't *that* bad. He just didn't want to share his bad dreams. They're probably about kinky sex stuff.

I go into the bathroom to pee. When I get back, they're still bickering. Yikes. Change of plans—I'll try harder next time. "I think I'm gonna head out," I say.

Lillia glares at Reeve. "You made her uncomfortable."

Reeve challenges, "DeBrassio, are you uncomfortable?"

"No—"

"See?" he says. "I've known this girl my whole life. She doesn't get uncomfortable like a normal girl." A sly grin spreads across his face. "Hey, remember that time in sixth grade when my parents had a Labor Day barbecue? You were wearing white shorts, and I made a ketchup bomb, and it exploded all over your butt, and I told everybody you had your period?" He busts up laughing.

"Reeve!" Lillia yells.

But I'm laughing too. I remember it like it was yesterday. What was embarrassing was I didn't even have my period yet, but I didn't want people to know that.

"You didn't give a shit," Reeve continues. "You just borrowed a pair of Tommy's soccer shorts like it was nothing. Ruined my whole prank."

"Yeah, and I frenched him in your bed that day too," I say, and Reeve's eyes go wide.

"For real?"

I nod.

"You ho!" he hoots.

Reeve and I both crack up so hard I'm coughing out a lung, and Lil says, "Um, that's sexist. Tommy's the ho! He hooked up with every girl on your block, even the old ones. There's such a double standard for guys and girls."

Still laughing, I say, "Lil, quit taking it so seriously. We're just kidding around."

"Thank you, DeBrassio," Reeve says. "She's always ragging on me. It's nice to have somebody on my side for once."

I point at Lillia. "You need to chill out." Reeve starts clapping, and then I point at him. "And you need to not be so full of yourself. It's annoying. You ain't that special." Reeve opens his mouth to protest, but I shush him. I say to Lillia, "Lil, if you want to hear embarrassing stuff from back in the day, here's something. In elementary school Reeve was too chickenshit to take a dump at school, so he used to ask to go to the nurse's office every day after lunch. We all knew where he was going. There was this one day—"

Reeve bellows, "Kat!"

Everyone in Scoops turns to look at us, and Lillia's giggling so hard she's stomping her feet. "OMG, tell me more, tell me more!"

Reeve grabs my shirt sleeve in a panic. "Please, DeBrassio, I'm begging you, do not finish that story. I swear I'll try to be less cocky!"

"All right, all right," I say, chuckling.

From across the table Lillia mouths, *Tell me later*, and I give her a wink and a nod.

When we get out of Scoops, Lillia and Reeve walk me to my

car. As we head down Main Street, I notice the way his eyes follow her wherever she goes. When she stops at a store window, or pauses to take a pebble out of her loafer. He can't take his eyes off her. And any excuse he can get to touch her, hold her hand, put his hand on the small of her back, the guy can't get enough. It's clear he's crazy about her.

I'm still not Reeve's biggest fan, but even I have to admit he adores her. And as her friend, that's all I really give a shit about. So long as he keeps treating her the way he does, Reeve and I are good.

Chapter Twenty-Nine

LILLIA

THE PROM COMMITTEE HAS ONLY MET TWICE SINCE the new year. Rennie was the head of the committee. I guess I've pretty much taken over her job, but only because I'm good at making lists and keeping track of things. Rennie never wrote anything down. I was basically her secretary.

I open up my notebook, start going down the checklist, and say, "So far we've only sold twenty tickets to prom. We really need to work on outreach, you guys."

"Actually, I'd like to address that," Alex says from the other end of the long library table.

I'm careful not to look directly at him. "What is it, Alex?"

He looks out at the table. "It's been brought to my attention that—"

Reeve chuckles, and it makes Alex's mouth snap shut. "Sorry. You just sound like Principal Tortola." Reeve looks at Derek and makes a smirky face, and Derek smirks back.

Alex continues as if Reeve didn't speak. "It's been brought to my attention that some people feel the price of prom is too expensive, and that some people who'd like to go can't swing it."

"What do you mean?" Ash asks, frowning. "Who's been telling you that? Your chorus friends?"

"It's just a lot of money, when you stop and think about it. Last year tickets were, what, fifty bucks? And now they're a hundred? That's crazy."

I speak up. "It's because Rennie changed the venue from the Water Club to that club in the city, remember?"

Derek groans. "It's gonna take us an hour to get there."

"Plus, the point of prom is to celebrate the end of high school with the whole class," Alex says. "I mean, twenty tickets? Half of those were bought by the people on this committee! If it's just going to be us like always, why are we even bothering?"

I press my lips together tightly. It wasn't my idea to move prom! I wanted to keep it at the Water Club so we could get nice pictures on the dock. "You guys were all sitting at this very table when Rennie brought up the idea of having the prom off island. Not one person objected."

"Rennie had a way of convincing people," Alex admits.

"Oh, wait up!" Derek says. "Speaking of Rennie, Lil, do you know if our flight back from Jamaica is direct?"

I frown. "What flight?"

"For spring break."

Alex groans. "Weren't we just talking about prom?"

I completely forgot about our spring break plans. We made those plans before Rennie's death, before everything. Rennie had found some package online through a travel agency that included airfare and hotel at an all-inclusive resort. We gave her the deposit money last summer, before school started. "Um, I don't even know if that's still happening," I say. Everyone's staring at me, slack-jawed. "I mean, I don't know if she ever gave the second half of the deposit or what. I don't even know which website Rennie found the deal on."

Reeve lifts his head off the table. Underneath he grabs my hand and gives it a quick squeeze.

Derek groans. "Are you serious? But you were, like, her right-hand man . . ." His voice trails off.

I bite my lip. This isn't my fault. It's not like I was in charge of the trip. Any one of us could have asked Rennie about it.

"Well, then, where'd the money go?" Ash demands.

Reeve and I exchange a look. I'm sure he's thinking what I'm thinking. That there is a very good possibility that Rennie used that money on something else—like, say, her over-the-top New Year's Eve party—and was planning on paying it back with the cover fee she charged that night for people to get in. She'd done it before with cheerleading money. But there's no way I'm saying it now when she isn't here to defend herself. "I have no idea."

Ash pouts, "If this trip is ruined, I don't know what we're going to do. Everything else will be booked up." She casts a dark look in my direction. "Thanks a lot, Lillia."

"Hey, how is this her fault?" Reeve demands. "If we lost our spot, we'll just go somewhere else."

"How?" Derek snaps. "I don't have money to put toward a new trip. I gave Ren everything I had saved."

Alex starts packing up his things. "Look, don't worry, guys. If we can't go to Jamaica, I bet my uncle Tim will let us take his boat." He turns his back on Reeve and me, and to the rest of the group, he says, "He'll hire a crew to take us. They'll cook for us and everything. Trust me, it'll be better than Jamaica."

Everyone starts talking at once, all excited, and I get up to throw away my lunch. Reeve follows me over to the trash cans. He whispers, "I have a feeling we're not going to be welcome on Tim's boat, Cho."

"Fine by me," I say, and I mean it. With everything that's happened this year, I really am fine to sit this one out.

Chapter Thirty

KAT

I'M IN THE FUNERAL PARLOR IN MY BLACK DRESS, black tights, black-patent leather Mary Janes—the same outfit I wore on my first day of school in sixth grade.

Dad puts his arm around my shoulders. "We've just got to make it through one more hour, and then we can go home."

Confused, I peer around him and see a long line of people waiting to pay their respects. Next to us is the polished mahogany edge of a casket, its hatch propped open for mourners to take one last look.

There's music playing somewhere.

This does not mean
I don't love you
I do, that's forever

I wipe a tear from my eye. The song is "Suite: Judy Blue Eyes." My mom said those lines to me over and over near the end of her life. I think the thing she feared most about dying was that she wouldn't be able to love us once she was gone. The song gave her comfort.

Oh my God. This is her funeral.

I snap my head around, fast. I don't want to see her like this. I don't want to see my mother's dead body.

Mrs. Tabatsky steps forward and takes my father's hand. She's crying. "Oh, Patrick. I'm so sorry." Reeve leans against her. The other Tabatsky boys, along with Reeve's dad, stand silently behind them in their suits.

I realize I haven't seen much of Reeve since summer ended and he transferred to the Montessori on the mainland for seventh grade. Before he left, I teased him about going to a fancy school full of nerds and how he was going to turn into a huge geek. He acted all cocky and told me that when he was a millionaire, maybe I'd be lucky enough to fix his Lamborghini. Reeve was always fun to fight with, because he had comebacks as good as mine, and the two of us could rag on each other for hours.

He doesn't make eye contact with me. He keeps his eyes down on his church shoes.

Wait a minute. Is this a memory? Or am I dreaming?

"It's a dream," Rennie confirms. She comes up beside me with a glass of water. "Isn't this dress the cutest?" she says, and does a spin. It's bright pink, sleeveless and short. "This was the one I wanted to wear to your mom's funeral, but you wouldn't let me."

I remember.

Earlier that morning Rennie called to see if she absolutely had to wear black. She had something else in mind. I got so mad and said, *Of course you do, stupid,* and I hung up.

"I'm sorry I yelled at you, but come on, Ren. Who wears hot pink to a funeral?" I ask her, laughing.

Rennie starts laughing too. "Okay, fine. But your mom told me I looked pretty in this dress once, so I was going to wear it as a tribute to her."

"After I hung up on you, I worried that you might not show up," I say. "But you did. You and your mom were the first people here, and you stayed with me the whole day. I remember you always made sure you were blocking my view of the casket, because I didn't want to look. I couldn't handle seeing her corpse, painted in makeup she would never have worn, surrounded by that ugly silk liner in the coffin. Judy wasn't silk. She was blue jeans. " I start to cry.

Rennie smiles tenderly and pulls me into a tight hug. "Of course I'd show up, dummy. I was your best friend."

Rennie was a good friend, mostly. And she was there for me when it really counted. "I'm glad we made up before you died," I tell her, hugging her back.

She groans, "Ugh. I freaking hate that girl."

As soon as I let go, Rennie disappears. "Wait! Ren!"

I turn and see that the next person in line is Mary. "Why are you crying?" she asks in a very curt voice. "Rennie made your life miserable, remember? You said you hated her. You said you were happy that she was going to finally get what she deserves."

"I—I know that. But we made up." I wipe my eyes. "And she didn't deserve to die."

Mary rolls her eyes. "You're such a traitor, you know that? You wanted this! Don't you remember our pact? You're a terrible friend who breaks promises, and you're a liar. I'm glad your mom gets to see who you turned out to be."

It kills me to hear her say that. "Mary, wait. Come on, let me explain." But she suddenly starts pushing me toward the casket. "No! I don't want to look! Don't make me look!"

But Mary is so freaking strong. And my shoes slip along the floor. I squint my eyes tight, because I can't fight her off. I feel myself hit the casket, the edge of it smacking into my stomach.

"Open your eyes!" she screams.

"No! Please!"

Her fingers peel apart my eyelids. "Look at what you've done!" I'm hysterical.

And then, suddenly . . . nothing.

"Kat, sweetie, it's okay."

I open my eyes, and there's my mother by my side. She looks like she did before she got sick. Healthy. And so beautiful.

"I don't know what's wrong with her," I say, clinging to my mom.

"She's lost, Kat. And that makes her dangerous."

I wake up in the den, sprawled out on the couch. Dad and Pat are standing over me with the weirdest expressions on their faces. Even Shep is there, barking like mad and panting his hot breath in my face.

"What?" I say, and wipe the drool off my cheek.

"That must have been some dream, daughter." Dad says. "You were thrashing."

It was a crazy-ass dream, and I know it ain't going to be in my dream dictionary. But as crazy as it was, I'm not happy to be awake. I wish I was still asleep with my mom next to me.

On my way to class the next day, Alex casually drops a paper hat onto the top of my head as he walks by.

It doesn't even occur to me that it's a note until I pull it off my head at the insistence of Mrs. Hetzel. That's when I see Alex's handwriting on the underside. I peel back the folds and find an invitation to join him and his friends on a boat trip for spring break. As part of his graduation present, Alex's uncle Tim hired a crew to sail his boat around and basically attend to our every whim. Alex can invite whoever he wants.

I find him practicing his guitar in the chorus room during his free period. Right away he grins at me and is like, "Are you in?"

"Maybe."

He's surprised. "Why not?"

"First off, I said maybe! Are Lil and Reeve coming?" Alex looks away. "Did you even invite them?" When he doesn't answer, I flick his ear, hard. "You invite all their other friends but not them? Oh my God, you know what, Al? This vindictive thing you're doing"—I wave my finger in a circle—"is not a good look on you. I get it. Reeve stole your dream girl and Lil picked another guy. But also, BFD. Don't hold on to this shit and let it turn you into something you're not."

He sighs. It probably is exhausting for Alex to keep up this level of anger. It's not in his nature. "Do you want to come or not?"

"I'm not friends with your friends," I remind him.

"They aren't that bad. Plus, I'm inviting a couple of kids from chorus too."

I roll my eyes. "Ashlin *is* that bad." Last week, as I was walking through the school parking lot, I spotted her picking the pennies and nickels out of her center console and tossing them out the window like they were old gum wrappers or something. I mean, I get that pennies are basically worthless, but nickels aren't. Who in their right mind throws away nickels? A homeless person would love him some freaking nickels.

Alex shakes his head, like I've got it wrong. "She's nice. And she'll be nice to you. I promise. It won't suck. I mean, you do remember my uncle's yacht, right?"

I have to laugh, because of course I remember. That's where we hooked up last summer. "Eww, dude. Please. You're like my brother. I don't want to think about kissing my brother."

"Fine, fine. I'm just saying. What else are you going to do?"

I open my mouth, but close it just as fast. I don't have jack shit going on for spring break, besides obsessively checking my mailbox for word from Oberlin. Danner said she'd send in my letter after the benefit, so I'm assuming I'll hear something soon.

"I'll think about it," I say. "But I want to talk to Lil about it first, because I'm not a jerkface." I emphasize the last part for Alex's benefit. It feels weird to say yes, to go away with Alex and his friends, when I know she isn't invited.

When I see Lil next period, I get right to it. I tell her about Alex's spring break invite and watch her face closely for any signs that she's pissed. But she doesn't give me any.

"Yeah, you should go," she says. "Definitely."

So, looks like I'm going. I guess it'll be fun.

I guess.

The only thing that sucks is that if Lillia was going, I know it'd for sure be a good time.

Chapter Thirty-One

LILLIA

THE VERY FIRST DAY OF SPRING BREAK, I GET THE
news—I got in to Boston College! My mom and I jump up and
down and scream our heads off when we see the big envelope.
Daddy's at a conference now, but he's flying in on Friday, so
we can do a celebratory dinner at Uni Sushi, which is easily
the most expensive restaurant on the island. There's only a
tasting menu, and it's incredible. I've been there once, for my
fourteenth birthday. My mom took Rennie and Nadia and me.
The best part is, my mom said I should invite Reeve too, so he
and Daddy can properly meet. It will be perfect, because my

dad will be in a good mood, and there will be amazing sushi, and it will just be really easy-peasy. Fingers crossed.

I spend the week riding Phantom nearly every afternoon and working on my tan. If I can't tan on a yacht, I can at least tan by my pool. I'll be damned if they come back all golden brown and I'm pasty like sugar-cookie dough.

One day Reeve and I go get mani-pedis at the salon, and the ladies at the salon go gaga over him. The whole time, Reeve flips through fashion magazines pointing out possible prom looks for me. He finds one I really love, so I rip the page out when no one's looking.

As soon as I get home, I start calling stores in Boston, and I find one that carries it—this fancy boutique on Newbury Street near our apartment. It's call C'est La, and it carries a lot of French designers. My mom buys all her bras there, because according to her, only the French know how to do lingerie.

The next day Reeve and I wake up extra early and head into Boston. We go straight to the boutique, and I run and try the dress on. It fits perfectly, but I'm still not sure.

Reeve knocks on the dressing room door. "Come on, lemme see."

"No, I want it to be a surprise," I say.

I'm still staring at myself in the dress, looking at it from every angle, when it occurs to me—what's holding me back. Why I'm uncertain. It's the first dress for a school dance that I'll have bought without Rennie beside me telling me it's the one.

I have to bite my lip not to cry. I look into the mirror and whisper, "Ren, what do you think? Do I have your okay?"

I close my eyes and imagine that Rennie is next to me, smiling, saying, "Yeah, beotch, you have my okay."

It's silly, but when I open my eyes, I know this dress *is* the one, because Rennie said so.

After we leave the boutique, I take Reeve to the place where all the food trucks park near the BC campus. Sausage-and-pepper sandwiches are Reeve's favorite, and supposedly this one cart serves up the best ones in the entire country. It's hilarious, watching him eat it. He keeps making these *Mmmmm* sounds. Then we walk around campus for a bit before we drive back to the ferry. I point out the dorms and the library, and we stop in the student store and I buy a BC sweatshirt. I imagine it'll be just like this when he's visiting me on the weekends when he doesn't have football.

On Friday I'm on my computer looking at pics people are posting from Alex's uncle's boat. Ash just posted one of some crazy chocolate dessert with whipped cream and cookie crumbles. There's another one of her with Derek. She's sitting in his lap, and she's got on a wide-brimmed hat, and her hair is braided in pigtails. I'm scrolling through Alex's feed when I see a picture of Kat in a bikini with a captain's hat on and a cigar hanging out the side of her mouth. She's super tan too.

I pause on a picture of Alex and Kat. They've got their backs to the camera, and they're dangling their legs over the water, cracking up over something. I'm glad she got to go on this trip. The old Kat would never have gone on vacation with any of those people.

I helped her pack the night before she left, and Kat kept saying how this was her first real spring break trip, how she'd hardly ever even left Jar Island. It definitely made me stop and think about how I've taken for granted the vacations my parents have taken us on—Paris, Hawaii, Japan, Korea, even just those weekend jaunts to New York. I doubt Kat's ever been to New York. Rennie had never been before we took her. The next time we go to New York, I'm going to invite Kat. It's her kind of city.

I snap my laptop shut and put on my favorite bikini, the one with the daisies. Then I grab an Orangina and a towel and head out to the patio. Nadia and her friends Janelle and Patrice are floating around the pool with the outdoor speakers on blast. It's not that warm out, but the sun is bright and our pool is heated. Janelle and Patrice chorus, "Hi, Lillia!"

"Hey, guys," I say. I go turn the music down, and Nadia rolls her eyes but doesn't say anything. She knows better than that. She can be mad all she wants, but she knows that if she dares cop an attitude with me in front of her little friends, I am not having it.

I've got my eyes closed when I feel someone picking me up. My eyes fly open, and it's Reeve grinning at me. He's in his swimming trunks and sunglasses. I thought he was at the gym! That's what he's been doing every day when I've been at the stables. Now that he's gotten his playbook and workout routine for Graydon, he's always in the weight room lifting weights. It shows, too. He has a serious six-pack now.

"Hey, you," I say.

"Hey, you," he says, and he scoops me up and carries me over to the pool like I weigh nothing.

"Don't you dare!" I scream, flailing my arms and legs.

"Do it, Reeve!" Janelle shrieks.

"I'm serious, you better not," I warn him.

Reeve winks at me. "I won't," he says, and then he jumps into the water with me in his arms. We land with a big splash, and I'm still screaming with my arms tight around his neck. Sputtering with laughter, he says, "You're choking me!"

I splash him right in the face and paddle away from him. "Everybody, get Reeve!"

Janelle and Patrice dive toward him, but Nadia hangs back. Reeve swims right for her and picks her up like he's going to throw her into the air. She's screaming her head off, and for a second I worry that she's mad. I'm about to tell Reeve to put her down, when she starts cracking up. And then everybody's splashing everybody. Us girls get him good, and Reeve starts circling like a shark, throwing all the girls around. They love it. I swim to the edge of the pool and hang off the side and watch. I haven't seen Nadia this happy since before Rennie died. "Lilli, help!" she screams, giggling so hard, she can barely stay afloat.

"Sister power!" I scream back, swimming toward them. I start trying to dunk Reeve, but it doesn't do any good, because pretty soon he's got me by the waist with one arm and Nadia with the other.

It's a really good day. It feels so nice to play, to feel young and free. Later Nadia and her friends are watching TV inside, and Reeve and I are wrapped up in towels watching the sun set. "Hey, can you maybe wear a tie to dinner tonight, and khakis?" Before Reeve can answer, I add, "And my dad will order sake for the table, but you definitely shouldn't drink any."

Reeve gives me a look. "Cho, I'm not a barbarian. I know how to act around parents."

"I know, I know, but please just don't act cocky. My dad hates when young men act cocky." That's a direct quote, too.

"Hey, you knew what you were signing up for when you got on this ride," Reeve says, grinning, and I shriek and slap him on the legs.

"Ow, ow! That hurts!" Reeve grabs my hands. "I'm kidding. I'll be a perfect gentleman. Don't worry so much."

I lean back against him and say, "Remember the first time we met? When the house was being built? You were here with your dad and we were playing tag, and you ran right into a room with fresh cement and ruined it." I burst into giggles.

Ruefully Reeve says, "My dad beat my ass for that. It was worth it, though. You had on a frilly dress like you were going to a piano recital, and you were such a little bitch." In a high-pitched voice he says, "'I'm rich and this is my house.'"

I slap him on the chest and he fends me off, and we just sit there, watching the sun dip away.

"I love you, Cho."

A smile spreads across my cheeks. "Duh," I say.

"You're such a brat," he says, pulling me closer.

"You knew what you were signing up for," I say.

He laughs, and then I say, "I love you, too."

Reeve's chest puffs up, he's so happy. "Hey, I was going to wait to give this to you tonight, but I'm already nervous about impressing your dad, and they might think it's weird, like I'm getting too serious too fast . . ." He reaches into his bag and pulls out a small box. "For you."

I don't know if Reeve has good taste in jewelry or not, but I recognize the red velvet box as being from Brightline's—the shop where I bought the necklaces for me, Rennie, and Kat—and they really don't have anything ugly. I open it already smiling. It's a beautiful necklace: an opal heart surrounded by a line of pavé diamonds, on a short chain. I can't stop staring at it. "I love it! But, Reeve, it must have been so expensive."

"Only the best for Princess Lil," he teases, and I lean forward and hold up my hair so Reeve can do the latch. Years from now this will be what I remember when I remember my spring break senior year. Not the missed trip to Jamaica, or not being invited on Alex's yacht with all my friends. It will be this moment right here. The smell of chlorine on his skin. The way the sun dips slow into the water before it disappears. The first time I ever told a boy I loved him.

Chapter Thirty-Two

KAT

THE SUN IS SINKING LOWER AND LOWER IN THE SKY. Even though I know it's bad as shit for your eyes, I've got my sunglasses perched on the top of my head so I can stare straight into it. The orangey pinks of the rays, sizzling out across the slate sky, lighting up the turquoise water in electric-blue streaks. The colors are just too beautiful, and to look at them through some cheap-ass drugstore plastic lenses would be a straight-up travesty. Plus we set sail back to Jar Island tomorrow, and I want to hold on to every single minute.

Clearly I screwed up. Forget Oberlin. I should have applied to some random school in the Caribbean to study marine biology so I could see this sunset every damn day.

Everyone else is below getting ready for dinner. I'm in my black bikini, cross-legged on one of the white sunbathing beds on the main deck. It was starting to get cold, and my suit was still wet from this afternoon—when me and the guys were taking turns jumping off the bow. Luckily, one of the boat staff brought me out a drink and set a super-soft blanket over my shoulders.

I've done jack shit for the past few days besides swim and sun myself, and my legs are almost as brown as the whiskey in my glass. I have to keep reminding myself to sip it slowly, because it's the smoothest, most quality shit in Uncle Tim's bar, and it goes down dangerously easy. I fear I'll never be able to drink cheap whiskey again.

Down on the deck below me, I hear the boat staff setting the dinner table for us, the clinking of glasses and silverware. We've eaten outside every single night, a gourmet meal with fresh seafood, on a big banquet table draped with white linen tablecloths. There's a chef working all day for us, breakfast, lunch, dinner, and desserts, while we fuck around.

I thought it would take some getting used to, this kind of life. But it hasn't. Like the whiskey, it's going down really, really easy. And I'm kind of bummed that this is my one and only spring break trip.

"Yo, Kat. Look what we found!"

I turn my head and see PJ walking over in a button-up shirt and board shorts, mirrored sunglasses hiding his eyes. He's holding a wooden box. Jonah, one of Alex's chorus friends, comes up beside him and lifts the lid, like a game show hostess showing off a prize. Inside are neat stacks of brown cigars, each one encircled with an ornate gold foil band.

I stand up and pull on my cutoffs. "Holy shit. Are you serious? Another box of Cubans?" I haven't smoked a cigarette for three weeks now, but I've made a spring break exception for a Cuban. Several spring break exceptions.

"Uncle Tim must have just come back from Havana," Derek says. He takes out two, cuts the tips with a silver clip monogrammed with Uncle Tim's initials, and passes around a lighter. "Yo, Al! You want one too, right?"

Alex comes up from the kitchen, followed by one of the hired boat staff carrying a tray in his hands loaded with four tumblers of whiskey and perfect square ice cubes. I quickly drain the glass I'm holding and then trade my empty for a fresh one.

"The chef is making some sick crab cakes! Should be ready in an hour, guys," he announces. After taking a few big gulps of his whiskey, he says to us, "What do you say we never go back?"

Though he's smiling, I know there's truth behind those words. This has been an escape for Alex, to not have to see Reeve and Lillia together.

In a way it's been an escape for me, too.

Right after we set sail, I regretted saying yes. First off, sailing on any boat when *Judy Blue Eyes* is gone depressed the shit out of me. And, as I expected, it was awkward on board for the first few days. We were definitely divided along class lines. Alex's chorus friends mostly hung out up on the deck, while the rest of us were in the lounge. Jonah spent the whole first night shuffling his magic cards, and Ivan didn't do much but stare down at his bongos and pat them quietly. Brianna, the girl who did the Christmas duet with Alex, has followed him around like a lovesick puppy. It was basically my worst fears come true.

But things took a turn when the captain found us a cove between some tiny sand islands, and the water was warm like a bath. Everyone took turns jumping off the bow into the water, even Ashlin, which impressed the shit out of me.

That was really all it took for us to be cool with each other. That night everyone hung out on the deck together. Ivan played his bongos, and PJ and Derek made up a rap, which was pretty decent for a freestyle and had me laughing my ass off. Ashlin had Brianna putting braids in her hair. And Alex, bless his heart, kept sitting between me and Jonah, because dude had his eyes on my boobs, like, 24/7.

All in all, not a bad time. In fact, it's been pretty great.

So my escape? I'm always so quick to shit on things . . .

people, experiences, different points of view. I get it set in my head that things are a certain way, and then I shut out anything that might contradict that perception. Except I couldn't pull that shit on this boat, and I'm better for it.

I go downstairs to shower and change for dinner. Ashlin is in the room, getting into this flowy caftan thing, and Brianna has on a 1950s housedress. I don't have anything dressy to wear for our last meal, so I put on my black tank dress. I should seriously get new clothes before I head to Oberlin. I mean, if I get in. That acceptance letter better be waiting for me when I get home.

Ashlin comes up behind me with a scarf. It's got a cool trippy pattern on it. She ties it around my head like I'm some kind of seventies rock star.

"Thanks," I say.

"You should totally wear a look like this to prom! Something vintage."

Prom. See? Another one of those things that I've shit on. Why shouldn't I go to prom? I'm a freaking senior, after all.

Ash looks over at Brianna. "Did you buy your dress yet?"

"Um, not yet," Brianna says. "I'm not sure if I'm going."

"That's crazy! You have to go."

"I'm in this show at the regional playhouse, and I had to

buy my own costume. So I doubt I'll have the money."

"Oh," Ash says, and I can tell she feels like a dummy. "Well, that stinks."

"It's no big deal," Brianna says, lowering her eyes.

"Wait," I say. "Prom tickets are that expensive?" If they are, I probably can't go either.

"They are this year," Brianna explains. "It's going to be at some club in Boston."

"That's a dumb idea." I turn and look at Ash. "Who's making these bonehead decisions?"

Ash points her finger at me. "Don't even. You have no right to complain. If you care, then come to a prom committee meeting. Don't just bitch about it."

Damn. Ash has some fire in her. "Okay, okay. Down, girl." I smile at her, and she smiles back.

It's crazy, the things that have happened this year. How much I've changed. How everything that I thought was set in stone isn't. It makes me excited for the future and all its possibilities. Anything can happen.

Suddenly I have the overwhelming urge to talk to Mary. I want to tell her how much better life gets, if you give it a chance. I want to tell her to let go of the Reeve drama once and for all. I want to tell her that I miss her.

Ashes to Ashes

Chapter Thirty-Three

LILLIA

IN THE CAR ON THE WAY TO THE RESTAURANT, I SMOOTH down the skirt of my silk dress and say, "Daddy, please be nice to Reeve."

He and my mom exchange a look. "I'm always nice."

In the backseat Nadia and I exchange a look of our own. "Not true, Daddy," she says in a singsong voice. "When you met James, you gave him the third degree about drinking and driving. And, hello, we don't even have our licenses yet! Now James is afraid to come over to the house."

My dad hides a smile.

I give Nadia a grateful look, and then she remembers she's supposed to be giving me the silent treatment, and she turns her head back toward the window.

When we pull into the parking lot, Reeve's sitting on a bench in front of the restaurant. He's wearing a tie and khakis, and even a navy-colored sport coat that he must have borrowed from one of his brothers, because I've never seen him wear it before. He quickly stands up from the bench and shakes my dad's hand. "Dr. Cho," he says. "Good to see you again, sir."

"Daddy, this is my friend Reeve," I say.

"Hi, Reeve," my dad says. The two of them are almost the same height. Reeve's just an inch or so taller.

Reeve kisses my mom on the cheek. "Stunning as always, Mrs. Cho," he says, which of course she eats up. My dad looks amused by this. To Nadia he says, "What's up, li'l pup," which she acknowledges with a wave.

When we get to the table, my dad pulls out the chair for my mom, and Reeve tries to pull out my chair, but he jerks too hard and it makes a terrible squeaking sound, and everyone turns around to look. I'm so tense, I feel like I'm going to give myself a stroke, but Reeve looks as relaxed and at ease as always.

My dad orders a bottle of sake, and when he offers some to

Reeve, Reeve picks up his glass and accepts with both hands. I shoot him a panicked look, like *What are you doing?* and Reeve says, "Dr. Cho, I read that in Korean culture it's rude not to accept alcohol from an elder."

My parents exchange impressed looks. "Absolutely correct," my dad says.

"And I'm supposed to drink it like this?" Reeve turns his head to the side and takes a small sip.

My dad hoots with laughter. Daddy never hoots. I can feel my stomach start to unclench.

"Wait, why is he drinking it like that?" Nadia asks.

"You aren't supposed to drink in someone's face, because it's considered disrespectful," my mom says. "You're supposed to turn your head slightly. Reeve, where did you learn about this?"

"I read a few articles, and I watched a YouTube video on drinking with elders," Reeve says.

"Oh, that's darling," my mom exclaims. "What else did you learn?"

Reeve sits up straighter. "Never pour your own drink. Never let someone else's glass sit empty. Always accept a drink with two hands."

My dad turns to me. "Do you know about all this, Lilli?"

"I know to accept with both hands," I say.

"What about you, Nadi?" my mom asks.

"I don't need to know about it because I'm not old enough to drink anyway," Nadia says with a frown, spearing a cherry out of her glass. We both like to drink Shirley Temples when we go out to eat.

My dad laughs. "Well, it's good to know anyway."

Though he doesn't say so, Daddy is also impressed by how much sashimi Reeve eats. My mom keeps putting more on his plate and he keeps eating it. It turns out he's also fine with chopsticks. When my dad asks him about his postgrad year, I get nervous again, but Reeve is prepared. He tells him he's been accepted to Graydon, that he's already training again.

"Where is Graydon?" Daddy asks him.

"It's about an hour outside Boston," Reeve says. "In Connecticut."

"Hm," my dad says, but he doesn't say anything else. He leans forward and says, "A colleague of mine's son did a post-graduate year. He ended up playing a year of football at UVA before he injured his knee. Then he had to transfer because his grades weren't good enough. What are your plans, Reeve?"

My mom gives Daddy a sharp look, which he pretends not to notice. I say, "Daddy, Reeve is really smart. He broke 2100 on the SATs!"

Reeve laughs an awkward laugh. "Lillia, you don't have to talk me up like that." To my dad he says, "I don't have any illusions about playing in the NFL or anything. I just want to go to a great college, and football is my way in. I'd like to double major in business and communications, sir."

That's news to me. I can tell my dad is satisfied by the answer too.

Then Reeve tells a story about how he sold seashells to tourists when he was a kid, and everyone laughs, even Nadia.

On the way home my mom winks at me in the rearview mirror.

Chapter Thirty-Four

MARY

I'M WAITING IN LILLIA'S BEDROOM FOR HER TO COME home from the dinner celebration with Reeve. I watched him all day from a safe distance, playing around in the pool with Lillia, saying "I love you," trying so hard to impress her family at their special dinner.

I could have stopped it at any time. Crushed his perfect day. I wanted to so badly.

But then I thought, *Why?* Let him have it. That way it'll hurt all the worse when I take everything away. I'll be so much stronger, and way more powerful, if I wait a little longer.

Tomorrow. That's it. Tomorrow's going to be hell on earth. My day of reckoning.

I've been in Lillia's room before, but tonight I really take time to look around. Lillia has so many pretty things on her vanity. Bottles of lotion and tubes of lipstick and a pink hairbrush from France, plus a big glass jar where she keeps her hair ribbons. Her closet is like you see in a fancy boutique—stacks of cashmere sweaters, rows of blouses and skirts and dresses, everything arranged by color, from light to dark. Even though I've hardly seen Lillia wear the same outfit twice, so many of them still have the tags on. There's one dress hanging on a special puffy hanger, and it's cloaked in plastic. I know as soon as I see it that it's her prom dress.

Lillia gets everything she wants. The boy, the college acceptance letter. She has a dream life. But not tonight. I'm going to ruin her dreams tonight.

I walk toward her dresser. Her necklaces hang on a silver tree, but she also has a jewelry box. There's a picture frame with a photo of a young Lillia and Nadia riding on the same merry-go-round horse. They both have their hair in pigtails, and Lillia is hugging Nadia so tight it looks uncomfortable.

I hear the family come home. Not one but two sets of footsteps hurry up the stairs. So I dart behind the chaise.

Lillia comes in first. Her dad calls out, "Good night,

college girl!" and she calls back, "Night, Daddy!"

Nadia comes in right behind her. She flops down on Lillia's bed as Lillia unzips herself out of her dress and slips on a soft gray nightie.

Lillia carefully takes off the necklace Reeve gave her this afternoon, hangs it on the necklace tree, and then takes a seat at her vanity and asks, "So, what do you think? Did Daddy approve?" She pulls open a drawer and takes out a couple of cotton balls.

"Are you kidding?" Nadia says. "I think Daddy loved him. That Korean culture stuff, Daddy ate it up! Reeve was so smart to do that."

Lillia smiles into the mirror. "I feel bad. I basically scared Reeve into his best behavior. I was so sure he'd do something . . . I don't know. Something that Daddy wouldn't like."

I shake my head. Reeve knows how to charm everyone. That's part of why he's so dangerous. It can happen, even when you don't want it to. Even when you are trying your very hardest to resist. Lillia should know that better than anyone else. She's known him for years. She's seen the way he treats people. And yet she doesn't recognize it. She refuses to see his true colors.

Nadia rolls onto her stomach and watches Lillia remove her makeup. It's clear Nadia adores Lillia. After a while Nadia says, "Lilli." She's trembling. "I'm sorry I was so terrible to you."

Lillia turns around in her chair. "Nadi, don't even."

But Nadia has started to cry. She smothers her face in the comforter.

Lillia immediately gets up and lies on the bed with Nadia and strokes her hair. "It's fine, okay? I understand why. You were upset. You loved Rennie a lot. We both did."

"Still. That's not what sisters do." She sniffles some, but it only makes the tears run harder. "And now you'll be going away to college, and I won't ever see you, and . . . and . . ." Her face wrinkles up like a baby's. "I'm going to miss you so much."

Lillia shushes Nadia, and lies down next to her, comfy-cozy. "I'll miss you too, Nadi," she whispers. "But I'm not going away forever! I'll come home a lot, or you can come and visit me. We'll go shopping, and eat at the food trucks. Boston's not that far away. " She reaches over to her night-stand and plucks out a tissue for Nadia. "I don't know what you're so sad about, anyway. You're going to have Phantom all to yourself now."

Nadia laughs, but she's still sniffly. Lillia pulls her blankets up over them, reaches for her TV remote, clicks something on, and the two lie in bed together. As snug as two bugs in a rug.

Lillia falls asleep first, and Nadia nods off a few minute after. I slide up next to Lillia and place my hand on her forehead.

JENNY HAN & SIOBHAN VIVIAN

Lillia puts on her daisy bikini and walks out to their backyard pool with a drink and her towel. Nadia and her friends are there, swimming and suntanning. Lillia leans back in her lounge chair and closes her eyes, as peaceful as can be. Finally Reeve arrives in his swimming trunks.

Lillia's dreaming about today. She's trying to relive it all over again.

That's not going to happen.

There's a splash, and Lillia opens her eyes, confused. This isn't how it went. Reeve should be scooping her up, jumping into the water with her.

She looks around. Nadia and her friends are gone. And Reeve's already in the pool.

With me.

Lillia screams a bloodcurdling scream. "Mary, no!"

I've got my hand on Reeve's head, holding it below the surface. It doesn't matter that he's got the body of a Greek god. His strength is no match for me.

Her hands fly to her mouth, her eyes wide and terrified. She darts toward the pool edge, but I make the pool stretch wider with every step closer she takes, so she never makes up any ground. She can't get close to us. "Please stop!"

"You've been a crappy friend to me, Lillia. You broke our

pact, you forgot about me, and you fell in love with the one person you shouldn't have."

She touches the necklace, her mouth agape. Then she runs to the diving board and falls onto her stomach. She's reaching out, trying desperately to get a hand on Reeve. "Mary, please! He'll drown!"

"Yes, he will. When Reeve dies tomorrow, remember that I'm the one who killed him."

I lift my hand from her forehead.

See you tomorrow, Lillia.

Chapter Thirty-Five

LILLIA

When I wake up, I know that I had a bad dream, but I can't remember what it was. I'm lying in bed trying to piece it back together when Reeve calls.

"Come over," I say, rolling onto my side.

"I'll stop by after I go work out my legs at the school pool."

Hearing that makes me nervous. I sit up in bed. "Your leg isn't hurting, is it?" Reeve's been working out so hard these last few weeks, following the coach's plan so he'll be fully ready for the prep school's summer session.

"Don't worry. It's fine. I'm just being proactive."

"You'd tell me, though, right? If it was hurting you?" I wonder if I'll ever not feel guilty for what happened to Reeve on homecoming night.

"You sound like my mom," Reeve says, laughing.

I make a *tsk* sound. "Well, we both care about you, dummy!" He's right, though. Mrs. Tabatsky and I are both on him about not pushing himself too hard. And we're both a little obsessed with Reeve's protein intake.

I know Reeve was just joking, but I'm still thinking about it an hour later, when I'm sitting in the kitchen eating cinnamon toast and fingering the necklace he gave me yesterday. No girlfriend in the world wants to be compared to her boyfriend's mother. That's the opposite of hot.

So I get an idea to surprise Reeve at the pool, for old times' sake.

If only I had a new bikini to wear. Something Reeve hasn't seen me in. Nadia's downstairs watching a movie, so I sneak into her room and go through her drawers. I find a brand-new one that she bought at the end of last season. It's a tiny triangle top and a skimpy bottom in iridescent lavender, the kind of bikini I've only ever seen girls wear in Miami. At the time, I tried to veto it, because I felt like it was a bit much for her, but she acted like I was being a prude. She clearly never wore it,

JENNY HAN & SIOBHAN VIVIAN

though, so she must have agreed with me deep down.

I change into it and check myself out in Nadia's mirror. I tug at the bottom so it covers a little more. It's definitely sexier than any bikini I've ever owned, but at least Reeve won't be comparing me to his mom anymore.

Chapter Thirty-Six

MARY

Many ghosts are motivated by a deep psychological issue, about which they tend to be single-minded and obsessive. Be warned that if a ghost makes him- or herself known to you and does not solicit your help, he or she likely means to do you harm.

Reeve doesn't see it coming, even though I'm there, kneeling on one of the diving platforms. Even though I got the idea from his very own dream.

He takes off his towel. After a few arm circles and knee

jumps to get warm, he hops into the water at the shallow end. He pulls a pair of swim goggles down over his eyes, sucks in a deep breath, and begins swimming a long straight lap, right toward me. I lean over the water and wait for him to come up and take a breath. His last. When he does, I'll be the final face he sees. And then we'll both be free.

To become visible a ghost must vibrate at the specific life frequency of the intended witness.

I close my eyes and use everything, every last drop of power, to set myself in sync with Reeve. A low buzz turns into the crystal-clear beat of his heart pumping him through the water in my empty shell. The in-and-out and in-and-out of his breath fills my atrophied lungs as he rotates his head from the surface to underwater. The bursts of blood coursing through his veins feel like thousands of electrical pulses waking up my numb extremities.

Reeve swims closer and closer. A few feet out from the wall, he sucks in a big last breath and takes the final stretch underwater. He starts rising back up to the surface, and I reveal myself like I read in Aunt Bette's book. We lock eyes before he hits the air. His face contorts.

Good-bye, Reeve.

I leap into the water and wrap my arms and legs around his body. Reeve flails and thrashes, but I squeeze him like a vise and sink him *down, down, down* to the dark bottom of the pool.

He's fighting me so hard, it doesn't take long for him to run out of gas. His hum quiets, quiets, quiets.

It's almost over. I'm so glad it's almost over.

And then, a shock of white before things come in flashes.

His mother's face.

Brothers throwing him up to the sky.

A hug from an old woman.

A dog snarling and snapping at his hand.

Running and sliding on wet cement.

His dad, drunk and swinging his fists.

This is Reeve's life, flashing before his eyes. And because we're in sync, I can see it along with him. Every bit of this mystery boy is unfolding for me like a movie of a billion different frames.

Baseball home run.

Hiding under a bed.

Walking into the Montessori lunchroom.

A flash of me, soaking wet on the ferry, bawling my eyes out.

Reeve running home, sobbing.

At the ferry the next day, looking for me.

Our teacher, breaking the news.

Reeve vomiting in the boys' bathroom.

Reeve inconsolable, my pocketknife in his hands.

Opening the blade, staring at it.

It's starting to hurt now. Feeling every emotion Reeve's ever felt, all at once.

At the Jar Island lighthouse. Climbing his way up to the peak.

Screaming he's sorry into the wind.

Staring over the edge.

Never in my wildest dreams did I think my death affected Reeve that way. Enough to make him do something so drastic, as drastic as I did. He did care. His skin burns in my grip, crazy hot. I fight the urge to let him go.

A park ranger grabbing him, pulling him down.

The show slows along with Reeve's heartbeat. He's dying in my arms. *Almost done*, I tell myself, because it's stinging me like fire to hold on. *Keep going. It's almost over.* The last image, brighter than bright:

Lillia Cho.

I can't bear it. I can't bear it for another second. I drop him.

When I open my eyes, I'm back at my house. Lying on the floor. My cheeks are wet. I'm crying.

I couldn't do it. After all this time, after all he's done to me, I couldn't do it. Through his eyes I saw everything. I felt everything. Pain. Joy. Despair. Regret. Everything. All the things I've forgotten how to feel.

Love.

I know now that I'll never be able to kill Reeve. That's why I haven't done it already, when I've had so many chances. I've been holding back. I'm never going to be able to kill him.

But he still has to pay for what he did. Otherwise I'll never be free. But if not me . . .

And then I remember.

Reeve was the one who tormented me into doing the unthinkable. Taking my own life. He's got to be the one to do it. There's no other way.

Chapter Thirty-Seven

LILLIA

I PUSH THROUGH THE POOL DOOR, AND THE FIRST thing I notice is how quiet it is. How eerily quiet. Then I let out a scream that bounces off every wall. Reeve's body is floating in the center of the pool, facedown.

Oh my God, oh my God, oh my God.

"Help! Somebody help!" I scream. Then I jump into the pool, thrash over to him, and drag him to the side.

As soon as the air hits his face, Reeve takes a guttural, bubbling breath. His skin is white. I try to hoist him out of the water, but he's too heavy, plus I am crying my eyes out. I'm just holding on to the edge of the pool, trying to keep us both afloat.

He takes another breath, and then another, and the color in his face slowly returns. He looks at me and starts coughing and wheezing and trying to get air into his lungs. He launches into a coughing fit. I push myself out of the water and drag him up with all my might. He helps hoist himself up, but he barely has any strength. He sits bent over, his legs dangling in the water, trying to get a good breath.

I scramble to my feet and run over to the bleachers, grab his towel, and drape it over his shoulders. He's shaking; he won't stop shaking. "I'm fine, I'm fine. I just—need a minute—to catch—my breath."

I let out a choked sob and sink down beside him on the ground. I thought he was dead. "Oh my God," I say, and then I'm crying so hard, I can't see.

"Cho, don't cry," he begs. "I'm okay. I'm fine."

Through my tears I ask him, "Wh-what *happened*?"

Dazedly he says, "I don't know. I—I must have passed out in the water."

I wrap his towel tighter around his shoulders. Last night's dream comes into focus. I remember Reeve in the water. Mary.

I dreamed that this would happen.

My eyes dart around the room. I can't shake this feeling

of unease. I rise to my feet; my legs feel weak and unsteady. "Can you stand up?"

"You're soaking wet," he says, touching my heavy sweatshirt hem.

I help him to his feet. I collect my shoes, his gym bag, my towel. We go out to the parking lot and climb into his truck, and Reeve looks at me and says, "Why don't you get changed first? You're freezing. Do you have any dry clothes?" He starts rummaging around in the back for my towel.

"Reeve, I'm fine! You're the one who almost drowned." I just want to get out of here.

Reeve starts up the truck. "Where are we going? Your house?"

Suddenly my home, my room, doesn't exactly feel safe. I spot the ring of keys in his console. "Take me to one of your dad's rentals," I say, and I grab his hand and don't let go.

We drive to the other side of the island, to Canobie Bluffs. It's starting to rain, and Reeve is driving one-handed because I won't let go of his other hand. I keep twisting in my seat, looking out the back, to the side, every direction. I don't know what I'm looking for.

Yes, I do. Mary. I keep expecting to see Mary, even though I know she isn't here, and it was only a dream, and there's no way she had anything to do with what happened at the pool.

But still. I'm afraid. More than afraid. I'm terrified.

We drive down an empty-looking street, all vacant rental properties with signs out front. Reeve pulls into the driveway of a gray Cape Cod cottage that faces the water. He has a grimace on his face. "Let's get you inside where you can warm up and dry off."

I look out the window. "Park the car in the garage."

Reeve obeys. We get out of the truck and walk into the house. It's dark. Reeve starts turning on lights, and I pull all the curtains closed. He goes over to the fireplace and starts stacking logs. "Go dry off. I'll have a fire going in no time."

I don't want to let him out of my sight, so I just take off my wet sweatshirt and wrap myself in the throw from the couch.

After the fire's going, he sits down on the couch next to me. He starts drying my hair with the edge of the blanket. "I don't want you to catch a cold," he says, with so much tenderness I start to cry again.

I have to tell him. About Mary, about the revenge, about everything. I open my mouth, but nothing comes out. Just a sob.

"I'm fine," he says. "I'm fine." Reeve wipes my eyes with his sleeve.

Sniffling, I say, "You always take such good care of me, Reeve." Why can't Mary see how good he is? He's not the monster she makes him out to be.

He takes off his sweatshirt. "Put this on."

I push it away and start kissing him. His cheeks are cool to the touch. I could have lost him today. That's what I keep thinking. And once I tell him what we did, what I did, I'll lose him for good. There's no way he'll still love me once he knows the truth. What we have now, it will be over. Because it's not just the drugs—that part he knows about, even if he's never let me say the actual words out loud. It's not just that I'm responsible for him losing his football scholarships and not finishing out the season. It's the fact that the only reason I went after him in the first place was to pull a prank on him. And that all this time I've known his worst, darkest, most horrible secret, the secret he's guarded so carefully.

I lean back against the couch so that I'm lying down, and I pull him with me. "I love you so much," I tell him, over and over. I run my hands over his back, down his spine. His back muscles flex against my hands. I feel frenzied with wanting him near. Proof he's here with me. I keep pulling him closer, closer. Our arms and legs are entwined, and we're both breathing hard.

"Lil," he groans. He tries to push away from me and sit up, but I won't let him. I cling more tightly.

I whisper, "Don't stop."

"Let's take a break for a second."

I shake my head. "I don't want to take a break." This could be it for us. Once I tell him the truth, who knows what will happen next.

"Are you—are you sure?"

"Yes."

I push the blanket away, and it drops to the floor. His head jerks up. "Wait—are you *sure* sure? Because I don't want to do anything if you're not sure. You're still upset from what happened at the pool."

I reach up and smooth his damp hair. "I've never been surer about anything in my life," I tell him. "Do you have—do you have a condom?"

He hesitates and then says, "There might be some in my truck. I've put them in there before because my mom cleans my room and sometimes she snoops in my drawers. But sometimes Tommy uses my truck too. I definitely wasn't assuming that you and I—I mean, they're from before—" His face is reddening, and he's starting to stutter. "They're from before we ever got together. They might even be expired."

It's sweet, how nervous he is. I'm not mad, not one bit. I'm glad he's prepared. "Can you just stop talking and hurry up and get it?"

Reeve jumps up and runs out the front door. He's back in, like, two seconds and is hovering above me.

JENNY HAN & SIOBHAN VIVIAN

And then he's kissing down my throat, my chest, my breasts. His breath is warm and it feels good. I close my eyes and hold on to his forearms. I can hear the rain falling into the ocean. I feel like I am in a boat, safe and sound at sea, where no one can hurt us. That's what I'm pretending right now. We are miles away from here, Reeve and me.

I feel him untying my bikini bottoms. "Is this okay?"

I'm nervous, my heart is racing, but I don't want him to stop, so I keep my eyes closed and say, "Mm-hm."

Then he's touching me, and my eyes fly open, and I jerk against his hand. For the first time I'm glad about how many other girls he's been with, because he's so good at this. At making me feel good. Nothing has ever felt better than this. I press my face into his shoulder so I don't gasp out loud. And then I feel him against me, and he asks one more time. "Are you sure? Because I love you and I'll wait as long as you want."

I look right into his eyes. With my eyes I tell him how much I trust him. How glad I am that it's him. "Yes. I want you to be the first. My real first."

He kisses me on the mouth, so sweetly, and he pushes inside me, and it hurts, just a little. I bite my lip. He kisses me again, and he's moving, and I'm moving with him, and the pain is starting to fade away, and I just feel joyous. So this is what it feels like to give yourself to someone you love. My eyes well up and I wipe them on Reeve's shoulder.

After, he rests his cheek on my chest and closes his eyes. I know what he's doing. He's listening to my heartbeat. "I want to be with you forever, Lillia."

On the way home Reeve keeps asking if I'm okay. I tell him yes, yes, I'm fine. With every second that passes, I lose my nerve to tell him the truth.

When I get inside, there's a note from my mom on the fridge saying she and my dad and Nadia went out for dinner and a movie, which makes me feel relieved. This sounds so silly, but what if they're able to sense that something is different about me? I heard that after you lose your virginity, you look different.

I feel different. When I catch a glimpse of my reflection in the foyer mirror, I see it. Flushed cheeks, shiny eyes. I look like a girl in love.

My lip starts to quiver. I am a girl in love. And I'm afraid of what that means for us.

I run upstairs to my room, my phone in my hand. It suddenly buzzes with a text from Reeve.

Home safe and sound. You?

I'm ready to text him back, just like he asked. I flip on the light switch, and then I let out a scream.

My room is completely trashed. Clothes are everywhere. My down pillows have been slashed open and feathers float through the air. The belly of my stuffed rabbit has been slashed too, and his beany insides spill out onto the carpet. My perfume bottle is shattered on the vanity table; glass is everywhere. My dollhouse is smashed.

And there is Mary, sitting cross-legged on my floor in the middle of it all.

Oh my God.

I back away from her, my whole body trembling. Taking deep, gulping breaths of air, I manage to get out the words "Why did you do this?"

"Why? Because Reeve killed me. He killed me, Lillia. You're in love with a murderer."

I reel backward. "Get out! Get out right now!"

"And go where? Reeve Tabatsky took everything from me." She lifts her head and looks at me and says, "I hung myself that day, just like I told you. But I didn't survive. I'm dead. You can go to the cemetery and see my gravestone. Elizabeth Mary Donovan Zane." And then she stumbles to her feet, walks through my bedroom wall, and walks back in.

I scream and scream and scream. I put my hands over my ears. "Stop! This isn't real. It isn't real." I'm dreaming. This is just another nightmare. This isn't happening. I clench my hands into the tightest fists, my fingernails piercing my palms. *Please wake up*, I tell myself. *Wake up, wake up.*

When I open my eyes, Mary is standing right in front of me. "Touch me," she says. "Think about it. You never have. You've never once touched me."

I squeeze my eyes shut and shake my head.

And then I feel something, some force pushing my arm up. I try to pull my arm back down, but I can't; the force is too strong. "Touch me," she says again. This time it's an order, one I can't refuse.

Even though she looks as alive as the day I met her, I reach out to her, my fingers trembling—and my hand slips right through her like she's made of mist. I scream.

My phone rings. It's Reeve.

I try to hide my phone behind my back, but in an instant Mary's next to me, looking down at the screen. "We made a pact. We said we'd see it through till the end, but you didn't, did you? No, you broke your word. You said you'd break up with him."

Dread seeps into my bones like a cold fog. "I'm sorry. I'm so sorry."

Mary stares at me for so long, I get chills all over. "So here's what you're going to do. You're going to tell him it's over. You're going to tell him you know what he did to me, that you could never love a person who would do something like that. You're going to say what you should have said in the first place. And Reeve will know it's because of me."

I shake my head. "No. No. I can't do that."

"Then I'll kill him."

"You wouldn't do that, Mary. I know you!"

"No, you don't. You don't know me at all. I could have done it at the pool today. Do you want to know why I didn't? It would've been too easy. Too merciful. I'd rather see him suffer."

The phone is ringing again.

"It's up to you," she says.

"I'll do it!" I cry out. "I'll tell him. I'll do whatever you want. Just please don't hurt him." I try to grab her arms, but my fingers slip right through.

A strange smile lights up her face. "Then answer the phone."

I let out a huge sob and swipe my finger across the screen. "Hello."

"Hey. What's wrong? Why do you sound like that?"

Tears pour down my cheeks. "I can't be with you anymore."

There is a stunned silence. "What? Why not?"

"I came to the pool today—to tell you—" I can't stop crying. "To tell you I know what you did to that girl."

Anguished, he says, "What girl?"

Mary whispers, "Big Easy."

"B-B-Big Easy," I repeat. I can barely get the words out, I'm crying so hard. "She died because of you."

I hear a sharp intake of breath, and he chokes out, "Alex told you, didn't he?"

"You're a b-b-bully. You bullied that poor girl to death. I can't—I can't be with someone so heartless. I can't. I'm sorry."

"Cho, please just listen to me—"

"It's over, Reeve."

"But what about today?" he whispers.

"That was to say good-bye. So—good-bye, Reeve." I hang up and power off my phone. "I did it," I gasp. "It's over. Is that enough for you? You'll leave him alone now, won't you, Mary?"

She nods. "But, Lillia . . . I'll always be here; I'll always be watching. If you ever go back on your word again, Reeve's life is over, and his blood will be on your hands, not mine."

And then she disappears.

It takes me hours to clean up the mess, but I finish before my parents and Nadia come back home. I'm tired but I can't sleep. At first it's pure adrenaline—every time I hear a noise, my whole body stiffens and I'm bracing myself, my heart racing out of my chest. But then the terror fades and I'm just thinking.

Thinking, thinking, thinking . . .

Thinking about what I know to be true and what I know to be impossible. It is impossible that Mary is dead. That she's been dead all along. But it's also true. My friend Mary is dead. She's dead, or I'm going crazy.

I'm not crazy. I'm not. If I'm crazy, then so is Kat. Kat's not crazy. So I can't be either. This is really happening.

If I look back far enough, I can see that everything that's happened up till now, it's because of Mary. Because of that day in the girls' bathroom. The revenge, Reeve getting hurt, Rennie dying, Reeve and me falling in love. Everything could have been different. Everything was *supposed* to be different.

Reeve and I were never meant to be. If not for Mary, we wouldn't have looked twice at each other, not in a million years. Not like that. But here we are.

Before Mary, I couldn't stand him. So I can't even regret it. I can't even say that if I could go back and do it all differently, I would. Because if I say that, then I erase the love I feel for him in my heart, I erase every perfect moment, every time he looked at me like I was the only girl in the room. In the world.

I can't do that. I wouldn't have done one thing differently, because what I did gave me him. What we had was perfect, and it was finite in the way that all good things are. Nothing gold can stay. I take off the necklace Reeve gave me and then I cry until the sun comes up. For what could have been and what will never be.

Chapter Thirty-Eight

MARY

HONESTLY, IT'S A GOOD THING THAT LILLIA'S SO IN love with Reeve and vice versa. It makes this whole plan so much easier. Threaten his life and she'll do anything I ask. Have Lillia spear him in his most vulnerable place and it's an instant mortal wound. Better than anything I could inflict, because it cuts him deepest.

I will myself to Reeve's bedroom, and when I get there, it's empty.

But then I hear a thud. And another. And another. They get harder and harder, these thuds, constant and steady like a metronome. They are so hard they vibrate through the bedroom, shake the change on his change plate, rattle the cup of pencils on his desk.

I follow the beating to just outside Reeve's private bathroom.

The water is on, and steam billows out past the partially open door. I know I shouldn't, but I can't help myself. I walk inside.

Reeve's shower has glass doors. They are rippled and frosted, so you can't see straight through them. But I can definitely make out his shape on the other side. The color of his skin. The shape of his butt. His fists pounding against the tiled walls.

I climb up onto the toilet, sit on the tank, and listen as the water falls. He punches and punches, and then, when I'm sure his fists must be so tender, he sink down and begins to sob.

I could almost feel bad for him, but I won't, because this is just the beginning.

Chapter Thirty-Nine

LILLIA

DADDY WAKES ME UP WITH A KNOCK ON MY DOOR IN the morning. I don't remember falling asleep. "Lilli," he says. "Reeve's outside."

He walks over to my window. I get out of bed and follow him. Down on the street, in front of our house, is Reeve's truck. He's sitting inside the cab, eyes looking up to my window.

I take a big step back.

Awkwardly Daddy says, "I saw him when I went out to grab the paper. I invited him in for breakfast, but he wouldn't come. I think he's been out there all night. Did you two have a fight?"

"We broke up."

Daddy's eyes widen. "Are you all right? Do you, um, want me to call your mom in here?"

"I'm fine," I tell him. "Can you tell him to go?" My dad nods and leaves.

I stand at the window and watch my dad send Reeve away. Then I turn my cell phone back on. It explodes with text messages, and each one breaks my heart.

Please don't do this.

I'm coming over.

Outside.

I'm not going anywhere. I'll wait here all night if I have to.

Cho, please. I love you.

And finally . . .

You're killing me.

No, Reeve. I'm trying to save you.

I watch him drive away. But the relief I feel is short-lived, because my phone rings again, and it's Reeve. I hit ignore, and I get back into bed. I lie on my side and cry and cry.

Nadia comes in at one point and climbs into bed with me. I keep my back to her, and she snuggles up against me. "Just talk to him," she says. "You guys love each other. Whatever it is, you can work it out."

But we can't. Not if I want him to live.

We both fall asleep, and then I hear my phone ring and I grab it and check to see if it's Reeve. But it's not him; it's Kat. She must be back from Uncle Tim's boat. I want to tell her everything so bad. She's the one person who would understand. But I'm terrified that if I make one false move, this whole thing will come crashing down and Mary will just kill Reeve.

The phone stops ringing, and then it buzzes. A text from Kat.

Ahoy! Land ho! Did ya miss me? Call me so we can hang.

I can't see Kat, not yet. Kat will question me, she'll press me for details, and I'm a horrible liar. She'll know right away that something's not right. I'll just have to avoid her until I figure out what I'm going to say.

Chapter Forty

KAT

THE FIRST DAY BACK AFTER SPRING BREAK, I GO looking for Lil as soon as I get to school. I can't wait to show her how sick my tan lines are. But before I find her, Ms. Chirazo stops me in the hallway and says, "We have a situation."

"Huh?"

She takes me by the arm. "Come with me."

I follow her quickly to her office with a terrible feeling in my stomach. "Is this about Oberlin?"

"Yes, I'm afraid it is," she says, closing the door behind me. "Have you heard anything from admissions?"

"No." It was such a bummer. Alex docked the boat, and I just had this feeling that I'd come home to news. But there was no letter, no e-mail. "I mean, I haven't checked e-mail yet today, but—"

"Here. Use my computer."

I sit down and check, and there's nothing.

She bites on the arm of her glasses. "That's good. That means they haven't rejected you yet."

"Yet?" I run my hands through my hair.

Then Ms. Chirazo has me log in to the Oberlin website and check the status of my application. *Incomplete.*

"Incomplete? What the f—"

"Katherine," she warns.

"I don't get it. I sent in everything they asked for."

"I checked your files today, just on a whim. And thank goodness I did. We never did get a hard copy of your recommendation letter. And I just had this feeling."

"I don't get it. Danner said she'd send it in after the benefit."

"Did anything happen that would make her rethink giving you a recommendation?"

"No."

"Are you sure?" she asks again, all distrusting.

"I swear, I've been a freaking saint. A perfect volunteer."

Ms. Chirazo leans back in her creaky chair. "Between this

and the smoking, it's almost like you're trying to sabotage your chances at Oberlin."

I shake my head emphatically. "No! I want off this island more than you know." Except, when I say the words, I know that's not true. I mean, I'm going to college, obviously. But after spring break, I don't know. I was actually excited to see Jar Island again, to be home with Pat and Dad, to come to school today.

It's crazy.

"Well, you're almost out of time, Kat." She points at the calendar. "That letter needs to be postmarked today if you want it included in your application. They make all their final decisions by April fifteenth."

Shit. Shit, shit, shit.

"Okay," I say. "I'm on it."

Chapter Forty-One

LILLIA

WHEN I DROVE INTO THE SCHOOL PARKING LOT THIS morning, there he was. Waiting for me right out front by the doors. He looked for my necklace, which I wasn't wearing. I tried to hurry past, but he stopped me and begged me to talk to him. To let him try to explain. I kept shaking my head, and by the end of it we were both crying. Alex walked by, and I could tell he was wondering what was going on, but he kept going. The bell rang and Reeve finally let me go, but then when I walk out of first period, there he is again.

"Cho, I'm begging you," he says. "Please, for God's sake, talk to me."

"I already told you I don't want to talk to you."

He throws his head back in frustration. "Fuck! I love you, Cho. And you love me, so let's just—let's just go somewhere and figure it out!"

People are slowing down and looking. They're looking at us. I grip my books harder. "There's nothing to figure out! Just leave me alone!" I start walking away, and Reeve runs in front of me and blocks my path. "Get out of my way," I say.

"No. Not until we talk!"

"You never want to talk, and now all of a sudden you want to talk. Well, it's too late, okay?" I try to move around him, but he blocks my way again.

I see Alex walking in our direction, and I think he's just going to keep going, but then he stops short. "Dude, let her go," he says.

Reeve's eyes practically go black. "It was you, wasn't it? You told her. You shady piece-of-shit motherfucker."

"What are you talking—"

And then Reeve punches Alex in the face, so hard that Alex goes stumbling backward.

I scream, and then I run over to Alex. His nose is bleeding freely, he's holding his arm to his face, and the blood is soaking through his shirt. "Oh my God, Alex. I'm so sorry, I'm so sorry," I say. My hands are shaking as I fumble in my bag for a tissue, and then I try to wipe up his face, but he moves away from me.

"You're crazy!" he yells at Reeve.

Mr. Mayurnik is already hustling Reeve away to the principal's office.

"I'm so sorry," I keep saying, over and over.

Chapter Forty-Two

MARY

FOR THE REST OF THE DAY, THE FIGHT IS ALL ANYONE can talk about. I roam the halls, eavesdropping on whispered conversations, looking over the shoulders of people writing texts. Reeve sucker-punched his former best friend. Obviously Lillia was involved somehow.

But no one can figure out why.

There are plenty of guesses. Reeve cheated on Lillia. Lillia cheated on Reeve with Alex. Her father said he wasn't good enough for her.

Every guess is bad. But not as bad as the truth.

Ashlin always asks to go to the bathroom near the end of her senior English class, which is the period right before her lunch. I know because I've been watching her for a few days. You'd think Mr. Malone, the teacher, would wise up or at least tell her no when he's in the middle of discussing a passage, but he never does. I think he has a crush on her. Whenever he has the students read quietly at their desks, I've caught him peering over his newspaper at her. And one time, as he was walking up and down the aisles handing back a quiz, I swear I saw him peek down her shirt.

Gross.

Anyway, Ashlin spends a good fifteen minutes at the mirror fussing with her hair and touching up her makeup. She wants to make sure she looks her best, because the second the bell rings, she's off to meet up with Derek at his locker so they can walk to the cafeteria together.

She's in love with him. I know it because of the way she acts around him, nervous. I can feel her heart beating faster whenever he's near her, fast like a hummingbird's. And her speaking voice gets a lot higher pitched. And because her notebooks are full of his name, doodled over and over again. Ashlin is very good at bubble letters.

Unfortunately for her, Derek doesn't feel the same way

about her. He flirts with her and holds her hand, and he'll sometimes carry her books for her. But I also know Derek sneaks notes to other girls in school, mainly freshmen and sophomores. He gets lots of texts from other girls too, but deletes them right away. I wasn't sure why, but then I saw Ashlin take his phone and check it once, when he went to get a drink.

Derek is shady. Just like Reeve.

Which makes Ashlin and me kindred spirits in a way.

When an emotional connection is forged with a spirit, the apparition will reveal him- or herself in his or her most vibrant state, one that is indistinguishable from the living.

I wait in the last stall until Ashlin comes in. She pulls a paper towel from the dispenser and lays it on the sink before setting her purse down, to make sure it doesn't get wet.

I close my eyes and concentrate really hard. I focus on Ash's insecurities until I can feel them inside myself. It's like two notes, and I make myself in harmony with her. It reminds me of that first time I met Kat and Lillia; it feels like that. Like we are completely in harmony with each other.

Then, when I open my eyes, everything around me seems

brighter. The white porcelain of the toilet, the graffiti on the stall walls, the light coming through the frosted window.

I'm visible.

I step out of the stall, and Ashlin's eyes move off her reflection in the mirror and onto me.

"Oh," I say with a smile. "Hey, Ashlin."

Ashlin smiles at me in the mirror. I can tell she's trying to place me, trying to remember if she should know my name or not. "Hey there," she says.

I walk up to the sink next to hers. "You don't know me, but I'm on the yearbook committee. A bunch of us were saying the other day how your senior portrait is the prettiest one of all the senior girls."

Ashlin turns around. "That is so sweet of you to say. I was actually choosing between that shot and another one where I'm not showing my teeth when I smile. I went back and forth for, like, weeks, but Derek said the one I picked made my hair look blonder, so."

"It's true." I make like I am going to walk out, but then I stop and turn back around. I bite on my pinky, like I'm deliberating something, and then I say, "I feel so bad for Alex. But then again, Reeve's been violent before, so maybe it's not surprising that he'd lash out like that when someone finally stood up to his bullying." Ashlin opens her mouth, like she's going to say something. But then she just nods, so I keep going. "Actually, it's almost exactly like what happened with him and that poor girl in seventh grade. Except less tragic, obviously." I shake my head. "No wonder Lillia doesn't want to be with someone like that. He's got blood on his hands."

She frowns and says, "What are you talking about?"

I look over both my shoulders and then lower my voice. "Reeve bullied a girl so badly she killed herself."

Ashlin's eyes widen. "What?"

And then I give her all the gory details. I tell her everything. Ash shakes her head a few times, but I know she believes me. I can feel it.

After Ashlin practically sprints out of the bathroom, I spend the rest of the day watching the story spread like wildfire. Some kids say they vaguely remember hearing about that girl. Big Easy. From church, or swim lessons. But after they hear what I went through, I bet none of them will forget me.

When I get to Reeve's house, he's having a full-blown fight with his mom in the kitchen. She's holding his fist in a bowl of ice water. I can see it's swollen and bruised on top of the old cuts he got punching his bathroom walls.

"You could lose your acceptance to Graydon. What do you

have if you don't get a fifth year? Nothing! All that hard work by you and Lillia will be for nothing."

"I'm not going to lose my acceptance."

"If they get wind of a three-day suspension, you think they'll be happy?" She shakes her head. "I keep debating calling over to the Linds and apologizing on your behalf—"

"Mom, stop, okay? It's not a big deal."

She glares at him. "It is a big deal. You've had a rough year. Your injury, Rennie's death, and now this," she says, lifting his hand out of the bowl. Reeve looks away. He doesn't want to see it. "I'm going to call Dr. Clark. I bet I still have his number."

"Mom!" Reeve shouts.

At that, Reeve's dad ambles in and digs around in the fridge. "Not this again. I'm not spending another couple hundred for some overeducated WASP to try to convince us that our son is depressed and possibly suicidal. Teen boys get into fistfights, just like seventh-grade boys want to climb on lighthouses and be little daredevil shits." He pops open a can of beer, and both Reeve and his mom look up at the sound.

When his dad walks out, Reeve clenches his teeth and says, "I hate him."

His mom puts her finger to her lips. "Reeve, please, don't start with your father. He's had a rough day. You know how it is when tourist season starts and the summer people come back in demanding this and that from him."

At that, Reeve pushes away from the table so hard the ice water bath sloshes onto the floor, and he stalks out. Mrs. Tabatsky grabs a towel and starts to cry.

Things in the Tabatsky house are falling apart, but for me it's all coming together.

Chapter Forty-Three

KAT

I WISH I COULD GO STRAIGHT TO LILLIA'S HOUSE AND find out what the eff happened between Alex and Reeve, but that scoop will have to wait. Instead I go to the Preservation Society immediately after school. I march right into Danner's office. I'm so mad I'm shaking.

"Where's my letter, Danner?"

"Excuse me?"

I sit down. "I want my damn letter of recommendation! I did everything you richy-riches asked for, including picking up your damn dry cleaning. Don't you get that you're screwing with my future?"

"I already wrote you one, Kat. I mailed it in a few weeks ago."
She narrows her eyes. "I told them how you were a woman of
great poise and promise."

Oh. Oh, shit. "Well, um, do you think I could possibly get
another copy? Like, now?"

Danner looks like she wants to throw me out onto the street.
And honestly, I'd deserve it, for the way I just spoke to her.
"Please. If I don't get this letter, I don't have a shot. Please don't
ruin my life because I'm a freaking idiot."

Danner opens her mouth, then closes it, then stands up.
Grimly she says, "Let me get another piece of letterhead into the
printer. I didn't save my original, so I don't know if I'll be able
to channel all the wonderful things I wrote about you the first
time around, but I'll try to pull something adequate together."

Thank freaking God.

Danner leaves the room, and a few minutes later old Evelyn
comes shuffling in wearing some amazing silk pantsuit and kit-
ten heels, even though she's ancient. I love Evelyn. The feeling
must be mutual, because when she sees me, she brightens like
her big honkin' diamond ring.

"Oh, Kat, good. I didn't realize you were working today."
She hands me a stack of papers. "Can you file these? I have no
idea where they go."

"Sure, Evelyn." It's the least I can do.

I walk out to the file cabinets in the hallway and start putting things where they belong. Press releases in the media file, contractor bids in the development files.

A power of attorney document? No clue where that goes. It's from Greenbriar Sanitarium.

> *In light of current medical concerns, Erica Zane has been awarded by the state full authority to execute all decisions, financial and otherwise, for her sister, Elizabeth [Bette] Zane.*

Underneath that is a deed transfer. Mary's house. Donated to the Jar Island Preservation Society.

I don't get it. That house has to be worth a mil. It's one of the oldest on the island, and a landmark. I figured Mary's family is well off, but not enough to give away a house like that for free.

I'm relieved, obviously, because clearly Aunt Bette, or Aunt Elizabeth, is getting the help she needs.

But what about Mary?

There are other papers too, stapled to this one. I set the rest of the pile of filing on top of the cabinet and take this stack back to Danner's office. I'm about to slide them into my bag to show Lillia, when Danner comes in.

"What are you doing?"

Shit. Think fast.

"Sorry. I was filing these papers but I thought I heard my phone ring." I stand up. "Congrats on the Zane house. I'm glad it went through."

Danner eyes me suspiciously. She takes the papers out of my hands and replaces them with an envelope. "Best of luck to you, Katherine."

Chapter Forty-Four

LILLIA

MILKY MORNING'S OATMEAL CUPCAKES WITH chocolate frosting are Alex's favorite. So I have six of those, and two chocolate chip cookies. I'm standing outside his pool house, working up the courage to knock on the door. I know he's home. His car is right out front. Maybe I should just leave the bag and go. He's not going to want to see me right now. It's my fault he got punched in the face.

I set the bag on the ground, and that's when the door opens. Alex is standing there holding a bag of frozen peas to his face. "Hey, Lil."

I take a deep breath and say, "Alex, I am so sorry for what happened today. You were just trying to help me, and then you got hit for it. I swear to you I wasn't trying to pull you into anything."

"I know that."

I let out the breath. "Really?" I bend over and pick up the Milky Morning bag and hand it to him. "Here."

Alex takes it and looks inside. "Thanks."

"Of course. I really am sorry, Alex."

"What the hell happened with you guys?" He shakes his head. "Never mind. It's none of my business. Thanks for stopping by, Lil."

I nod, and then I run back to my car. As I'm driving home, I have to force myself not to turn around and go to Reeve's. I heard he was suspended for three days. I know he's suffering right now too. I wish so badly that I could be the one to comfort him.

When I get home, Kat's waiting for me on my front steps. Crap. I was able to avoid her at school today by hiding out in the library, but now here she is. She jumps up as soon as I reach the steps. "Why haven't you been answering your damn phone?"

"Sorry—"

"Never mind that. What the hell happened today, dude? I heard Tabatsky sucker-punched Alex in the freaking face!"

"Um . . . yeah." I sit down on the steps, and Kat joins me. What do I say? I want to tell her the truth, but I'm afraid, because of Reeve and also because if Mary's leaving her out of it, there's no reason to get her involved. It's safer for her not to know. "Reeve and I were fighting, and Alex stepped in, and then Reeve punched him." Kat's eyes go huge and she opens her mouth to ask another question, and I speak before she can. "Reeve and I broke up."

Her jaw drops. "Are you serious! Why? You guys are crazy for each other!"

What reason can I give that she'd believe? "He . . . he cheated on me."

"Motherfucker!"

I nod my head. "Yup."

"Who'd he cheat on you with?" she demands.

"Just some random girl. She . . . she doesn't live on the island. I found some texts on his phone."

"That's it. I'm gonna kick his ass." Kat starts to stand up, and I quickly grab her arm and make her sit back down.

"Please don't go over there, Kat," I beg. "It's so humiliating. I don't ever even want to think about it again."

"But he can't just play you like that, Lil—"

"No! Swear to me you won't say anything to Reeve, Kat. Swear it."

"*Fine.*" Kat starts chewing on her thumbnail. "You're all right, though?"

"Yes. I mean, I'm sad. But I just want to forget any of this ever happened." I force a smile. "Your tan looks amazing. Did you have a good time on Tim's boat?"

"It was killer," she says. "But don't change the subject. You sure you're okay?"

"Yes, I swear! I just don't want to talk about it anymore. It's been such an awful year." My eyes fill with tears.

"Okay, okay. Don't cry. I'll change the subject." Kat squeezes my knee. "I have something crazy to tell you about Mary."

I think I stop breathing.

"It's literally crazy. Mary's aunt is in the loony bin!"

"What?"

"Dude, it's a long story, but basically I found a power of attorney form at the Preservation Society office! Mary's mom had her committed!"

"Oh my gosh," I breathe.

"Yeah, so mystery solved. Mary's back with her parents and away from her freaky aunt."

"Right," I repeat. "Mystery solved."

Chapter Forty-Five

KAT

INSTEAD OF GOING STRAIGHT HOME AFTER LEAVING Lillia's, I drive to Mary's house.

As I get out of my car and walk up the path, I almost can't believe the state of it. Mary's house is rotting at warp speed. Strangely, it looks way worse than the last time Lillia and I came here to look for her, which was only three months ago.

The grass in the yard is overgrown. There are mushy leaves everywhere, and it gives the whole front lawn that decaying smell. Every window in the house is dark. The mail slot in the front door is stuffed full, and the overflow is in a messy pile on the front step, waterlogged and brown and pulpy. The biggest tree in the yard must have fallen in a storm or something. It's gone. Only a stump is left, but the perimeter bushes where it fell are crushed and aren't growing back. I watch a bird fly from a telephone wire into a small hole in the attic vent.

I guess I get why Mary's mom was cool with giving the house away. There isn't much left to save.

It looks like that old Volvo was towed away. And in its place the Preservation Society has parked two big Dumpsters, and they are full of Mary's family's stuff. A floral armchair, a couch, some paintings. I'm looking for a recent photograph of Mary, but they're all of when she was younger, when I didn't know her. I lift up an old curtain and find a huge stack of books underneath. Weird old books with cloth covers.

The first one is titled *The Sleeping Mind: The Power of Dreams and Semiconsciousness.*

Hells yeah, that's my jam. Underneath that are other ones, occult-type shit, spirits and whatnot. Some aren't even in English. Real Wicca-type stuff, the kinds of books you can't find in a regular bookstore. Bet I could make a killing off them on eBay.

After checking over both my shoulders, I lift a couple of them out, the ones that haven't been rained on and ruined. I put them into my trunk.

Chapter Forty-Six

MARY

ON HIS FIRST DAY BACK AFTER HIS SUSPENSION, REEVE spends an hour getting ready. Clean shave, some product in his hair, and a couple of different outfit changes before he decides on jeans, a polo, and a pair of aviators. I can tell he's nervous, because he applies deodorant three times. I get why. No one has called him since his fight with Alex. Not one of his friends. A few times Reeve scrolled through his phone, probably to reach out, but he never went through with it.

Before he backs his truck down the driveway, he stares into his rearview mirror and touches the puffy dark circles under his eyes.

He hasn't been sleeping well. I've made sure of that.

When we reach the school parking lot, Reeve turns up his car stereo loud and sticks his arm out the side window, like he's out for a springtime joyride. The weather has turned nice, and there are lots of kids hanging around the fountain. It's been turned on again.

I can't help but think of that first day of school, of confident, cocky Reeve hanging with his friends, not a care in the world.

Reeve tries to project that same attitude, but I can see the cracks. His pace is too quick. He keeps looking around, waiting for someone to see him and give him a wave or a "What's up." But it's as if he's invisible.

Actually, worse. No one wants to see him.

I know, because that's how it was for me, after Reeve came to the Montessori. And I bet Reeve realizes the shift as quickly as I did. He's a smart cookie.

Derek and PJ are tossing a Frisbee back and forth on the lawn. Reeve sees them, hustles over, and steals the catch in midair. "We gotta take advantage of this weather and get an ultimate game going stat. Maybe after school?" Reeve cocks back the Frisbee to join in the toss, but instead of holding out a hand, both Derek and PJ walk over toward him somberly.

"Look, I know what you guys are going to say. And you're

right," Reeve says, holding up his hands. "Me versus Lind was never going to be a fair fight. But—"

"Hey, man, is it true, what people are saying?"

Reeve's smile doesn't waver. "What are they saying?" he says lightly. Derek and PJ share a weird look. Neither one wants to say it. "What?" Reeve asks again, though this time his voice has changed. It's quieter. Scared.

Reeve walks to homeroom with his head down. He immediately opens his notebook and starts writing a note to Lillia. He works on several versions of it all day. Sometimes it's defensive, sometimes apologetic, sometimes rambling. He's so distracted that his teachers have to say his name two and three times before he'll hear them.

They are the only people who speak to him.

When the final bell rings, he jumps out of his seat, folds up his note, and runs to Lillia's locker. She doesn't show up.

As we ride back home, Reeve doesn't even put the radio on for show.

"Do you get it now?" I ask him. "Do you see what's happening?"

He doesn't answer me, of course, and I don't need him to. I know he understands.

Reeve comes through the kitchen like a bull. His mother is

trying to ask about his day, but Reeve doesn't answer. Instead he opens the fridge, grabs a six-pack of beer, and takes it up to his room. He drinks them all.

Before I leave, while Reeve is peeing in the bathroom, I take the pocketknife out of his top drawer. With all the force I can muster, I ram the blade straight down into the wood.

He comes out of the bathroom at the sound. My present to him, quivering, the blade half into the wood.

He walks over and tries to take the knife out. But it's stuck in too deep, and he has to work at it to get it free. He rubs his finger over the splintered wood, the gash in his dresser top. I can feel his heart racing as he says, "Tommy? Dude, what the hell?" His voice is slurry from the beer.

Tommy doesn't answer.

Reeve turns the pocketknife over in his hands, examining it. As he does, I lean into his ear and whisper, "The sooner you do it, the sooner you'll be out of your misery. Because I'm not going to stop until you're gone, Reeve. That I promise you."

Chapter Forty-Seven

KAT

I DROP INTO THE SEAT NEXT TO ASHLIN, AND I WISH I had my freaking camera out, because the face she makes is classic.

"What are you doing here?"

"Hey, Ash." I glance around, faking like I'm confused. Alex has just walked through the doors into the library, with PJ and Lillia right behind him. I hear Derek shouting out to someone down the hallway. "Oh, shit. Wait up. Is some kind of meeting happening here right now?"

"Yeah," Ash says. "It's prom committee—" She swats my arm. "Kat!"

I crack up. "What? You told me that I'm not allowed to bitch unless I show up to a meeting, so . . ."

Ash shakes her head. Derek and PJ both slap me five as they settle into their seats. It's been like this ever since spring break. We're friends.

Lillia gives me a smile, but then looks down at her lap when Ash leans across her to talk to Derek like she's not even there. Those two are still on the outs, I guess.

We shoot the shit for a few minutes until Alex clears his throat and asks, "Does anyone know if Reeve's coming?" Everyone shrugs their shoulders and avoids looking at one another.

Lillia keeps her eyes down, sweeping invisible crumbs off the tabletop. Neither of us have a clue how people found out about what Reeve did to Mary. I've been telling as many blabbermouths as I can to get their facts straight, the girl didn't actually die, but it hasn't really helped stem the tide. Gossip has a life of its own, and people are going to believe what they want. It's hitting Reeve harder than hard. I feel bad for the guy, but what else can I do? He did do some effed-up shit. The thing I can't figure out is who let that secret out. It definitely wasn't Lillia. And even if Alex knew, he wouldn't do that.

Finally Derek says, "Um, he might not be in school today. Or, if he is, he skipped our English quiz."

Alex twists in his seat so he can see the clock on the wall.

"Okay. Well, we'd better get started." Alex opens the meeting by using his empty soda bottle as a gavel. "Let this meeting of Jar Island prom committee officially come to order. It looks like we've got someone new with us today. Would you care to introduce yourself?"

Lillia laughs, and I roll my eyes. Alex is so corny sometimes. "Shut up, Alex. Look. Basically I'm here because I think it's a stupid-ass idea to have prom at a freaking nightclub all the way in Boston. I think we should have it here, on Jar Island, like we do every year."

PJ shrugs his shoulders. "I doubt we'll be able to get a new location. It's already crawling with tourists again. This stuff needs to be reserved a year in advance."

I fold my arms. "Well, then no one's going to come."

Ash sighs. "I hate to say it, but Kat might be right. Nobody's buying tickets because they can't afford it."

Lillia says, "Even if we did find another location, we don't have any funds to reserve it. We'll lose our deposit on the club for sure. They made us sign a contract and pay them in full."

"What about our gym?" PJ suggests. "I bet the school would let us use it."

No one says anything. Me either, actually, because a high school prom in our ugly gym sounds lame.

Lillia, being a good sport, clears her throat. "I mean, sure. I guess we could ask the janitors to clear out the mats and light some scented candles to get rid of the smell."

Ashlin moans, "OMG, this is going to be the most low-rent prom in history. Even worse than the time they had prom at that nursing home rec room a couple of years ago. Remember it smelled like Depends? I wonder if they're booked. . . ."

I glance across the table at Alex. "What about your house?"

"Huh?" He snorts. "My house is big, but we can't fit the entire senior class in it."

"Then we'll rent a big tent and pitch it in the backyard. Didn't your uncle have his wedding there?"

"Third wedding. Yeah. And he invited a ton of people." He cocks his head to the side. "This could work. My mom loves to put on an event. She was talking about throwing me a big graduation party. Maybe she could do this instead."

"All right, cool," I say. "But we're going to have to kick planning into high gear to get everything ready. I'll take the lead." I open up my notebook and start delegating work and subcommittees and all that shit for the next thirty minutes straight, and everyone's nodding their heads, totally on board with me taking over.

A few weeks ago I planned on graduating without ever attending prom, and now I'm basically running the show.

The bell rings, and we head out. Ash drops her makeup bag

on her way out of the room, and Lillia picks it up and runs it to her. Ash takes it and quietly says thank you, but it's not exactly warm.

If I've learned anything this year, it's that life's too fucking short. I wasted too much time being angry and bitter. I wish I could go back in time and say a thousand things to Rennie. It's too late for that, but it's not too late for Ash and Lillia.

Chapter Forty-Eight

LILLIA

KAT TEXTS ME ABOUT AN EMERGENCY PROM COMMITTEE meeting at Ash's house, seven p.m. It makes sense. We've got so much to do. It's already April.

So after dinner I drive over to Ash's. I must be the first one to arrive, because there aren't any other cars in the driveway. Their housekeeper, Sheila, lets me in, and I go straight up to Ashlin's room. The door is closed, so I knock. She doesn't answer, so I poke my head in. She's asleep under the covers. Ashlin has always loved an after-school nap. I clear my throat. "Ash?"

Ashlin stirs and rolls over. "Lil?"

I stand in the doorway awkwardly. "Sorry I woke you up. Is anyone else here yet?"

Groggily Ash sits up. She's in one of her big cheerleading T-shirts and pink-and-green polka-dot underwear. Her fluffy blond hair looks like chicken feathers in the back. She looks so—Ash. I didn't realize how much I missed her until this moment. She checks her phone. "What are you talking about?"

"The emergency meeting." That's when I realize—this is Kat's doing. She's trying to bring Ash and me back together. I can't believe it. I step in and perch at the edge of her bed. "Sorry. I guess I heard Kat wrong."

Yawning, Ash eyes me. "So is it true you and Reeve are done-zo?"

I nod. "The whole thing was a mistake from the start."

"I don't blame you for breaking up with him. You think you know somebody . . . I mean, bullying a girl so bad she kills herself?" Ash shakes her head.

"I know," I say quietly. "Who told you?"

"Some girl from yearbook. She went to school with him at Montessori."

My heart is beating wildly. "What's her name?"

"I don't remember. She has blond hair. Pretty. Kinda soft-spoken."

Chills tickle my spine like piano keys. It's Mary. It has to be.

Ash continues, twirling her hair around her fingers. "When Reeve transferred back from Montessori, he seemed totally fine, like no big deal. You'd never have known a girl had just died because of him."

"He was young," I say, my voice thin. "And I think it hit him a lot harder than anybody knows. He just didn't let anybody see."

"True. That's how he deals, right? He doesn't." She leans back against her pillows. "When Ren died, I don't think I saw him cry once, and he knew her the longest of everybody. He just keeps things locked up inside. Like, I think that being with you might have been his way of not dealing with his pain."

"We never should have been together in the first place." Saying it out loud makes me feel like crying, but I know it's true.

"I don't know. I still think what went down was a betrayal to Ren. Like, no matter what, it was effed up, what you guys did. But I think you and I both know that Reeve never saw her that way. They never would have ended up together. And he's always had a thing for you, and Ren knew it."

"No, he hasn't," I say. "He hated me."

"Maybe so, but freshman year he told Derek that you were the hottest girl in our class and he wanted to hit it." Ashlin scratches her neck. "You've always had a love-hate thing. I've been thinking about this a lot. I wonder if Rennie's dying isn't what finally brought you guys together."

I let this idea roll around in my head for a second. "What do you mean?"

Slowly she says, "Well . . . I don't know. I mean, you guys knew her best. So maybe it was a natural thing for you to reach out to each other when she died. Maybe that's why it was so intense and crazy."

The thought never occurred to me. Because Reeve and I started having feelings for each other before Rennie died. But now I'm starting to wonder if things would've gotten so serious with us if Rennie hadn't died. We were both grieving for our friend, and then everybody was shunning us and all we had was each other. It was us against the world. I never knew Ash had such a perceptive side. But she's making sense.

My eyes well up. "I miss you. I know I messed up. But, Ash, high school's almost over, and I don't want to leave it like this, with you hating me."

Ash looks down at her comforter. "I don't *hate* you."

"You don't?"

"No. I've missed you, too," she admits. "Spring break wasn't the same without you and Reeve. Kat was so annoying. It's like, okay, we get it, you're a badass. You can stop walking around the boat in a wifebeater with a cigar hanging out of your mouth. But I did have fun with that girl Brianna."

I wipe my eyes with the back of my arm, and Ash offers me

the corner of her comforter. "Kat's actually really cool when you get to know her," I say. "The badass stuff is just a front." And then I say, "I'm sorry I didn't tell you about me and Reeve. I didn't want to keep it a secret from you. Things just got so complicated."

Ashlin nods. "You want to get nachos at Greasy Spoon?" And just like that, our fight, and this conversation, is over. It's so her. And I'm grateful for that.

Chapter Forty-Nine

MARY

I APPEAR IN THE DOORWAY TO SHOP CLASS AND SET my sights on Reeve. He's off to the side of the room by himself, sitting on a stool in front of the table saw, his shoulders hunched, staring at a pile of sawdust on the floor near his feet. His project, a birdhouse, is only half completed. It's missing a roof and a perch.

"Reeve!"

Reeve slowly lifts his head and looks over at the shop teacher, Mr. Werther. Everyone else in class has finished with their birdhouses. The projects are in a line on Mr. Werther's desk, and he's going through and assigning them each a grade.

"What?" Reeve says snottily, without looking up.

"You've got twenty more minutes before you get a zero."

Reeve shakes his head and sneers, "Like I care about a fucking birdhouse," barely under his breath. Then he turns on the saw blade by stepping on the floor pedal with his foot.

The students look at each other and murmur. Mr. Werther looks momentarily stunned that one of his students would be so rude. He shouts over the sudden burst of noise, "That's ten points off for operating the saw without your safety goggles."

"Awesome," Reeve deadpans.

He presses his foot down more on the saw pedal, and the blade whirls so fast, it turns into a silver blur and lifts up the hair away from his forehead.

I stroll over and lean in to Reeve's ear.

In a singsong voice I say, "You deserve everything that's happening to you, Reeve. Every single terrible thing." I know he can hear me. "You are not a good person. And now nothing good will ever come to you. I will make sure of that."

Reeve closes his eyes. He hears me. I know he does.

"You're a murderer." I walk around the table so that I'm directly in front of the saw, lick my lips, and say, "You killed me. You've got blood on your hands."

Reeve's eyes pop open. I can see the hair on his neck stand

up. I smile and say it a little louder. "That's why Lillia left you, Reeve. She saw the real you. She knows you're a monster. And she couldn't ever love someone like you."

Reeve takes a deep breath, like he's trying to push my voice out of his head.

I skip around the room, all around the room. "Murderer. Murderer. Murderer."

Reeve presses harder on the pedal, and the saw whirs louder. But not as loud as me. I keep skipping, keep taunting him. I can do it forever.

Reeve reaches over the top of the whirling saw blade to grab his piece of wood. His hands are shaking. He tries to line up a cut, but he can't concentrate. Not with me screaming. He squeezes his eyes shut.

And suddenly Mr. Werther comes running over. I try to stop him, but he pushes right through me, grabs Reeve by the back of the shirt, and pulls him away from the saw.

"What the hell are you doing?" Mr. Werther screams.

"I'm building my damn birdhouse!" Reeve shouts back, but he's clearly shaken. Reeve shrugs Mr. Werther off him. As he does, his arm flails and he hits one of the saws behind him. "Shit!" he shouts, and pulls the hand in close to himself. He's cut his finger, not too deep, but it lets out a slit of the darkest, deepest red. I swear I feel it. The warmth of his blood.

Ashes to Ashes

Mr. Werther has had enough. "Forget the birdhouse. You've got yourself a failing grade for not following safety protocol. You're practically falling asleep! Now get out of here and down to the nurse."

Reeve picks up his birdhouse and bleeds all over the wood. On his way out of the shop class, he throws it into the trash can.

I can hear the other kids whispering as he stalks down the hall. I know Reeve can hear them too. He pushes through one of the metal doors and heads toward the parking lot.

"Are you going to cry?" I ask him. "Go ahead and cry, then. Cry your freaking eyes out. But it's not going to change anything."

Reeve straightens up, and it's almost like he hears me. He goes over to his truck and gets in. But he doesn't turn the key in the ignition. He just sits there. Then he drops his head onto the steering wheel and cries, just like I told him to.

Later that night I'm there when Reeve falls asleep. As soon as he does, I'm in his dream.

It's always a surprise where I find myself when I land there. Sometimes it's a memory of Lillia, sometimes it's him and Alex in happier times. Tonight he's apologizing to Alex. The two guys are in Alex's pool house, playing video games. Reeve reaches for a soda and says, "I regret it, man. I really do. And

I know you've loved her forever. But I have too."

Then he looks up and sees me there. He's scared.

"Please."

I grab his hand, and we're at the top of the lighthouse. I'm not Mary. I'm Big Easy. And Reeve's a seventh grader. I'm perched on the cap, just a few feet above where Reeve is, on the catwalk surrounding the part of the tower that holds the bulb.

I bring him here, every night, and tell him there's nothing left to live for. That everything he loves is gone. I repeat it like a script, like a play I'm acting in.

Eventually he'll hear me. And then he'll do what's right, what he should have done the first time he came here. He'll jump.

Chapter Fifty

LILLIA

THE SPORTS BANQUET WAS SUPPOSED TO BE A NIGHT for all of us, but especially for Reeve. He was the star. Just like Rennie was.

I didn't think he'd show up. I thought for sure that he'd skip it. I hoped he would, because every time I see him, it hurts. But there he is, sitting at the end of the banquet table, wrinkled shirt untucked, sipping from a water bottle. Whatever's inside, I know it isn't water. Reeve is drunk. And I have this sinking feeling something bad is going to happen.

I'm at the other end of the banquet table, between Alex and

Ash. Alex and I are accidentally matching—I'm in a pale pink silk dress, and he's in a pink tie. When we saw each other, we laughed.

The girls on the junior squad present us senior girls with roses, per tradition. Coach Christy presents a plaque for Rennie, and all the girls on the squad cry. I do too.

Wiping tears from her eyes, Ash whispers to me, "I can't believe everything's about to be over."

I whisper back, "Me either."

"I just wish—"

I give her hand a squeeze across the table. "I know." She doesn't have to say, because I'm wishing the same thing. That Rennie was here.

Some of the football players get up and make speeches, and everybody cheers. When they call out Reeve as MVP, he doesn't get up, and my stomach twists in a knot. He acts like he doesn't even hear. Derek has to pull him up and push him onstage. Oh, Reeve. I'm terrified that he's going to trip and fall up the steps, but he doesn't. He accepts the trophy, and as he walks away, he mutters, "This is bullshit," which the mike picks up. Thank God his parents aren't here. I bet he didn't even tell them.

After the awards and speeches, everyone gets into the buffet line. As is the tradition, the PTA moms made lasagnas. Alex offers to get our lasagnas, but I tell him I'm not hungry. I go to the drink table to get our drinks. I'm pouring two lemonades when I feel a tap on the shoulder. I turn and look, and it's Reeve.

"What up, girl." His voice slurs on the word "girl." "Aw, you and Lindy look so cute together tonight." He waves a hand at my dress. "Did you guys color-coordinate so everyone would know you're a couple?"

"We're not a couple." It comes out quick and defensive, but I can barely look him in the eyes. Not because it isn't true. It just hurts too much.

"Yeah, right." He snatches one of my lemonades and takes a swig.

"Sorry, there's no alcohol in there," I say.

He waggles his eyebrows at me. "You're feisty tonight. That's okay. I like you feisty."

Taking a shaky breath, I say, "You're being really belligerent. If you're going to act like this, you shouldn't be here. You could get expelled!" I pour myself another lemonade and turn to make sure my parents aren't seeing this. Thankfully they are deep in conversation with Ash's mom.

Reeve reaches out and stops me. "So I'm a piece of shit and Lind is your knight in shining armor. That's already been established. And you know what, you can go off to Boston with the kid, you can wear his fucking varsity jacket, you can even marry him and have perfect mixed babies. But you're never gonna love

JENNY HAN & SIOBHAN VIVIAN

him." His eyes bore into mine. "Not like you do me."

My body goes hot and then cold, and then back to hot. I open my mouth, but I don't have any words.

And then Alex appears at my side, flanked by Derek and PJ. To the guys Alex says, "Get him out of here before the teachers see him."

"You afraid that if you leave Cho alone with me for one second, she'll come running back to me?" Reeve throws his head back and laughs uproariously. "Alex, man, you gotta get some balls."

"Let's bounce," Derek says, trying to push Reeve toward the door. "The lasagna sucks."

"Get off me," Reeve says, shrugging Derek away. People are starting to look. Teachers. Parents.

Desperately I look at PJ and Derek and say, "Please, get him out of here, you guys."

PJ throws his arm around Reeve and says, "Come on, man. Let's go outside for a second."

They're forcing him out the door when Reeve twists around and calls out, "You know I'm right, Cho."

I go sit back down at the table, and I don't look up when he calls my name again. People are looking at us, whispering, which I ignore. Alex sits down next to me, and I start cutting into my lasagna, but my hands are shaking so badly, I can't cut through. I knew Reeve was going to be upset about the breakup, but this is so much worse than I ever could've imagined.

"Lil."

"Hm?"

"Are you okay?"

"Sure." I want to run outside and go to Reeve, but I can't. Mary could be here; she could be watching. I have to play my part.

"Yeah, I'm worried about him too." Alex sighs heavily. "He's had a shitty year, that's for damn sure."

"I know." Because of me.

I don't say the words out loud, but the guilt on my face must give me away, because Alex says, "Don't do that. Don't blame yourself. This is a long time coming. Reeve's got demons, Lil. You can't do anything for him. He's gotta face them himself."

Chapter Fifty-One

KAT

I COME DOWNSTAIRS AND WHIP PAT WITH MY HOODIE. He's on the couch in his boxers, eyes closed, sleeping while Dad watches some fishing show on the TV from his La-Z-Boy. "Where's my charger, scrub? My phone's dead."

Pat rolls over and groans. "Kitchen table. Nobody's calling you anyway."

I trade my dead phone for Pat's on the kitchen countertop. As I do, I spot an envelope from Oberlin tucked inside one of Pat's racing magazines. As soon as I see it, my heart explodes. I run back into the living room, screaming, "How long has this been here?" It isn't a huge envelope, but it's not a small one either.

Pat shoots straight up. The left side of his mouth glistens with drool. "What? Kat, what?"

"Why didn't you tell me that I got a letter from Oberlin!" It's postmarked March 31, but it's practically the middle of April.

Pat rubs his eyes, hard. "What? I told you about that."

"No, you didn't!" I scream.

Dad clicks up the volume. "Kat, relax. It's probably some dorm information."

Whoops. I forgot all about the fact that I never told Pat or my dad that I haven't actually been accepted into Oberlin yet. "Never mind," I say, and I go back to the kitchen and sit down at the table with the envelope.

I squeeze my eyes shut, trying to black everything out as I slide my finger along the envelope seal. But I don't see blackness. I see my mother.

Dear Katherine,

Oberlin is delighted to welcome you ...

I'm in. I'm fucking in.

I walk back to the den to apologize to Pat. I was a bitch.

But he's back asleep, and Dad's nodding off himself.

This is how it'll be next year. The two of them here, without me.

I start to cry. I've spent years dreaming about getting off this island, but I don't know if I really understood what it will take to do it. What am I going to do without these guys?

I'm out walking Shep through the piney forest when I hear what sounds like loud music. I follow it and find Reeve's truck parked in a clearing. There's no road leading to this spot, just a dirt bike trail. He's shaking his head back and forth, windows rolled up, the music of his radio blasting. He tips a bottle to his lips.

Poor dude. Day drinking is not a good sign. Day drinking by yourself in the woods is a very, very bad sign.

I approach slowly. I don't want to give the kid a heart attack. I cut a diagonal through the woods so he can see me through his windshield.

And that's when I see Mary, sitting in the passenger seat next to him. Her head is turned, and she's watching him like she's a hungry lion and he's a bloody piece of meat.

What the hell?

Shep starts going absolutely nutso. The dog's so old, he barely has the energy to wag his tail, but suddenly he's yanking me forward so hard I have to use both hands to hold on to his leash. I let him pull me toward the truck. Over his barks I call Mary's name.

Reeve keeps his eyes closed. I don't think he can hear me over the blaring music. But Mary hears me. She suddenly turns her head and meets my eyes. I'm up to the truck now, my hand on the door handle. And just as I pull it open, she disappears.

I swear to God, she just fucking disappears!

Shep lets out one more bark. And then he quiets down and sits next to my feet.

Reeve's eyes fly open, startled. He quickly shuts off his radio. "Jeez, Kat!"

I stare at him. Did he not just see Mary sitting freaking next to him? "What? What the hell is going on?" I look all around me, over my shoulders.

"Nothing. I'm just trying to be alone."

Alone?

But Mary . . .

Maybe I'm dreaming? I've had so many weird dreams about her lately.

Reeve cracks open a new beer, tips it to his lips, and chugs it down in about four gulps.

"Reeve." Damn. What the hell is going on here? Shep is amped up, sniffing around and growling. I let Shep up into the truck, climb in, and lock the door. "I . . . need to talk to you."

Reeve gives me a sour look. "Dude, I just want to drink. I don't want to talk."

"You've got to stop this. I mean, come on. You're destroying yourself!"

I figure he'll call me out for being dramatic, but instead he says, "There's nothing left to destroy. It's over." Reeve throws his empty bottle into the woods, and it shatters off a tree. He pops open another beer, turns to me, and says bitterly, "All thanks to Alex. He's obsessed with her. That's why he ratted me out."

Reeve lifts the bottle to his lips, but this time I grab his arm and stop him. "For cheating on Lillia?"

Reeve stares at me. "What? I never cheated on Lillia. Are you crazy? He's the one who told everyone about what happened in seventh grade." He looks up at me, waiting for me to say something. "I know you've heard about how I bullied that girl until she freaking killed herself, so don't pretend like you don't know what I'm talking about."

I can hear my heart pounding. "Who cares what those dummies say? Rennie made up lies about me for freaking years, remember? Yeah, it was shitty what you did, but it's not like the girl died. It was a suicide *attempt*."

"She did die."

"No, she didn't."

Reeve punches the steering wheel. "I don't know why you're

arguing with me about this, Kat! I'm telling you she died, okay! She freaking died because I was an asshole! I can't blame everyone at school for thinking I'm a big piece of shit, because I clearly am."

I can barely breathe.

"What was this girl's name?"

"Elizabeth Zane." He chokes on the words. "I used to call her Big Easy." He looks at me and blinks a few times as his eyes fill with tears. "Get it? Big *E-Z*. Aren't I so fucking clever?"

Holy shit. There's no way. No fucking way. "What did she look like?"

"Blond hair. Heavy."

That sounds like Mary, back before she lost the weight. And she did say Reeve used to call her Big Easy.

"Are you sure she's dead?" I whisper. "I mean, are you one hundred percent positive?"

Reeve looks at me like I've lost my mind.

Maybe I have. Mary is . . . dead?

No. I mean, that's impossible.

But then I think about the occult books I took from Mary's house. A bunch of them were dog-eared on the pages that talked about communicating with spirits, spirits who think they are still alive.

I can't see; I can't hear; I can't breathe. I feel for the door handle and tumble out of the truck.

"Wait, where are you going?" Reeve asks.

"I—I—I need a ride. And you're too drunk to drive me." I walk around to Reeve's side and pull him out of the driver's seat.

"What? Come on, dude."

He's got a few more beers left in the truck. I dump them all out and say, "Just shut up and pass out."

There's only one person who can tell me, for sure, what the hell is going on with Mary. I take out my phone and look up directions to Greenbriar Sanitarium.

Chapter Fifty-Two

LILLIA

"Do you think we made the right call with this font?" I ask. I'm at Alex's, mounting on an easel the picture of Rennie we had blown up. I picked up the picture of Rennie from the copy shop and brought it right over so we could see how it looked. It's her senior photo, and at the top it reads *Rennie Holtz, Prom Queen In Memoriam* in a scripty Edwardian font. "Should we have gone super clean, like, minimalist?"

Alex looks up from untangling twinkle lights. His mom had a bunch left over from his uncle Tim's wedding, and the guys on prom committee are going to string them up all over the backyard tomorrow morning. "Nah. Rennie's always liked bling. The fancy font was the right choice."

"I hope so," I say. Prom queen was Rennie's dream. I want it to be just right. After all, homecoming should have been hers.

"Don't worry, it looks great," Alex tells me. "It's exactly what she would have wanted." Like always, his words have a way of setting me at ease. Which is a feat these days. I hate being at school, seeing Reeve fall apart. I have such crazy anxiety that he's going to say or do something he won't be able to take back. Make some kind of scene, like he did at the sports banquet.

Lately it's been good between us. Almost like old times. I know I don't have to say anything, but I blurt out, "This year's been crazy, but the one thing I'm grateful for is that you and I can be friends again. I really missed you, Lindy." Alex looks taken aback. Before he can say anything, I say, "Wait. I know I haven't been a good friend to you. I took your friendship for granted, and I led you on because I liked the way you made me feel. You made me feel—so special . . . and I didn't want that to end. But it was wrong. And I'm sorry, Alex. I'm so sorry." I hold my breath, waiting for him to answer.

"It means a lot that you'd say that."

"I mean it."

"So, then, apology accepted."

I stare at him. "Just like that?"

"Yeah. We're cool, Lil. I mean, we've been friends for a long time. That counts for something. It does to me, anyway."

"To me, too." I lean over and give him the biggest hug I can. Then Alex goes back to the twinkle lights and I say suddenly, "Hey, what do you think about us going to prom together? I don't have a date, and you don't have a date, and you know our moms are going to be all about us getting pictures together either way. You don't even have to buy me a corsage!" Alex takes so long to answer that I add, "As friends, of course."

At last Alex says, "As friends. Sure. But don't worry, I'll still get you a corsage."

I beam. I feel lighter already. "Then I'll get you a boutonniere."

Chapter Fifty-Three

KAT

ABOUT AN HOUR LATER I PULL UP THROUGH THE wrought-iron gates. The place is a huge brick mansion from another time, with beautifully manicured gardens. It could be a spa, if not for the bars on the windows.

Reeve passed out cold before we even pulled onto the ferry, and he's been snoring ever since with Shep in his lap. I park in one of the visitor spots and walk quickly up through the front door.

"Can I help you?"

"Yes. I'm here to see my aunt. Her name is Bette Zane."

"You mean Elizabeth Zane?"

"Um, yes. Sorry."

I sign in as Mary Zane, and then I'm pointed down a long hallway. It takes all my self-control not to run down there as fast as I can.

As beautiful and tony as this place looked from the outside, the inside looks exactly like a hospital. White walls, beeping machines, sterile.

The hallway ends at a large room with a glass ceiling. It could have been a greenhouse or something back in the day, and it's filled with sunlight. It's now a rec room, and patients here are quietly going about their business—a few are watching a television in the corner, one is working on a puzzle, three are playing cards. One lady is just staring off into space like she's catatonic, but then she catches me looking at her, and she glares.

I see two nurses who are manning a pill cart look at me with suspicion and share a whisper. Probably thinking if I'm here to see someone, why am I just staring around, casing the joint? Shit.

And then, to my right, I see a woman painting at an easel.

A painting of a lighthouse.

It looks exactly like the ones in Mary's house. Except it's blurry. Unfocused.

I race over to her side. "Um, excuse me. Elizabeth?" She

doesn't even blink. I lay a hand on her arm. "Bette?"

She turns and looks at me, confused. Not in the *Oh! Why, I wasn't expecting company!* way. In the *I'm hopped up on so many drugs, I can't see straight* way. Who even knows if she'll be able to tell me what I need to know.

Her hair is almost entirely gray, and the ends zap out, fried and dead, like she hasn't gotten a haircut in a long time. Years, I bet. She's thin, almost sickly-looking. She's got on a pair of sweatpants and a sweatshirt that are two sizes too big. She's got the same pale complexion as Mary, and the same little nose.

"I'm sorry to bother you, but can I ask you a couple of questions?" That's all I say because I don't know whether I should call her Mary or Elizabeth or Big Easy.

She turns back to the canvas and smacks the brush against it.

"I'm hoping you can tell me what happened to your niece."

A shock of panic bolts through her. Her paintbrush tumbles handle over tip, until it hits the floor with a splat of red. Aunt Bette grabs me and tries desperately to make her eyes focus on mine. "Why? What happened to Mary? Did she hurt someone?"

I shrink back and try to wriggle my arm out of her grip, but she won't let go. "No. I don't know." Panicked, I start looking around for help. What the hell was I thinking coming to a damn mental asylum? They don't lock people up for nothing!

"She's here because of that boy. She won't let him go. She

won't ever let him go." The hairs stand up on the back of my neck. Reeve. "But you've seen her too?"

"Yes . . . I . . . We're friends."

The next thing I know, Aunt Bette is dragging me out of the room, her bony fingers digging into my skin. "You have to tell them! My sister, she made them think I was crazy! She didn't believe me that Mary was back from the dead!" She's making such a ruckus that everyone's turning to stare.

My knees buckle. "Mary's really dead?"

But before Aunt Bette can answer me, a voice calls out my name. "Kat! Kat, what the hell? How long are you going to make me wait out there?"

Aunt Bette turns her head. It takes a second for her to drop her hold on me and lunge at Reeve, snarling like a wild animal. Before she can get to him, a bunch of people restrain Aunt Bette. She's not making any sense. She's foaming at the mouth. And Reeve, he's as white as a ghost.

I grab his hand, and together we run down the hallway.

"What the hell was that all about?" He's still drunk. I can tell.

"Family business," I pant.

After I drop Reeve off at his house, I walk Shep home then jump into my car and head over to the Jar Island cemetery. It's dusk, and the groundskeeper will be locking the gates soon, but I make zigzags down the lines of gravestones until I find it. The Zane obelisk.

I crouch down and touch the cold marble slab.

ELIZABETH MARY DONOVAN ZANE

I glance around. Is she here right now, watching me?

I take out my phone, snap a photo of the grave, and send it to Lillia along with a text.

I'll be outside your house in ten minutes.

Chapter Fifty-Four

MARY

I'M IN REEVE'S ROOM WHEN HE COMES STUMBLING home. I watch from behind a curtain as Kat parks his truck in the driveway, helps him up the stairs, and then runs down the street with her dog.

She knows my secret. I didn't mean for her to see me. Even though it was only for a second, it made me feel . . . naked. Exposed.

But it doesn't matter.

Reeve comes in and passes out cold on his bed. I put my hand to his forehead, enter his dream.

He's already at the lighthouse. He's there, ready to jump.

I see that, and then I lift my hand. I let him have a bad dream all on his own. And when he wakes up, that's when it will happen. I can feel it.

Chapter Fifty-Five

LILLIA

WE'RE OVER AT ALEX'S WATCHING A MOVIE—ASH, Derek, PJ, and the junior girl he's been dating. We hang out here a lot lately. I don't think any of us want to risk getting into it with Reeve somewhere in public. We're all avoiding him. Alex fell asleep thirty minutes into the movie, his head on my shoulder. I've tried to hold as still for him as I can.

My phone buzzes with a text from Kat. Maybe I can convince her to come over. It's an action movie that PJ picked, and it's not like she needs to see the beginning to be able to follow along. I see the picture, and I feel my heart stop.

I write back, *I'll be out front at Alex's.*

I slide away from him. As I do, he opens his eyes and smiles up at me. "Where are you going?"

I whisper, "I'm going to the house to make popcorn," and fluff up a pillow for him to put under his head.

"Mmm. Popcorn." Alex closes his eyes and immediately falls back to sleep.

"Make enough for all of us!" Derek yells.

I grab my bag and my car keys and slip out the door.

I'm on the curb when Kat pulls up.

"Get in." Kat glances around her. "We don't have much time."

There's a stack of old books in the passenger seat. I climb inside and put the books on my lap.

"I saw her, Lillia. She was in Reeve's car . . . haunting him. And then she fucking disappeared." Kat forces a swallow. "You didn't break up with Reeve because he cheated on you, did you? Mary made you do it. Just like before." My mouth is dry. I want to tell her, but I'm afraid. "The secret's out, Lil. And she knows that I know!"

For a split second I think about denying it, even now, even with all that Kat knows. That's how scared I am of Mary, of what she can do. But then I look at Kat, and I can't even try. "I'm sorry. I thought it would be safer for you if I left you out of it. And . . . I couldn't risk anybody else finding out, not with Reeve's life at stake."

"It still is. I saw Mary in his truck today, basically torturing him, trying to get into his head. I called her name, and she straight-up disappeared."

I gasp. "Could Reeve see her?"

"No. But I think he could feel her next to him. Or hear her voice. I'm not sure, but she's definitely getting to him. Think of how crazy he's been acting lately, drinking twenty-four seven, not sleeping." Kat fumbles in her pocket for cigarettes but comes up empty. "After that I went to the mental hospital where her aunt Bette's been locked up. Yo, it was crazy. She kept asking me if Mary had hurt anybody. I had Reeve in the car because he'd passed out and I didn't have time to drop him off. He came in looking for me, and she went ballistic."

I feel my bottom lip quiver. "God, are we really talking about this? That ghosts are real?"

"I don't know. I mean, yeah. This is insane, but . . ." Kat drags her fingers through her hair. "What's that quote? Once you eliminate the impossible, whatever's left, no matter how improbable, must be the truth. So it must be true."

"Why can we see her?"

"I've been thinking about this, about the day we first met her. She came back for revenge, right? And you and I both wanted revenge too, so maybe that's the connection. Maybe she needed us to help her finish whatever it is she's here to do. Whatever it is, it's got to do with Reeve." Kat lets out a long sigh. "Now that we both know her secret, I don't think we have much time."

My whole body starts to shake. "Is there a way that I could somehow convince Reeve to leave Jar Island and never come back? I can't tell him the truth, because Mary will kill him for sure."

"Kill? She said 'kill'?" I nod, and Kat shakes her head. "That sounds batshit crazy. Did we know her at all? She was so sweet. She was like a little kid. I can't even believe it." Kat grabs one of the books from my lap. "I found these in the Dumpster outside Mary's house. Her aunt used them on her. They have spells in them. Protection spells."

I wipe my eyes with my sleeve. Kat flips the book to the page she's looking for. In the margins there are notes written in pencil.

—Arrowhead root sold at Nature's Bounty in Canobie Bluffs.
—First spell attempted October 1st, lasted 3 days.
—Second spell October 7th (doubled ginger powder), lasted 5 days.
—Research possible anger diluents?

Kat grabs another book and then bites her fingers on one hand while flipping with the other. Suddenly she stops on a page and thrusts the book into my hands. "Look at this! It's a binding spell. We could use it to bind Mary to her house!"

"But what if she isn't there?" I drag my finger across the page. "Wait. Okay. It says that she doesn't have to be, so long as the spirit has an emotional connection to the place." I shake my head. "This is crazy. I mean, do you really think this can work?"

"It has to. It's our only shot."

There's a knock on my window. It's Alex. He makes a motion for me to roll down my window. "Yo, Kat! Come inside."

"Can't," she says. "Sorry." With her eyes locked on mine, she says, "I need to run to the store and get some stuff for dinner. But, Lil, I'll text you later, see if you're still hanging out *tonight*."

"Great," I say, with all the fake enthusiasm I can muster. "I'll see you later."

JENNY HAN & SIOBHAN VIVIAN

Chapter Fifty-Six

KAT

READING AND DRIVING IS SOME DANGEROUS shit, but so is a damn ghost, so it ain't like I got a choice. I get my ass to the health food store as fast as I can, and I start grabbing whatever shit I see. I found a couple of other spells in the books, for protection. We have to take every precaution.

First thing I do is race home and put a chalk perimeter around my house. I grab Shep and throw him into my car, because he's turned out to be a good guard dog, at least where Mary's concerned. Thinking back, I realize that he always barked like crazy when Mary was around.

Then I go to Reeve's. Thankfully, it's pretty dark, so none of the neighbors can see me doing the outline around their place. Even the garage, just in case. I move fast, and a couple of times I think I hear a noise, and I jump, but it's just the wind. I hope.

With Reeve, I want to do extra. I feel like I need to fortify his room, too.

Mrs. Tabatsky lets out a gasp when she sees me standing on her doorstep. "Kat!" She grabs me for a hug. "What are you doing here, honey?"

"Hi, Mrs. T. I'm here to see Reeve. Is he home?" I'm talking so fast, the words run together.

"Yes, yes. Come in," she says, pulling me through the front door. She pats me on the butt. "Go on upstairs. I'll bring up a snack."

"Thanks, Mrs. T!" I scramble up the carpeted stairs, two at a time, my book bag bouncing against my shoulders. It feels so familiar. Even his house smells the same, like potpourri and casserole.

I'm heading toward the attic stairwell when a hand reaches out and closes around my wrist. It's Tommy Tabatsky, in basketball shorts and no shirt. His body looks pretty good, too. I think all the Tabatsky boys were born with six-packs. The last time I saw him, he was making out with some random skank at the Greasy Spoon.

"What are you doing in my house, DeBrassio? You here to see me?"

I shake him off me like he's a gnat. "Tommy, I don't have time for this."

I turn to leave, and Tommy says, "You know I got my own place now. You should come by sometime." He winks at me, and I flip him off, and he laughs. "Same old Kat."

Reeve's door is slightly ajar, so I just barge in. He's in bed with his laptop in his lap, no shirt. Do he and his brothers just never wear shirts? "What the hell!" he yelps. He jumps up and grabs a T-shirt.

Shutting the door behind me, I say, "Nice boxers." I walk over to his desk and start opening his drawers.

"Quit snooping around my stuff! What are you even doing here? You dropped me off hours ago."

I find an almost empty bottle of vodka and a bottle of whiskey in the bottom drawer. "You look like hell. You need to eat something, get some sleep."

He puts a pillow over his head. "So then leave so I can sleep."

"I'm about to, so shut up!" As I'm running around his room, I almost trip over an empty bottle of whiskey. I pick it up and shake it at him. "What, are you an alcoholic now? Are you trying to drink yourself to death?"

"That's none of your business." Reeve gets up and snatches

the bottle out of my hand. His eyes are flat; there's no light in them. He looks . . . hopeless. Who knows how long Mary's been torturing him, but it has clearly taken a toll.

"Your mom said she was gonna make us a snack. Go get it."

"God, you're so bossy," Reeve grumbles. But he goes.

As soon as he's out the door, I unzip my book bag and grab the sea salt. Reeve has two windows, so I pour a stream along the sill of each one, and then I do his doorway. Next I get the sage bundle, light it up with my Zippo, and start waving it around. I hope I'm doing this right.

I'm smudging the shit out of the space around his bed when Reeve comes back with a tray. "Please don't burn your goth girl incense in here," he says, setting the tray down on the bed. "It gives me a headache."

"It's not incense. It's sage. I'm clearing negative energy, you ignorant ape." And with that, I run out the door.

"Hey! My mom just made you a snack!"

I'm burning rubber to White Haven. I call Lil, and she picks up on the first ring.

"Kat. What's taking you so long!"

"I found a spell that's supposed to protect our houses. I did mine, and I stopped by and did Reeve's. We can do yours before we leave."

"Thank God!"

"There's one more thing. To do the most powerful binding spell, we both need to bring something that's precious to us to sacrifice—as, like, an offering. I think we have to do it. We don't know how strong Mary is, and I ain't doing this twice."

"So, like, the pearl necklace my dad gave me for my sweet sixteen?"

"No, you dummy! Nobody cares about your pearl necklace. You don't even care about your pearl necklace."

"What did you bring?"

"My Oberlin acceptance letter."

She gasps. "Kat! No!"

"Mary knows how badly I want to go there. I'll give it up for her."

"Well, you don't need the letter anyway. You can still go."

"It's what the letter represents. I ain't going to Oberlin." Damn, it hurts to say the words out loud.

"But you didn't apply anywhere else! That means you'll be stuck here for another half year at least."

"I'll figure something out. We can't fuck around, Lil. Who knows how far Mary's going to take this! Come up with something good. Be outside in five!"

Chapter Fifty-Seven

LILLIA

I OPEN THE JEWELRY BOX ON MY DRESSER AND TAKE out Reeve's necklace. I hold it in the palm of my hand. I couldn't bring myself to give it back to him after we broke up.

I'll never be able to separate Reeve from Rennie's dying, and Mary, and all of it. There hasn't been a time in our relationship that wasn't weighed down with secrets and lies and pain. And the longer I hold on to him, the longer I'll be haunted by the what-ifs and the what-could-have-beens. It's too late for that. We don't have a future. But if I do this, if I set him free forever, he will.

* * *

After Kat makes sure my house is safe, we head to Mary's. Kat goes through the plan with me, and then we ride in silence. We're both too scared to talk.

To comfort myself I reach into Kat's backseat and pet Shep. He's coming along as protection. Kat figured out that animals sense ghosts, so he'll be our lookout. When she said that, I realized what must have happened that day at the stables with Phantom. Mary had to have been there.

She could have killed me.

I still have trouble believing that Mary, my friend Mary, would ever hurt me. But I can't think like that. She has become something else. She's not the girl I met on the first day of school.

We park the car, and I let Shep out of the backseat. He sniffs around in the grass and then sits down and tries to give me his paw.

"Good sign," Kat says. She turns to face the house. "Come on. Let's get this over with."

It has to work. We have to contain her. With prom two weeks away, I can't shake the feeling that Mary's just lying low, waiting to make a big move. Like the homecoming dance, only way, way worse. What if more people get hurt because of us? I couldn't live with myself.

I have to force myself to move, to put one foot in front of the other and walk toward this dilapidated old house and not away from it. As we walk up the front steps with Shep at our heels, Kat quips, "God, I need a cigarette. Quitting smoking during a freaking ghost exorcism was a dumb-ass move on my part." Her hand shakes as she turns the knob of the front door. "Here we go."

We step inside, and the house is dark and empty. And freezing cold, which feels impossible for May. I wish I'd brought a jacket.

"Is cold a thing mentioned in the books?" I whisper.

Kat whispers back, "I don't know. I didn't have time to read everything."

Shep sniffs around, and I turn on the flashlight on my phone and hold it out so we can see. We stay huddled together, taking tiny steps. Then we hear something creak, and we both shriek. It's just Shep tripping over a raised floorboard. I clutch her arm tighter.

"Lil, I'm gonna go upstairs and do the—"

"Shh!" I mouth, *Mary could be here.*

Kat nods and rummages around in her book bag. She takes out a container of sea salt. It's already almost empty, and I have a sick feeling we won't have enough. Next, a roll of twine. She lifts her eyes toward the staircase, and I give the thumbs-up.

And then we get to it. We go from door to door in the house, starting with the second floor, wrapping each doorknob six times with twine and then putting a line of salt before each threshold.

When we reach Mary's bedroom, her door is open and the room is pitch-black.

If Mary is already in there, would she come out and talk to us? Would I be able to see her like always?

Suddenly I feel prickles go up my spine. Someone's here. Watching me. I can feel it. The spell's working. It's called her home.

"Lil," Kat hisses. She has her length of twine ready. I reach out, wrap my hand around the doorknob, and start to slowly pull the door closed. Shep starts growling, low and long, and I freeze. "Keep going!"

I close it fast, and Kat winds the string while I throw down the salt.

Kat looks up at me and smiles.

And then the bedroom door starts to quiver and shake, like someone on the inside is trying to rip it off the hinges. Shep lunges forward, teeth bared, fur standing up on end.

"Oh my God!"

"Come on!"

Each door we pass starts to do the same, as if there is a spirit behind each one. Or maybe Mary's just everywhere.

Kat goes down the stairs, and I follow after her, shaking salt on each one. Kat has one of the books open in her hand, and she starts to chant. But I can barely hear what she's saying. Shep's barking like crazy now, deep and throaty, as if he were a pit bull. The doors upstairs sound like they're going to break open any second.

The temperature is even colder than before, like it's the dead of winter. Our breaths come out in little white clouds.

Kat takes out her Oberlin acceptance letter. "Give me your thing!" she screams. I fish the necklace out of my pocket and drop it into her hand.

I watch as tiny cracks begin to break along the walls. They're like spiderwebs. Pieces of plaster chip and fall onto the floor. Mary's in the walls, in the ceiling. The floorboards start to buckle up and snap one by one, like toothpicks.

Kat lights the corner of her letter on fire with her Zippo, and the whole thing goes up in a flash.

I swear I see someone streak past me, from the living room to the kitchen. Shep breaks free from Kat's hand on his leash. "Shep! Shep!"

Kat lunges to grab his leash, but it slips through her hands. He only gets a few feet away from us before the floor splinters violently. A board snaps in half and slices him straight through his belly like a wooden sword. He makes a sickening cry, and the sound goes right through me.

Oh no. No. Kat falls to her knees and lets out a moan. She picks him up in her arms and sobs. "Sheppy. Sheppy, I'm so sorry."

I go to her. Tears blind my eyes. "Kat, we have to go."

She's crying too hard to get up. Her sobs rack her body; they fill the whole house. They're all I hear. I pull on her arm. "Kat, please," I cry. "We have to go." She lets me pull her up. We pick Shep's body up together and then we run for the door.

Kat has my necklace dangling in her hand. I grab it, hang it on the front doorknob, and pull the door closed.

And just like that, it's quiet.

We run as fast as we can to Kat's car. We put Shep in the backseat, and Kat sits back there with him, her head bent close to his, tears falling onto his coat. She has blood on her shirt, blood on her arms. So do I.

I get into the driver's seat and gun it out of the driveway. I look up, and I see Mary in the window, expressionless, sedate. Trapped.

Chapter Fifty-Eight

KAT

FOR THE NEXT TWO DAYS I POST UP AT REEVE'S HOUSE, just to make sure Mary doesn't figure out a way to come and get him. Also, it's easier to sleep here than at my house, where Shep would have been trying to climb into my bed with me all night. He might've been as old as hell, but he died like a champ, protecting me. My poor puppy.

I take out my Shep grief on Reeve and basically order him around like crazy. His room is disgusting. I make him throw out the booze, take a shower. The essentials. That first night after Mary's bound to her house, he sleeps like a baby. An overgrown snoring baby. The stuff at school eases up on him too. He catches as break when two juniors get stoned during lunch and then go swimming in the fountain nude, and that becomes the thing everyone talks about.

Reeve's mom has tears in her eyes when she thanks me for looking out for her Reevie. God. I almost tear up too, been super emo ever since Shep died. I had to make up some shit to Pat and my dad about him running in front of a car on the road.

I do drive past Mary's house once, to make sure the spell worked. As soon as my car pulls along the curb, she runs up to the window in her bedroom and puts her palms up to the glass. It scares the shit out of me, and I burn rubber the hell out of there.

The hardest part for me, really, is to go back to normal life, to pretending I don't know what I now know to be true. I go over every minute in my mind of the time since I met Mary, looking for clues. There are plenty, and the books help me understand why people could see her on Halloween, but I still don't know if I'd ever have figured it out on my own. And since that's the case, the only thing to do, really, is to try to forget.

Lil and I basically have a new unspoken pact. We haven't talked about Mary once since that night. It's easier that way.

At school Lil asks me if I've bought a dress for prom yet, and

I tell her I already have something, and she gives me this dubious look. "Send me a pic," she says.

So when I get back home, I put on the one semi-fancy dress I own, a black strapless bandage dress. I look like a hooker. Why didn't I realize I looked like a hooker when I bought it a year ago?

Now I'm wondering if I shouldn't just wear black pants and a button-down and a bow tie, and go for an androgynous formal look. I'm pretty sure I've seen the more edgy actresses wearing tuxedos at awards shows.

But I just end up looking like a waiter. So I put the dress back on and figure I'll wear a blazer on top of it.

I text Lillia a selfie, and she writes back, *UM NO. Come over right now.* I tell her thanks but no thanks, but damn, that girl can be persuasive when she wants to be.

So that's why I'm sitting on Lil's bed in my bra and leggings, tearing up my nails while she's taking her sweet time sifting through her ginormous closet. From inside, Lillia calls out, "Close your eyes, Kat. I'm going to present you with two different but equally striking options. Whichever one you gravitate toward first will be the right one. Just follow your gut."

I roll my eyes. "Lil, it ain't that deep." Lillia steps out of the closet holding up two dresses. One is a floor-length teal silk halter dress that drapes in the front and dips low in the back; the other is a corseted canary-yellow cocktail dress that nips in at the waist and hits right above the knee. I let out a low whistle. "Holy shit. Why do you have such fancy stuff?"

"This one was for a black-tie wedding of a family friend, and, um . . . this other one I just had."

I reach for the long one. It still has tags on it. Six hundred and ninety-five dollars from some store called C'est La! Holy shit. "I can't wear this. It's too expensive. I'll be scared of spilling something on it. Give me the other one."

"The yellow one was even more expensive," Lillia says.

"Well, I don't want to wear this one if you haven't."

She shoos my hand away. "Don't worry about that. Which one do you like better?"

"I don't know!" I feel suddenly insecure—what if I look like I'm trying to be something I'm not?

Lil holds the teal dress up to my face, then the yellow. "You'd be a knockout in either . . . but the teal one brings out your eyes, and it's more grown-up. I think you should wear that one. Try it on."

I slip it on over my bra and leggings, and Lillia helps me with the zipper. She ties the halter neck into a bow, and the ends float down my back like streamers.

I stand in front of the full-length mirror, and Lillia and I stare at my reflection. "It's perfect," she breathes. She pulls my hair up and away from my face. "You should wear your hair up. It might not be too late to get a hair appointment at Cut. You'll probably get stuck with a super-early time, but that's better than nothing. I have the perfect shoes for this dress too. Suede, criss-cross with a hidden platform." She pulls her hair into a ponytail. "What size shoe do you wear again?"

"Eight."

"Darn. Why are your feet so big?"

I glare at her, and she giggles. Then she screams, "Mommy! I need your help!"

Mrs. Cho appears in Lillia's doorway a minute later. Breathless, she says, "Lilli, you scared me half to death. Don't scream like that—" Then she notices me standing by the mirror, and her face lights up. "Oh, Kat! You look gorgeous!"

"She's wearing it to prom," Lil tells her.

Confused, Mrs. Cho says, "I thought you—"

"Can she borrow a pair of your shoes, Mommy?"

I break in. "Wait. Mrs. Cho, I don't need—"

"I've got the exact right pair," Mrs. Cho says, nodding to herself. She disappears into the hallway and comes back with a red shoe box. Valentino. Shit.

They're gunmetal gray, studded, with a pointy toe. Rocker chic. Brand-new. I'm pretty sure these shoes are worth more than my car. They're freaking gorgeous.

Lillia pouts when she sees them. "I'd die for those shoes. God, I wish I had big feet like you guys."

At the same time Mrs. Cho and I say, "Size eight isn't big!"

I strap my feet in. Suddenly I'm four inches taller, and the dress even hangs on me differently. "What if I mess them up? Mrs. Cho, do you have a cheaper pair of shoes I could borrow? Like, Aldo or Nine West?"

Mrs. Cho smiles at me. "Honey, you were made to wear these shoes with that dress. No arguments."

When she leaves to go get me a clutch, Lil says, "Just promise me you won't smoke in my dress."

"I won't. I've been really good lately."

Lillia gives me a look like she doesn't believe me. "Smoking gives you wrinkles around your mouth, did you know that? Plus, and I'm sorry to say this, but it makes your clothes stink."

I groan. "Stop with the lectures, Lillia!"

As prim as can be, she says, "Fine, but please just don't smoke in my dress, that's all I ask."

I roll my eyes.

We're going back and forth over how to do my hair and what color lipstick, when I notice Nadia standing outside Lillia's door with her arms crossed. Reminds me of when she was a kid and she would spy on Lil and Rennie and me. Our eyes meet. She says, "That color lipstick isn't right for her. It's too bright. It should be darker. Richer. More like burgundy."

Surprised, Lillia says, "I don't know if I have anything that dark."

"I do," Nadia says with a begrudging sigh.

I wink at her. "Thanks, beotch."

She gives me a tiny smile back and disappears to find the lipstick. Lil falls back onto her bed and says, "I'm sad that high school's almost over. It feels like you and I just found each other again but we already have to say good-bye."

"Lil, we have the whole summer! Let's just make it amazing, all right?" Lil nods a teary kind of nod. I go sit next to her on the bed, and in an instant we're hugging and crying. Over Rennie, over Mary, over everything.

Chapter Fifty-Nine

LILLIA

"MOVE CLOSER TOGETHER, YOU TWO," CELESTE URGES as Alex's dad snaps away with his fancy Leica camera. She's at his side, directing every shot. We're outside by our pool, and my parents are sitting on a chaise, drinking champagne and smiling at us fondly.

We've already done shots with us by ourselves, with our parents, with each other's parents, pretty much every combo you can think of, all at Celeste's behest. The way Celeste is acting, you'd think this was our wedding day. She had Alex's dad take like fifty shots of Alex putting on my wrist corsage. It's a calla lily. Just like his boutonniere.

I've got on the white Hermès bracelet Alex gave me. I showed it to him as soon as I walked in the door. He started to compliment my dress, but I kept holding up the bracelet in front of his face and saying, "Isn't it so cute?" which made him laugh.

I do love my dress, though. It could be a wedding gown, if it was white. I borrowed it from my mom—it's mint-green silk chiffon with a keyhole in the pleated front. The straps are twisted into ropes, and the back is completely open. My mom bought me a crystal belt to wear with it. My hair is up, away from my face in soft waves. I couldn't have worn the dress I bought with Reeve. It wouldn't have felt right. That was a dress for another girl, another night. I doubt I'll ever wear it. I should just tell Kat she can keep it.

Alex's arm tightens around my waist. He looks more handsome than I've ever seen him. His hair is freshly cut, and his tux looks like it was made for him. Which, knowing Celeste, it probably was. Her philosophy is that every man should have a custom-made tux.

"Lillia, find your light," she calls out. My mom and I exchange a look. I swear, just because Celeste watches reality shows about modeling and photography, she thinks she's an expert. My mom's the one who actually used to be a model!

Through my smile I whisper to Alex, "Can you say something? We're going to miss the whole prom if we don't get out of here. Which would be weird, since it's at your house!" Thank God Celeste is spending the evening here, instead of chaperoning the prom. I can only imagine how she'd follow Alex around all night. I hold back a giggle. She'd probably want to slow-dance with him.

Alex nods, drops his arm, and says, "I think we've got enough pictures, Mom."

"But we didn't get one with just you and Nadia." She pouts.

Nadia's long gone, back up to her room. She posed for a few shots and then got bored.

"Mom," Alex protests.

"Just go get her," I say with a sigh. "And then we'll go."

Alex bounds off, and Celeste comes over and puts her arm around me. "I get so happy thinking about the possibility of you and Alex in Boston together," she says. "Your mom and I can do a girls' weekend and visit you guys every—"

"What do you mean? Isn't Alex going to USC?" I saw the acceptance letter on his desk last week.

She shakes her head. With a knowing smile she says, "You never know!"

My cheeks flush. Alex could be in Boston with me. I am

flooded with memories of our great weekend there together, when we almost kissed. I don't want to assume he'd be going for me, obviously, because we're just friends. The one thing I do know is that Alex giving up his dream is the last thing I want.

Chapter Sixty

KAT

I WRAP THE LAST SECTION OF MY HAIR AROUND THE barrel of the curling iron as quickly as I can without burning the shit out of my arm, which I've done twice already. I flip my head over and shake out the curls and then give my whole head a spritz of hair spray. My hair is still damp from my shower, and the curl isn't holding great. It's looking more beach waves than vamp curls, but whatever. It'll have to do. I'm in my black strapless bra and underwear, no makeup on, and I'm supposed to be at Reeve's house in five minutes to take pictures. I suck at time management.

I race around my room shoving shit into Mrs. Cho's beaded clutch. Nadia's lipstick, a couple of Band-Aids. I've got one smudge stick left from what I made to burn in Reeve's room, and I stick that in there too, just in case.

I hurry downstairs. The house is empty. I have no idea where Pat and my dad are. Maybe working on one of Dad's canoes. Business has picked up again now that the tourists are back. He already has enough orders to last him through summer. Dad's been training Pat for the last few weeks, which is good. Pat needs a long-term plan. He can't ride bikes and fuck around in Dad's garage forever.

I slip on Mrs. Cho's stilettos. They are so freaking hot, I almost wish this dress was short, so I could really show them off. Then I head out the front door. On the landing I quick light a cigarette and take a few puffs. I know Lillia told me not to smoke in her dress, but I need something to calm me down. I'm nervous, about tonight going well, and of course about Mary. I'll get the thing dry-cleaned. She'll never notice.

Dad and Pat are standing in the driveway. Pat wolf-whistles, and Dad blinks like I might disappear. He says, "You look beautiful, Katherine."

"I'd better. This dress cost more than our mortgage."

Dad hurries to meet me at the stairs. "Come here, daughter," he says quietly. He takes away my cigarette, and even though it's only half smoked, he tosses it into the grass. Then he tucks me under his arm. "My beautiful girl," he says, and then closes up my hand inside his.

That's when I notice Dad's in a nice button-up shirt, a pair of slacks, and his motorcycle boots. He shaved his beard. He looks younger.

"What are you dressed up for?"

"I want to take a prom picture with you."

Dad motions to Pat to come over. He's got Dad's camera around his neck, an old one that takes real film. He and my mom bought it the year Pat was born.

Pat hands Dad a plastic container, which Dad opens for me. Inside is a white rose corsage. "Dad!"

"I know you said that you and Reeve are going as friends, so I wanted to make sure someone bought you flowers." He slides it onto my wrist.

It's a good thing I don't have any makeup on yet, because my bottom lip begins to shake, and my eyes fill up. I kiss his face. He smells like aftershave. It's cheap shit he gets from the drugstore, but I love the smell.

The three of us walk over to Reeve's house. While Reeve's posing for a picture with his mom and dad, I take out Nadia's maroon lipstick, bend down to Reeve's truck's side mirror, and quick apply a coat.

Tommy comes outside and throws his arms around Pat, and they pound each other's backs like they're old war buddies. Tommy gives me a quick once-over, and I act like I don't notice, but I pop my chest out a little.

When my dad and Pat go to say hi to Reeve's parents, I'm about to follow, but Tommy grabs my wrist. "You look good. When you coming to my place for a sleepover?"

"Shut up, you tool! My dad's right there!"

I ended up hooking up with Tommy one night while I was sleeping over at Reeve's. He fell asleep in the recliner and . . . I don't know. I might have climbed on top of him. I was in mourning or something. And he is hot.

Reeve comes across the lawn and puts his arm around my waist. "Leave her alone, Tommy." Tommy trots back to the house, and at the last second he turns around and waves at me. "Not bad, DeBrassio," Reeve says. "Where'd you get that dress from?"

"I borrowed it from Lil brand-new," I brag. "Had the tags on it and everything." He gets a funny look on his face, like something's dawning on him. I elbow him. "What?"

He shakes his head. "Nothing."

"You look good too." Reeve's body was meant for a tux. Even

though it's a rental, it fits him perfectly. He has his hair wet and combed back, and with his strong jaw and bright smile—which was missing for so long that I forgot what it looked like—he looks like a leading man from some black-and-white movie.

He grins and puts his thumbs in his suspenders. "I feel good. I feel like myself again."

We pose for pictures on his front lawn. I make sure to get some nice ones of me, Dad, and Pat. I'll put one in a frame and take it with me to wherever I end up going to college, now that Oberlin's out. No matter where I go, I'll carry my dad and brother with me forever.

Chapter Sixty-One

LILLIA

WHEN WE FINALLY GET OVER TO ALEX'S HOUSE, THE prom is in full swing, and honestly, it's even better than if we'd had it at the Water Club. The white tents and the twinkly lights look elegant, Gatsby-esque even. While Alex goes around saying hello to people, I make my way over to Ash and everybody. We're exclaiming over each other's dresses when I spot Kat and Reeve on the dance floor. Reeve's behind Kat. She's tucked up against him, she's leading him by the suspenders, and they're dancing in sync, laughing their heads off. It's been so long since I've seen him happy. He looks so handsome and full of life. He looks like the old Reeve, and I'm glad. Even though it's over between us, I still want to know that he's okay.

I'm stepping onto the edge of the dance floor just as Reeve's walking off it, sweaty and flushed and out of breath. Smiling. When he sees me, his smile slips.

"Hi," I say, trying to keep my voice from shaking. I'm scared he's going to be cutting, or mean, or indifferent. "You look good, Reeve." I try to say it warmly, kindly, the way an old girlfriend would.

It feels like whole minutes go by before he says, "So do you."

I lick my lips. They feel very dry. "I'm—I'm glad you came."

"Yeah, I wasn't going to but Kat dragged me here." Reeve takes a step closer to me, and without thinking I back away from him. He sees me do it, and his eyes go straight to his shoes. We're standing in the shadows of the trees that surround Alex's house now. The prom suddenly feels far away. "Can I just say something?"

I'm afraid to say yes. I just look at him.

"I'm sorry for what I said to you at the banquet. It wasn't right. It was out of line." Reeve's looking at me steadily, waiting. "I wanted to tell you about what happened between me and that girl. And you know, what? I should have. It should have come from me, not from Alex or whoever. The only reason I didn't was because I was scared that if you knew, you wouldn't want to be with me." He shoves his hands in his pockets. "Which is exactly what ended up happening, so . . . yeah."

My eyes fill up. I want to tell him that I knew. That I loved him anyway.

"It's all right. I'm sorry too—for the way things turned out." The words come out thin and without conviction. "I would like us to still be friends."

Reeve shakes his head. "I don't think I can do that." He says it so softly, almost a whisper. "I'm sorry, I have to be honest. All night I'm thinking how it was supposed to be you and me. I know you don't want to hear that. But we were supposed to be at prom together, Cho."

"Reeve, please. I—"

"I'm never going to not want to be with you. I mean, I still love you, despite all the shit that's gone down. I would do anything to be with you. So no, I can't be"—he chokes—"your *friend.*"

"Reeve," I whisper. I touch his face. He grabs my hand, holds it tight in his.

"I know why you can't be with me now. What I did, what people here think of me. I get it. But school's almost over and in a couple of months, we'll both be off Jar Island. I'm still going to Graydon in the fall. I'll be an hour away from BC. I'm not giving up on you. On us." And then he's pulling me against him, and his mouth is on mine, and I'm kissing him back. I can't not be kissing him back. The smell of him, the way he tastes, I'm drowning in it and how right it feels. How good.

Between kisses, he says, "Please. Please find a way to forgive me for what I did. I love you. I love you so much, Lillia."

It wakes me up.

Mary.

I push him away, my fingers fly to my lips. Oh my God. What have I done? "Don't ever say that to me," I gasp.

"Cho, wait—" His arms are reaching for me.

"Don't ever come near me again." I turn tail and run, run as fast as I can away from the party, to Alex's pool house.

I can't be near Reeve. It's too dangerous. I won't go back to school, it's pretty much over for the seniors anyway. Or . . . or I'll go to Boston, stay in our family apartment until Reeve leaves for training. Whatever it takes to not be near him.

My purse. I need my purse.

I race into the pool house. I stashed my purse and my coat in Alex's closet for safekeeping. Outside the sliding glass doors, the music is blasting, and I hear the rest of our senior class shouting and clapping along to the music. Flashing lights from the DJ booth speckle the floor.

I slip out the door and hurry down the path, toward the front of Alex's house. I'm searching for my car keys when I remember that Alex drove us here. Maybe I'll call my mom to come and pick me up.

No. What if Reeve tries to find me?

I'll just walk home.

I'm about to pass through the fence gate when I slam into Alex. Alarmed, he says, "Lil, what's wrong?"

"I have to get out of here right now." I'm shaking. "I'm sorry." I try to push past him and get on the other side of the fence, where the valet guys are all sitting on the hoods of the parked cars lining Alex's driveway and street.

But Alex won't let me go. "Whoa, whoa, whoa. What's going on? Did something happen with Reeve?"

I start to cry. "I don't want to be near him, Alex. It's just too much. He makes it so hard for me. He's outside my house, he's drunk at the banquet screaming things, he's telling me he loves me and that he's never going to let me go. I—I can't breathe." I'm gulping for air. Every single day since I made that promise to Mary has been a struggle. How can I live like this? Pushing away the boy I love forever. "Alex, I can't breathe."

Alex puts his hands on my shoulders. "It's okay. It's okay. Try to take deep breaths, Lil."

I breathe deep. Raggedly I say, "He won't let me go. How am I supposed to do this if he won't let me go?"

Alex's face changes, and I look over my shoulder. Reeve is

JENNY HAN & SIOBHAN VIVIAN

standing behind us, valet ticket in his hand, white-faced and wretched. "I'll never bother you again," he manages. "You don't have to worry anymore." And then he's gone.

"Oh no," I whisper. "No, no, no."

I'm about to run after him when Alex steps in front of me. "Lil, this is just what he wants, to pull you back into his drama. He's sick. You can't help him."

"Alex, you don't understand." I'm practically screaming in his face. "It's not just Reeve. There are other people involved."

"Lillia! Calm down! Let's go get Kat. Talk to her."

Kat.

The spell.

I don't say anything. I just turn and run back toward prom.

Chapter Sixty-Two

MARY

I'M ON THE BEDROOM FLOOR, JUST STARING OFF INTO space, when my bedroom door suddenly swings open. I run toward it and stare down the hall.

Are Kat and Lillia back here to do something else to me? I can't let them catch me off guard again. I was so close to getting Reeve, so close to being free of this place. And again my supposed friends chose his life over mine.

As I walk out of my room and downstairs, I see the strings tied around the doorknobs, the salt on the floor.

It's all perfectly done.

I know exactly the spell they used on me. They had to sacrifice two things they loved. I don't know what Kat's was, but I do see blood on the floor from her dog, Shep. She did give up something, unintentionally anyway.

There's a necklace hanging from the front doorknob. I pick it up and immediately recognize it. The necklace Reeve gave her during spring break.

So she gave Reeve up to bind me. How poetic.

One of them must have gone back on their sacrifice if I'm free. There's no doubt in my mind who I have to thank.

Kat and Lillia are dangerous. They know my secret, and worse, they now know how to control me. I can't let them do that again. I won't be bound here for all eternity. I'm leaving. Tonight. Before they know I'm even gone.

I close my eyes and try to feel him, find him.

Chapter Sixty-Three

KAT

I SPEND PROM THINKING A LOT ABOUT DEAD PEOPLE, even though I dance ten songs straight with Ashlin. The girl can dance; I'll say that for her.

I think about Rennie and if she's watching us. I can imagine her gagging over some of the uglier dresses and the one girl who's wearing a freaking tiara. And I'm sure she thinks the jumpy castle is immature. Which, okay, yeah. I hear that. But a jumpy castle is also as fun as hell, and there's been a line to get in it all night long.

Maybe it's just me being sentimental, but I honestly believe that if Rennie were still alive, I could have sold her on the idea of ditching the Boston club to have prom here. She definitely had a rebellious streak in her. She liked shaking things up.

I think about my mom. I hope she thinks I look beautiful in my fancy dress. If she is somewhere out there, I know I've made her proud. A bunch of people have grabbed my arm tonight, kids from different social groups, thanking me. She would have loved that everyone was invited. That nobody was left out because they didn't have the money.

And, of course, I think about Mary. Every girl with long blond hair makes my heart skip, but it's never her, thank God. Our spell worked. She's trapped in her house. But it makes me sad that we're all here having the time of our lives when Mary should be with us. Not Mary as she is now, but as she used to be. She should be alive. I wish she were alive.

My stomach growls. I need to get on that buffet while the getting's good. It was Mrs. Lind's genius idea to get our prom catered, and I insisted we do Antoine's. Balsamic glazed chicken breasts, roasted red potatoes, those green beans I love.

I head over to the buffet and see that it's been pretty well picked over. If I want to eat, I'd better get to it. I get a plate and a soda and am heading back to the table when Lil grabs me by the arm so hard, I almost drop my plate. Frantically, she says, "I think I broke the spell. I'm sorry. I'm so sorry. Reeve kissed me and I kissed him back and something's wrong. I can feel it."

"Shit," I breathe. "Where is he now?"

"He overheard me saying all this stuff to Alex and he said—he said he wasn't going to bother me anymore and now he's just *gone*. I'm afraid he's going to do something crazy." A sob escapes my throat.

"Calm down, Lil. I'll drive by her house and check that she's still there. You go find Reeve."

The last thing I tell Lillia is that everything will be okay.

I hope Mary doesn't make a liar out of me.

Chapter Sixty-Four

LILLIA

I RUN DOWN ALEX'S DRIVEWAY AND ALONG THE ROAD, where the valets have parked the cars. My heart is pounding in my chest, but I don't stop running.

I finally spot Reeve's truck. *Please be inside it. Please.* But when I get closer, I see that he's not. It's empty. He's gone someplace by foot.

And then I spot his keys on the seat. I get in and tear down the roads. Where could he have gone? Maybe he went home? I check, even park the truck and run up to the house, but he's not there. His bedroom windows are all dark, his mom and dad are watching TV alone in the den.

He's nowhere, and I'm wasting time. I should go check on Mary's house. Kat might need me.

I'm halfway to Middlebury, speeding up the road that rides along the edge of the cliffs, when I nearly run over him.

He's wobbling along the edge, a bottle of liquor in each hand. I slam the brakes, and he stumbles. And a ways up the road there's Mary, sitting on the cliffs, watching him.

I lean across the cab and jerk the passenger door open. "Get in!"

"Cho, what the—"

"Just get in!" I scream.

He stares at me in shock, but he gets in. When I put my eyes back on the road, I see Mary there, standing in the middle of the street. Reeve still can't see her. I drive his truck up and onto the other side of the road, to pass her.

Reeve says, "What the hell is going on? What are you doing in my truck?"

"It's Mary. Mary Zane. Elizabeth!"

Reeve's eyes bulge. "What did you say?"

"She's been trying to hurt you, Reeve. Her spirit—she's—she's a ghost, Reeve. She's come back here for you." We're speeding along. "We have to get off the island. She can't leave."

His face is stark white. "Oh my God. I thought I was going insane. You've actually seen her? Oh shit. Shit, shit, shit."

I glance at the clock on my dashboard. The next ferry leaves in four minutes. We have to make it. We have to. "When you get to the mainland, don't come back until I call you."

"I'm not going anywhere without you."

"Reeve, don't argue with me! You aren't safe here."

His jaw sets stubbornly. "I'm not leaving you."

We pull into the ferry parking lot, and, thank goodness, the ferry's still there. There aren't any cars waiting to board, just us. We're pulling forward when I see her.

Standing in the parking lot, right in front of us, in that gauzy white dress, looking like an angel. Face twisted up and screaming for me to stop.

There's only one thing I can do. I hit the gas. The dockworkers shout and wave their hands at us. "No more cars!" they shout. This time I drive straight through Mary and up onto the ferry.

I spin around and look through my rear window. She's staring back at me. She doesn't move. She just watches Reeve and me and then disappears as the drawbridge is lifted and the ferry pulls away from the shore.

Chapter Sixty-Five

KAT

I DRIVE A MILLION MILES AN HOUR TO T-TOWN. DAD and Pat are back working in the garage, the hatch door lifted high. They see my headlights bounce up the driveway, and they wander out.

Dad flops a rag over his shoulder. "Kat? Why are you back so soon?"

I don't answer him. I just run as fast as I can to my room and grab Aunt Bette's books, the candles, the spices, and the salts, and the rest of the shit we used on Mary. I throw it all into my book bag. Just in case. I have no idea what we might need, or if any of it will work if our spell is broken.

I glance at the clock on my way out. God, I really hope this is a false alarm.

When I'm back outside, I find Pat blocking my car door, arms folded. "What's going on?"

"Move, Pat!"

"Come on. Just tell me—"

"Move!" I push him out of the way, which isn't easy in heels and a prom dress. He tries to stand his ground, and we wrestle for a second, but then Pat must see that I am so not fucking around right now, because he steps back.

"Okay, okay."

I jump into my car, put it in reverse, and hit the gas so fast, the tires spin smoke. Then I'm flying down the street, Dad and Pat left bewildered in my taillights. I drive, drive as fast as this piece-of-shit car will go, across Jar Island to Middlebury. The movie theater, Java Jones, all the tourists are colored streaks out my window.

A few minutes later I pull into Mary's driveway. Her house is as dark as the sky. I hike up my dress and tiptoe through the moonlit yard, on high alert, glancing around.

Is Mary here? Is she watching me right now? Or maybe Lillia was wrong. Maybe she didn't break the spell.

The crickets and my pounding heart are the only noises until, far off in the distance, the ferry horn sounds. I stand underneath Mary's bedroom window and wait for her to come, like she did once before. When she doesn't, I get this feeling, this sick-ass feeling that someone's going to get hurt tonight.

Maybe Reeve.

Or maybe us. Me and Lillia. Mary knows what we've done, that we tried to cage her spirit. I hold tight to my bag. I've got to fix this, or we're all done for.

I walk through the front door. Though it's dark, I can see that Lillia's necklace is gone, the salt disturbed. Every door we bound shut upstairs has been opened wide.

I go into Mary's bedroom, fall to my knees, and unzip my bag. With trembling hands I set out the candles and start lighting them with my Zippo so I can see. And then I open one of the spell books and try to figure out what the fuck to do.

Then the moonlight disappears and an icy wind blows through the room. The candles flicker out, and I feel so, so, so cold, colder than the coldest winter day. I relight my Zippo to start over and I nearly scream when the glow falls on Mary, sitting on her windowsill, staring down at me with accusing eyes.

"If at first you don't succeed . . . quit and try something else?" she says.

My mouth drops open. The wick of the candle sends up twirls of gray smoke. I squeeze my hand tight around my lighter.

"You almost had me. I'll give you an A for effort."

I fall to the floor and frantically flip through the book.

Mary makes a movement with her arm, and the spell book flies across the room, away from me. And then she holds up Lillia's necklace. "Too bad Lillia didn't keep up her end of the bargain."

I quickly bring out the lighter and rub my thumb over the metal wheel a couple times. Finally the flint sparks into a flame. As soon as it does, I go flying backward and slam into the wall with the force of a truck. Then gravity pulls me down into a crumpled heap on the hardwood floor.

Mary hops down from the windowsill, and she lands on the floor in her bare feet. I slowly lift my head as much as I can, but my entire body is wrecked and throbbing. My lighter has slid across the floor and is now near where I have the spell book open. I crawl on my belly toward it, squinting my eyes to try to push away the pain. When I'm close, I reach my arm out as long as I can and try to grab it. My fingertips just graze the lighter. But as soon as I make contact, Mary raises her arm and lifts me right up off the floor again.

"Stop doing that! Why aren't you listening to me?" She flings me against the wall another time. I can hear the plaster crack, or maybe it's my bones.

I cough and gasp for breath, the wind entirely knocked out

of me. When I open my eyes, the whole room is a watery blur. I grit my teeth and try to get to my knees. I can't see where Mary is, but I plead with her anyway. "This isn't you, Mary. You're not like this." Finally my vision sharpens and the spell book and my bag come back into focus across the room. I crawl toward it, gasping for breath. "Let us help you."

Mary steps between me and the candles. "Lillia is still in love with Reeve. He's all she cares about. That's why the spell was broken, that's why she's on a ferry with him right now, saving him and leaving you to die right here, right now." She spins around and lifts her arm. The rest of my stuff falls out of the bag. The salt and the lavender fly around the room, the candles roll in opposite directions. I keep crawling, but then I feel myself being lifted up again.

And then everything goes black.

JENNY HAN & SIOBHAN VIVIAN

Chapter Sixty-Six

LILLIA

I JUMP OUT OF THE TRUCK AND RUN OUT THE EXIT to the next level so I can make sure Mary's gone. She is. Where did she go?

We're going to pull away from the dock soon. I have to get off this boat. I can't leave Kat to deal with Mary by herself.

Reeve comes up behind me. He's shaking his head, dazed. "I can't believe it."

"Let's go up to the deck so we can talk," I say.

We walk up to the deck, and people are staring at us in our formalwear. I say, "Go inside and get us some seats. I have to go to the bathroom. I'll be right back." Reeve nods, still looking like a scared kid. This might be the last time I see him. So I get on my tippy-toes and hug him tight. His face breaks into a relieved smile.

"That stuff you said to Alex. You didn't mean it, right?"

"Mary. She told me to stay away from you."

"But how did—"

"I'll explain everything in one minute. Promise."

He nods and goes inside, and I take off in the other direction. I push open the exit and fly down the stairs to the lowest level. I run down the length of the ferry, pushing people out of the way. It's too late. We're already pulling away.

I stand at the guardrail. We've barely left shore. I could make it. I could jump. It's not so high up from here. I start taking off my shoes before I can stop to really think about it.

I pull myself up to the railing, and my heart is pounding out of my chest. I'm so scared. I'm so scared. And then I hold my nose, and jump.

It feels like I'm falling forever before I hit the water. It smacks into me so hard it knocks the wind out of me. The water is freezing, and I swallow gallons of it, up my nose, down my throat. Water all around me. I forget everything I learned about swimming, and I'm just panicking, because this feels like drowning. I'm drowning. My dress is like a funeral shroud, weighing me down, making every movement that much harder.

And then I'm fighting my way to the surface, and it just kicks in. The fight to live. I'm swimming. My body knows how.

I swim all the way to the dock. My arms burn, my throat burns, everything burns. I swim until I have nothing left. Two ferry workers spot me and fish me out of the water. "What the hell were you thinking?" one screams at me.

My whole body is shaking from cold and exhaustion. They go to get me a blanket, and I take off before they come back. I'm running out of the ferry parking lot, up the hill to Mary's house. My feet are bare and my dress is soaking wet and clinging to my body, but I don't care.

Hurry, hurry, hurry. Before it's too late.

My throat burns; my chest burns; every muscle in my body burns. But I have to keep going. I have to.

I don't stop running. I run up her driveway and to the front door. As soon I open the door, I hear Kat and Mary yelling, and then there's a thud, and it goes quiet. "Kat!" I scream. I take the stairs two at a time, tripping over my dress.

When I get upstairs, I push at Mary's bedroom door, but it won't open. "Kat!" I scream. I bang on the door as hard as I can. "Mary! Let me in!"

I'm screaming myself hoarse when I hear footsteps pounding up the stairs. I turn around, and there is Reeve, wild-eyed and out of breath. I gasp. "What are you doing here?"

"I got them to turn the boat around—"

"Kat's inside," I croak.

"Move," he tells me, and then he throws himself against the door just as it opens.

Kat's in a heap on the floor, cradling her arm, and Mary's standing over her. Looking at us. At Reeve. "You're here," she says.

In wonder he says, "It was you all along."

Chapter Sixty-Seven

MARY

NOW I GET TO BE THE GIRL HE CAN'T STOP STARING AT. "Look at me, Reeve." Reeve has dropped his head, and I hold out my hand and jerk his chin up, painfully high. "I said look at me. I want to show you what Lillia gave me." I dangle the necklace in front of him. "It's pretty, isn't it?"

Lillia makes a gaspy sound; she's crying, hunched over, trying to light a candle. Kat's got the book open in her lap, and she's muttering under her breath. They still think they can stop me. They think they can trap me here forever. With one flick of my hand I scatter their things across the room.

Then I turn my attention back to Reeve. "I'm sorry," he says. "I'm so sorry, Elizabeth. This is all my fault. Don't hurt them. They don't have anything to do with this. Let them go. Let's talk, just you and me."

"Shut up," I tell him. I use my fingers to push his lips together. "You don't get to be the hero, do you understand me? That's not you. You're the bully. You're *my* bully. That's who you are to me. You're why I didn't want to live anymore."

Reeve gets down on his knees. He tries to say something, but he can't, because I'm holding his mouth closed. I release it. He sucks in a breath. "Please. Forgive me, Elizabeth. I'm begging you."

"It's too late for that," I tell him.

He gasps for air. "I've been running from you ever since that day on the ferry. I've been so scared. That people would know what I did. What kind of person I was. And now it's here. You're here. I can finally tell you how sorry I am."

"I already know you're sorry. But sorry doesn't change anything." I lift my hand and push Reeve so hard he does a backward somersault and cracks his head on the floor. Cracks it like an egg. Blood trickles down his forehead. "Sorry doesn't bring me back to life."

Lillia tries to go to him, but Kat holds her back. Reeve looks up, stunned and woozy, and it takes him a second to get his bearings. Once he does, he keeps going. He inches toward me on his knees. "Elizabeth, please—"

"Who is Elizabeth? I was never Elizabeth to you. I'm Big Easy, remember? Say it."

He shakes his head and begins to cry.

"Say it!" I scream so loudly, the glass in the windows rattles.

"Big Easy," he chokes out.

"There you go," I say, kindly now. "Feels good, right? Feels natural."

I take my empty bookshelf and toss it across the room at Reeve. He throws his arms up and ducks out of the way, just in time. I do the same thing with my dresser. I send it flying across the room at Reeve, and it breaks into a thousand splinters.

I feel myself begin to change. Lillia, Kat, and Reeve, they see it happen. Their faces are white with shock. The prom dress, the long blond hair, it all goes away. I become Big Easy, fat and dripping wet.

"There's only one thing you can do for me now, Reeve."

He inches toward me on his knees. "I'll do it. Anything."

With a flick of my hand, the pocketknife, the one I gave Reeve, appears out of thin air and hovers in front of his face. "Kill yourself."

Lillia screams "No!" as Reeve takes the knife into his hands. Reeve tries to push both of them out of the bedroom. Kat breaks free easily, but Reeve's got a better grip on Lillia. She fights him with all her might. "Please, Mary! Don't do this!"

I lift my hand and send Lillia and Kat flying into the hallway. Then I close the door, lock the lock. And it's just me and Reeve. At last. The way it was supposed to be.

They pound and pound their fists on the door. They scream for him as loud as they can. But Reeve keeps his eyes on me. It's like we're the only two people left in the world.

"Do it," I tell him, and make the knife drop into his hand. "Do it and this will all end."

He opens the knife and lays the blade against his wrist. His hand is shaking. He sucks in a deep breath and slashes the skin on his left side. The red comes so fast, I think it takes even him by surprise. And then he does the other side, a cut to match. Shaking, he sinks down to the floor.

I watch the red grow, the color drain from his face.

And I feel nothing.

His heart slows; it must be slowing. I take a few steps forward.

I feel nothing. There's no white light, no door that suddenly appears.

Reeve is dying. And I'm not going anywhere.

He whispers, "I hope this sets you free, Elizabeth."

But it's not.

It's not! I'm still here.

The knife is lying on the floor next to me, blade out and streaked. I gave him that gift with all the love in my heart. It wasn't supposed to be for this.

I reach up to my neck and touch the gnarled blistered skin. It burns hot like fire. I feel the squeeze of the rope choking away the last bit of me that still feels like I could be real.

I'm the one.

I did this to myself. Nobody made me do it.

I open my mouth and scream. Hands fly up to cover ears. The windowpanes shake and shake and shake from my decibels, until they explode and shower the room in crackling shards, and the door bursts wide open.

Lillia and Kat rush inside. Kat tears at her dress, and the girls try to stop Reeve's bleeding.

I watch, motionless, as the flames flicker and hop to my bare mattress, what's left of my dresser. The room begins to fill with the blackest smoke.

I never meant for this to happen.

The floor opens up, and my burning bed drops down to the first floor. Sparks fly up through the hole. Kat screams and nearly falls through, but Lillia pulls her out of the way just in time. They try to pick up Reeve, to carry him to safety, but he's too heavy. And the fire is too hot. And the smoke is too thick. I can feel it blackening their lungs.

They will die if I don't do something.

They will die just like I did. For no good reason at all.

I killed myself to teach Reeve a lesson. To show him how badly he'd hurt me, to punish him for what he'd done. Only I was the one who was punished. I did it to myself. And I'd give anything, everything, to go back and do it over again.

The flames are an orange wall closing in on them. Lillia and Kat. My friends. The only real friends I ever had. And Reeve, the only boy I've ever loved. The boy who is so sorry for what he did to me. Who'd take it back if he could.

He can't.

But I can. Not for me, but for them.

I concentrate as hard as I can, and I hold back the fire for them. The flames hiss away from me as if I were a force field. I wrap myself around the three of them and carry them to the window, the heat on my back.

And then, the warmth and the light, they move through me. They envelop me.

I'm changing again. This time into something new.

And I'm gone.

Chapter Sixty-Eight

LILLIA

WE FALL ONTO THE COOL GREEN GRASS. I CAN'T STOP coughing, I can't get air into my lungs. I can hardly even see, my eyes are so watery.

Beside me Kat is doubled over, heaving and spitting black soot into the grass. Her face is streaked with ash and sweat. "Mary!" she screams, hoarse. We stare up at the burning house.

In that moment Mary's house becomes a fireball. Every inch of it is embers. The house lights up the whole sky like a second sun. I see Reeve in the grass. He's still moving. I crawl over to him and press on his wrists as hard as I can.

Sirens wail in the distance. Whatever brought Mary back, whatever brought us together, it's over. Mary is gone. Kat sobs against me, full-body racking sobs, and I hold her tight. I can hear the sirens, getting closer and closer. I feel Reeve's pulse. He's alive.

He's free. We all are.

Because whatever Mary was in the end, she saved us.

Epilogue

LILLIA

WHAT HAPPENED THAT NIGHT CHANGED US FOREVER, Reeve, Kat, and me. None of us would ever be the same again.

In the fall, when everyone else left for college, Kat stayed behind. She reapplied and went to college in the spring. Not to Oberlin. Instead she chose NYU. She said New York would be good for her, a better scene than Ohio. But we both knew the truth.

Reeve needed twenty stitches in each wrist. He was still in bandages for graduation. Everyone at school thought he'd tried to kill himself over me, and he never denied it.

He was pretty scarce that summer. Reeve moved to Connecticut only a few weeks after graduation to do summer sessions. I thought I might hear from him when I started at BC, the way he said he would at prom, but he never called. The following year he played football in Florida, then reinjured his leg his sophomore year, and that was that.

Alex waited until the last minute of summer to decide where he was going to college, but he eventually said yes to USC and went out to California. I cried when he left.

I had a couple of boyfriends throughout college, nothing too serious and nothing close to being in love. Alex and I would e-mail every so often, and he'd always send me something on my birthday. After Nadia graduated from high school, my parents moved back to Boston, but we kept the house on Jar Island. We turned into summer people again.

Kat's dad died of a heart attack a year after college graduation. We all went back to Jar Island for the funeral. Everyone who cared about Kat was there by her side—Reeve and his family, Alex, me. During the service I thought I saw Mary, sitting in the balcony, and then I blinked, and she was gone. I guess it was a trick of the light.

When Alex and I took the ferry back to Boston together, I asked him if he was seeing anyone special, holding my breath all the while. Alex half smiled in a sardonic sort of way and said, "You've ruined me for other girls, Lillia. No one else comes close."

I let my head fall onto his shoulder. "That was my whole plan."

We haven't spent more than a few days apart ever since. Some things are just meant to be, I suppose.

Kat hasn't set foot on Jar Island since her dad's funeral. She lives in Brooklyn now, which is probably where she was meant to be all along. Pat moved there too, after selling the house. It went for an insane price; real estate on Jar Island is in such high demand. Now they share a loft space in an old factory. I want to visit Kat, see what her life is like. Maybe Alex and I will go sometime this year.

I still go back to Jar Island for holidays and during the summer. And sometimes I'll see Reeve driving around in his truck. He and Luke took over his dad's business.

I remember how he used to look in his football uniform. No boy has ever been as handsome as Reeve in that uniform, on that field. I remember what it felt like to fall in love for the first time. You think you'll never love like that again. But you do.

Life is long if you let it be.

I only wish Mary had been able to find that out.

I hope she got off Jar Island.

I hope she found her peace.

Ashes to Ashes

Here's a sneak peek at

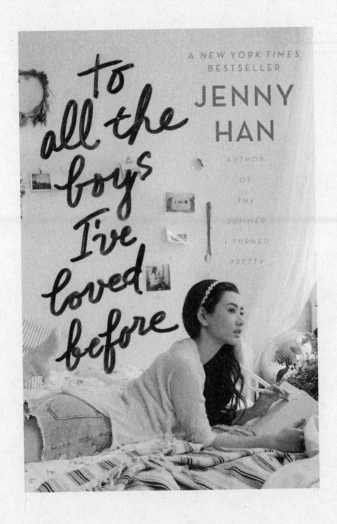

I like to save things. Not important things like whales or people or the environment. Silly things. Porcelain bells, the kind you get at souvenir shops. Cookie cutters you'll never use, because who needs a cookie in the shape of a foot? Ribbons for my hair. Love letters. Of all the things I save, I guess you could say my love letters are my most prized possession.

I keep my letters in a teal hatbox my mom bought me from a vintage store downtown. They aren't love letters that someone else wrote for me; I don't have any of those. These are ones I've written. There's one for every boy I've ever loved—five in all.

When I write, I hold nothing back. I write like he'll never read it. Because he never will. Every secret thought, every careful observation, everything I've saved up inside me, I put it all in the letter. When I'm done, I seal it, I address it, and then I put it in my teal hatbox.

They're not love letters in the strictest sense of the word. My letters are for when I don't want to be in love anymore. They're for good-bye. Because after I write my letter, I'm no longer consumed by my all-consuming love. I can eat my cereal and not wonder if he likes bananas over his Cheerios too; I can sing along to love songs and not be singing them to him. If love is like a possession, maybe my letters are like my exorcisms. My letters set me free. Or at least they're supposed to.

JOSH IS MARGOT'S BOYFRIEND, BUT I GUESS you could say my whole family is a little in love with him. It's hard to say who most of all. Before he was Margot's boyfriend, he was just Josh. He was always there. I say always, but I guess that's not true. He moved next door five years ago but it feels like always.

My dad loves Josh because he's a boy and my dad is surrounded by girls. I mean it: all day long he is surrounded by females. My dad is an ob-gyn, and he also happens to be the father of three daughters, so it's like girls, girls, girls all day. He also likes Josh because Josh likes comics and he'll go fishing with him. My dad tried to take us fishing once, and I cried when my shoes got mud on them, and Margot cried when her book got wet, and Kitty cried because Kitty was still practically a baby.

Kitty loves Josh because he'll play cards with her and not get bored. Or at least pretend to not get bored. They make deals with each other—if I win this next hand, you have to make me a toasted crunchy-peanut-butter-sandwich, no crusts. That's Kitty. Inevitably there won't be crunchy peanut butter and Josh will say too bad, pick something else. But then Kitty will wear him down and he'll run out and buy some, because that's Josh.

If I had to say why Margot loves him, I think maybe I would say it's because we all do.

We are in the living room, Kitty is pasting pictures of dogs to a giant piece of cardboard. There's paper and scraps all around her. Humming to herself, she says, "When Daddy asks me what I want for Christmas, I am just going to say, 'Pick any one of these breeds and we'll be good.'"

Margot and Josh are on the couch; I'm lying on the floor, watching TV. Josh popped a big bowl of popcorn, and I devote myself to it, handfuls and handfuls of it.

A commercial comes on for perfume: a girl is running around the streets of Paris in an orchid-colored halter dress that is thin as tissue paper. What I wouldn't give to be that girl in that tissue-paper dress running around Paris in springtime! I sit up so suddenly I choke on a kernel of popcorn. Between coughs I say, "Margot, let's meet in Paris for my spring break!" I'm already picturing myself twirling with a pistachio macaron in one hand and a raspberry one in the other.

Margot's eyes light up. "Do you think Daddy will let you?"

"Sure, it's culture. He'll have to let me." But it's true that I've never flown by myself before. And also I've never even left the country before. Would Margot meet me at the airport, or would I have to find my own way to the hostel?

Josh must see the sudden worry on my face because he says, "Don't worry. Your dad will definitely let you go if I'm with you."

I brighten. "Yeah! We can stay at hostels and just eat pastries and cheese for all our meals."

"We can go to Jim Morrison's grave!" Josh throws in.

"We can go to a *parfumerie* and get our personal scents done!" I cheer, and Josh snorts.

"Um, I'm pretty sure 'getting our scents done' at a *parfumerie* would cost the same as a week's stay at the hostel," he says. He nudges Margot. "Your sister suffers from delusions of grandeur."

"She is the fanciest of the three of us," Margot agrees.

"What about me?" Kitty whimpers.

"You?" I scoff. "You're the *least* fancy Song girl. I have to beg you to wash your feet at night, much less take a shower."

Kitty's face gets pinched and red. "I wasn't talking about that, you dodo bird. I was *talking* about Paris."

Airily, I wave her off. "You're too little to stay at a hostel."

She crawls over to Margot and climbs in her lap, even though she's nine and nine is too big to sit in people's laps. "Margot, you'll let me go, won't you?"

"Maybe it could be a family vacation," Margot says, kissing her cheek. "You and Lara Jean and Daddy could all come."

I frown. That's not at all the Paris trip I was imagining. Over Kitty's head Josh mouths to me, *We'll talk later*, and I give him a discreet thumbs-up.

It's later that night; Josh is long gone. Kitty and our dad are asleep. We are in the kitchen. Margot is at the table on her computer; I am sitting next to her, rolling cookie dough into balls and dropping them in cinnamon and sugar. Snickerdoodles to get back in Kitty's good graces. Earlier, when I went in to say good night, Kitty rolled over and wouldn't speak to me because she's still convinced I'm going to try to cut her out of the Paris trip. My plan is to put the snickerdoodles on a plate right next to her pillow so she wakes up to the smell of fresh-baked cookies.

Margot's being extra quiet, and then, out of nowhere, she looks up from her computer and says, "I broke up with Josh tonight. After dinner."

My cookie-dough ball falls out of my fingers and into the sugar bowl.

"I mean, it was time," she says. Her eyes aren't red-rimmed; she hasn't been crying, I don't think. Her voice is calm and even. Anyone looking at her would think she was fine. Because Margot is always fine, even when she's not.

"I don't see why you had to break up," I say. "Just 'cause you're going to college doesn't mean you have to break up."

"Lara Jean, I'm going to Scotland, not UVA. Saint Andrews is nearly four thousand miles away." She pushes up her glasses. "What would be the point?"

I can't even believe she would say that. "The point is, it's Josh. Josh who loves you more than any boy has ever loved a girl!"

Margot rolls her eyes at this. She thinks I'm being dramatic, but I'm not. It's true—that's how much Josh loves Margot. He would never so much as look at another girl.

Suddenly she says, "Do you know what Mommy told me once?"

"What?" For a moment I forget all about Josh. Because

no matter what I am doing in life, if Margot and I are in the middle of an argument, if I am about to get hit by a car, I will always stop and listen to a story about Mommy. Any detail, any remembrance that Margot has, I want to have it too. I'm better off than Kitty, though. Kitty doesn't have one memory of Mommy that we haven't given her. We've told her so many stories so many times that they're hers now. "Remember that time . . . ," she'll say. And then she'll tell the story like she was there and not just a little baby.

"She told me to try not to go to college with a boyfriend. She said she didn't want me to be the girl crying on the phone with her boyfriend and saying no to things instead of yes."

Scotland is Margot's yes, I guess. Absently, I scoop up a mound of cookie dough and pop it in my mouth.

"You shouldn't eat raw cookie dough," Margot says.

I ignore her. "Josh would never hold you back from anything. He's not like that. Remember how when you decided to run for student-body president, he was your campaign manager? He's your biggest fan!"

At this, the corners of Margot's mouth turn down, and I get up and fling my arms around her neck. She leans her head back and smiles up at me. "I'm okay," she says, but she isn't, I know she isn't.

"It's not too late, you know. You can go over there right now and tell him you changed your mind."

Margot shakes her head. "It's done, Lara Jean." I release her and she closes her laptop. "When will the first batch be ready? I'm hungry."

I look at the magnetic egg timer on the fridge. "Four more minutes." I sit back down and say, "I don't care what you say, Margot. You guys aren't done. You love him too much."

She shakes her head. "Lara Jean," she begins, in her patient Margot voice, like I am a child and she is a wise old woman of forty-two.

I wave a spoonful of cookie dough under Margot's nose, and she hesitates and then opens her mouth. I feed it to her like a baby. "Wait and see, you and Josh will be back together in a day, maybe two." But even as I'm saying it, I know it's not true. Margot's not the kind of girl to break up and get back together on a whim; once she's decided something, that's it. There's no waffling, no regrets. It's like she said: when she's done, she's just done.

I wish (and this is a thought I've had many, many times, too many times to count) I was more like Margot. Because sometimes it feels like I'll never be done.

Later, after I've washed the dishes and plated the cookies and set them on Kitty's pillow, I go to my room. I don't turn the light on. I go to my window. Josh's light is still on.

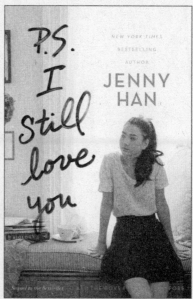

Because *summer*
should last forever.

Some loves last beyond a lifetime.

"A beautiful, haunting read."
—Tahereh Mafi, *New York Times* bestselling author of *Shatter Me*

SUBLIME

Christina Lauren
New York Times Bestselling Author

From *New York Times* bestselling author **Christina Lauren**